Praise for the Thicker than Blood series

Thicker Than Blood
Series

"With careful attention to detail, emotion, and ton scores with her debut effort."
JERRY B. JENKINS, *New York Times* best-selling author and owner of the Christian Writers Guild, on *Thicker than Blood*

"Darlington's setting in the fascinating world of antiquarian bookselling is clever . . ."
Publishers Weekly, on *Thicker than Blood*

"Great job! You kept me turning the pages."
FRANCINE RIVERS, *New York Times* best-selling author, on *Bound by Guilt*

"C. J. is a wonderful, talented writer . . . extraordinary. . . ."
BODIE THOENE, best-selling author of the Jerusalem Chronicles series, A.D. Chronicles series, and more.

"A true page-turner, this tale uses the mystery and suspense to keep readers entertained. But it's the characters who will enthrall."
Crosswalk.com on *Bound by Guilt*

". . . a fresh tale . . . every reader will find a part of his or her own life within these covers."
TOSCA LEE, best-selling author of *Iscariot, Havah*, and the Book of Mortals series with Ted Dekker, on *Bound by Guilt*

"a tension filled, heartfelt book.. . . . This is a book that will touch your heart, mind, and emotions.
The Suspense Zone on *Bound by Guilt*

"Darlington's stellar storytelling rivals that of any seasoned pro!"
RT Book Reviews, on *Bound by Guilt*

". . . [A] delightful inspirational story. *Ties that Bind* is a winner!
Fresh Fiction

"C. J.'s characters remain real, honest and incredibly powerful."
LORI TWICHELL, RadiantLit.com, on *Ties that Bind*

TIES THAT BIND

Also by C. J. Darlington

Thicker than Blood
Bound by Guilt
Running on Empty
Jupiter Winds

TIES
THAT
BIND

C. J. DARLINGTON

Mountainview Books, LLC

For Papa

Acknowledgments

Mom—thank you so much for your tireless help editing and reading over this manuscript. It's because of you that I'm living my dream of bringing stories to readers. Your work ethic is amazing and inspiring. Love you so much, squeeze, and I love you!

Tracy—you're always interested, always ask meaningful questions, and always get just as excited (if not more so!) than I do. You're a fantastic listening ear, and your encouragement has helped me on the days when writing words felt like pulling teeth.

Amy Livengood, Lori Fox, Deena Peterson, Candace Calvert, Lori Twichell, and Jennifer Erin Valent—for taking the time to read this story and offer terrific feedback.

April High—for so graciously allowing me to ride and enjoy the real-life Lacey. I will never forget your generosity, and I based all the good parts of my fictional horse on your Lacey!

Above all, thank you to my Father, who's made all this possible and loved me even when I don't deserve it. He is the father to the fatherless.

1

When Brynn Taylor was released from prison, she didn't expect anyone to be waiting for her.

"There she is!" a voice shrieked from across the parking lot, and a woman with a head full of tight, black corn rows and a toddler hugging her hip jogged toward Brynn. Following on her heels was what looked like a parade procession of extended family, all dressed in bright, starched clothes they could've just worn to church.

Brynn froze, a coyote in the headlights of a Hummer. Recognition flashed in the woman's face, but Brynn didn't have a clue who she was. The gal let out another squeal running toward her, the kid's head bobbing.

But then the woman and her entourage whooshed past Brynn, and she swung around to see another inmate emerging from the doors of the Denver Women's Correctional Facility. Within seconds, the whole crew swallowed their loved one in a group hug, and Brynn couldn't see her through the mass of family.

She heard the cries of joy.

Brynn stuffed her hands into the pockets of her new jeans. They felt stiff and scratchy against her skin, and her t-shirt was a size too large. In at nineteen, out at twenty-four, and she'd gained less than five pounds. She probably could've still fit into the clothes she'd come in here with, but they'd no doubt been dumpstered years ago.

"Thank you, Lord!" Someone's hand shot up to the sky, waving gratitude.

She wondered how long the other inmate had been inside and what crime she'd committed. Was she a druggie caught making a buy? A hooker who'd propositioned the wrong john? The majority of the women here were low-risk offenders, but many had been inside before. Most would be again.

For a second, the sea of family parted and Brynn caught sight of the newly released prisoner, her face streaked with glassy tear lines. She was clinging to an older woman.

"I'll do better, Mama. I promise," she sobbed.

Brynn turned away, her second-hand sneakers silently carrying her across the parking lot away from the huddle. Their happiness swirled around her, a slicing reminder there were no welcoming arms for her.

She lifted her face to the sky where gray clouds threatened to dump much-needed June rain. She hadn't expected to cry, but standing in the open air free of steel doors and walls, unwanted tears came.

No more would her world be defined by gray cinder blocks scratched with obscene words. There'd be no more violating strip downs from guards searching for contraband, and exercise would no longer mean walking the perimeter of a pen topped with razor wire.

There also wouldn't be anyone to keep her out of trouble. Everything was up to her now, which scared her more than anything. The last time she'd been on her own she'd ended up handcuffed in the back of a police car.

Brynn closed her eyes. Everyone assumed she'd refused parole and maxed out her sentence for the assurance of three squares a day. But really, fear was why she'd stayed. At least behind bars she knew what to expect and what was expected of her. Out here . . .

She blinked a couple times and pulled in a deep breath. Reaching into her pocket, she fingered the lone silver key they'd returned to her along with her empty wallet and expired driver's license. Out here she was free all right—to wreck her life all over again.

⌁

Brynn walked briskly through the gate of Ames Self Storage and made her way to the last unit with the green, garage-style door. She had no idea how her mother had managed to pre-pay for this spot years in advance, but Brynn was sure glad she did. She'd have nothing without it.

She unlocked the door and wrenched it open. When they'd moved from their country house into the smaller rental in town to be closer to the hospital, anything that didn't fit had ended up here.

She pictured the unit as it had once been—crammed with treasures like the family-sized dining room table Mom hadn't been able to part with, the decorative chairs that matched, Grams' antique set of silverware she'd received as a wedding gift, and a carved wooden chest that had belonged to an ancestor who crossed the Atlantic from Germany.

They were all gone now. Years ago, Brynn had scattered those precious heirlooms her mother and grandmother had hoped to pass on to her across the city's pawn shops. She tried not to think about that as she gathered up their old camping gear, some of the few items she'd managed to hang onto. It was no-name stuff, but it had served Mom and her well on their numerous hikes and weekend trips. Luckily, most of it was compact hike-in stuff they'd gotten cheap at a going-out-of-business sale. She'd pawned anything of real value, and what was left was the bare minimum—sleeping bag, two-person tent, and a few cooking utensils.

Kneeling on the cold cement, Brynn stuffed her hand into the sleeping bag's pouch. Still tucked safely between the down layers, she found her grandfather's Smith & Wesson .22. She'd pawned it twice but always went back for it.

Brynn ran her fingers across the tooled leather holster, then unsheathed the gun, flipped open the cylinder, and spun it. She could still smell the oil from the last time Mom cleaned it, and a wave of grief washed over her. If she'd kept her promise to her mother she would've avoided all the heartache of the last six years.

Slipping the gun back into its sleeping bag cocoon, she made sure the half-full box of bullets was with it. One more thing to grab, and she could escape from the memories this place entombed.

She found the old book inside a file box of ancient tax records. The boards were a blue/gray paper over something like thick cardboard, and the tan spine had a pinkish label that said: *Sense and Sensibility*, with the number "3" beneath that.

Brynn carefully slipped the volume into the folds of the sleeping bag with the gun. This book was all she had of her father, a man she couldn't even remember.

It was also her only hope to find him.

2

Brynn stared out the Greyhound bus window and watched the cookie-cutter houses zoom by. Six years ago, she never would've dreamed she'd end up here. She was a budding artist on the cusp of great things. Someday her paintings would grace the walls of galleries, and Mom would stand proudly beside her beaming and telling everyone the famous artist was her daughter. Now those dreams were as far away as Africa.

Brynn pulled the Jane Austen from her newly purchased backpack and opened it to read the full title:

Sense and Sensibility
A Novel
In Three Volumes
By A Lady
Vol. III

The publication date was 1811. She turned to the first page where people often wrote inscriptions, reading again the words she had memorized:

To my daughter Brynn,

One of my biggest regrets is that I never got to see you take your first step or do any of the "firsts" a child does. I wasn't there for you, and I'm sorry. I hope someday you can forgive me. I'll always love you.

Love,
Dad

Brynn rested the book on her lap, barely noticing the brown and barren fields passing by the bus window. She knew her father's name was Peter Williams, but not much more. Her only clue to finding *her* Peter Williams was the name and address in tiny script at the back of the book.

Edna Williams, 1052 Mountain View Drive, Monument, Colorado.

Her father had given this book to Mom when Brynn was only four years old, and Mom held onto it for years before finally surprising her with it as a gift for her twelfth birthday. Brynn's reaction probably hadn't been the one Mom expected. Her mother had hoped the book would quench some of the curiosity she had about her father, but Brynn only saw it as a tease. Because of him, Mom had to work two jobs just to put food on the table. Brynn would often wait up till eleven just to spend ten minutes with Mom before they both collapsed into their beds.

Leaning back in her seat, Brynn sighed. Was it the pressure of being a father that had driven him away? Even as a child she'd wondered. Had she been that much of a burden?

When they pulled into the Colorado Springs bus stop, Brynn stepped off with the rest of the passengers. After a pit stop to use the bathroom and buy some vending machine snacks, she headed out with Monument on her mind. According to Google maps, if she could get a lift she'd have a chance to reach Edna Williams's house in Monument before evening.

That's how she found herself thumbing a ride at the freeway on-ramp. The first few cars didn't even slow, and she wondered what she must look like to these drivers. Probably pathetic. And young. And female. She should load the gun and make it more accessible.

After a few minutes, Brynn sensed the presence of the car before she saw it. She turned around and walked backwards a few paces as a blue boat of a Cadillac with at least five antennae bristling from its roof slowed beside her. She ducked down to see the driver through the open passenger window.

The gray-haired old lady behind the wheel waved a bony hand at her. "Are you completely senseless, girl?"

Brynn stepped closer.

"Don't you watch the news? Hitchhiking's dangerous."

"Yeah," Brynn said.

"Then why you doing it?"

She rested her hand on the warm metal of the door. The smell of berry air freshener drifted through the window. "Need a ride up to Monument."

The old woman shook her head. "And I'm completely senseless to pick you up, but get in."

Brynn obeyed, and the old lady gave the Cadillac enough gas to send her flying backwards into her seat. She introduced herself as Gladys Joette and spent the next five minutes telling Brynn about the news story she'd watched last night in her hotel room about another hitchhiker girl who'd been abducted by a trucker. Yeah, that made her feel better.

"So . . . are you from around here?" Brynn asked.

"Heavens no." Gladys zoomed around a pickup going sixty-five, and Brynn hung onto the door handle. She glanced behind them half expecting to see a police cruiser swooping in for the kill. That would be just what she needed. Released and stopped in one day for speeding with a wild grandma.

"Topeka's my home base," Gladys said.

With a wave of her hand, Gladys gestured to the back seat. Brynn twisted around and took in the tangle of wires, computer screens and cameras.

"I chase storms," the old woman said, pride in her voice.

That would explain all the antennae. And perhaps Gladys, who quickly launched into a story about photographing a tornado in Castle Rock last summer.

"So what's *your* story?" Gladys zoomed around another truck.

"On my way to Monument."

The woman cackled.

"That's funny?"

"You're very good at evasion."

She stared at Gladys. Her no-nonsense manner was refreshing.

"I didn't fall off the turnip truck yesterday, you know."

"I'm looking for my father," Brynn finally said.

"He lives in Monument."

"I hope so."

Gladys nodded.

Brynn suddenly realized how much of a long shot the whole trip was. What were the chances this Edna Williams woman even knew her father? Maybe they weren't relatives at all and their same last names was pure coincidence.

She'd tried to confirm it before coming in person, but the only phone number she found for Edna Williams had been disconnected. Since people often ditched land lines for cells, she couldn't assume the woman had moved, but she was now starting to wonder.

Before Brynn knew it, the exit for Monument was upon them, and Gladys waited until she was nearly past the turn before actually taking it.

She swung the wheel and Brynn almost landed in Gladys's lap as she silently begged God to keep a cop from noticing this crazy old woman's driving.

Gladys flipped on her turn signal at the light. "Where to, now?"

Brynn pulled the directions from the back pocket of her jeans, reading them off.

"Easy breezy," Gladys said.

Within five minutes the Cadillac pulled up to the curb of a rancher with two huge pine trees towering over it. Brynn stared, suddenly content to stay in Crazy Gladys's car.

Gladys peered out the window too. "Want me to wait?"

Her offer was kind, but Brynn needed to do this alone. She took a deep breath and swung open the door, giving the old woman as much of a smile as she could manage. "Thanks, but you have storms to chase."

"As do you," Gladys said with a wink. "Godspeed, girl."

And then the Cadillac was gone with a squeal of tires, and a wave out the window.

Brynn took quick steps up the driveway, hoping Edna Williams would give her some answers. But any confidence she'd managed to muster dissolved as she faced the front door. What was she going to say? Could she do this without immediately revealing who she was?

She forced herself to knock. And then waited.

The lock clicked and a woman only a couple years older than herself answered. A baby cried in the background.

"Yes?"

Her cue.

"Is Edna Williams home?"

"Who?"

"Edna Williams."

The woman shook her head. "We just moved in six months ago. She doesn't live here now. You might try talking to Jack." She pointed at the house across the street. "He's been in this neighborhood for over thirty years."

Brynn thanked her, then found herself standing in front of yet another strange house. She rang the doorbell, only this time there was no response. She rang it again. As she turned away, a white-haired man poked his head from around the side of the house.

"Can I help you?" He came toward her with a slight limp, garden gloves hanging out of his back pocket.

"Are you Jack?"

"I was this morning." He smiled, reaching out his hand.

She shook it. His calloused skin felt rough against her fingers.

"Was out back weeding," he said. "Just happened to hear the bell through the window."

"I'm looking for Edna Williams. She used to live across the street?"

Jack's eyes brightened.

"You know her?"

He quickly turned somber. "Unfortunately, she died a couple years ago."

Brynn almost swore. Edna was her only clue, her only hope. She had no money to hire a private investigator. Even if she stretched her cash, she'd barely have enough to survive for a week.

But what had she really expected? To find her father the first day she went looking?

"Can I help in some other way?" Jack asked.

"I think she knew someone I'm trying to find."

"I see. You might try her great-niece, May Williams," Jack offered. "She lived with Edna for many years."

Brynn perked up.

"She moved down to Elk Valley a couple years ago, but came up here to visit Edna often." Jack pulled out his gloves, and dirt rained to the pavement at his feet. "She might be able to point you in the right direction, at least."

"Do you have an address? Phone number?"

Jack scratched his head. "Don't believe I have any of that. But she lives on a ranch, I think. Nice girl. Always helped me plant my flowers."

Brynn thanked him for his time, regretting she hadn't let Gladys wait for her. Somehow she had to get to Elk Valley.

3

Roxi Gold flipped off the shower water and grabbed a towel. Stepping out onto the bathroom tile, she almost tripped on her dog Selah, who lay sprawled across the bath mat.

"Don't let me get in your way," Roxi muttered, reaching down to give the sleek black pooch a stroke on the ear. Selah thumped her tail. She was an odd cross of whippet and terrier that, strangely, fit in perfectly here at Lonely River Ranch. They made a good team, both abandoned and now rescued.

Roxi stared at herself in the mirror, twisting to examine the scars two bullets had carved into her. Thankfully, the one on her shoulder was only visible if she went sleeveless, and the one at her temple was usually covered by her straight, brown hair.

She slipped into her Wranglers and tank top, barely giving the older scar on her arm a second glance. She'd gotten it as a kid falling out of a window. Not that long ago, it was all she saw when she looked at herself, but things had changed a lot in the past two years.

"Come on, girl." Roxi snapped her fingers, and Selah was instantly by her side. She'd overslept big time and would have to make it up to Jan and Keith Mercer, the couple who owned this ranch.

She expected to find herself alone in the house, but as she

walked down the stairs she heard female voices in the kitchen. One of them was Jan's, the other Roxi didn't recognize.

"Will you please keep it down?" Jan said.

"Shouldn't she be up?"

"She can sleep as late as she wants."

"You should wake her."

Even from the stairs she heard Jan's sigh and the tap of a cup being set on the table. Roxi held onto Selah's collar to keep the dog from flying into the kitchen and giving her away.

"If you don't set boundaries now, who knows what—"

"She's eighteen, Morgan."

"And living in your house."

"Exactly."

"When my kids are in my house," Morgan said, "they live by my rules."

"How about we start over and leave Roxi out of this?"

"She's why I'm here."

Jan sighed again.

Roxi crept down the rest of the stairs with Selah until she was right outside the kitchen entryway. Keith had a sister named Morgan. Was this her? Careful not to make a sound, she strained to hear the rest of the conversation.

"I'm just concerned about her and our kids."

"They'll get along fine."

Morgan cleared her throat. "That's not what I mean. With the barbeque next weekend, I just . . ."

A cup hit the table again, this time a little harder. "Is that what this is about?"

"You aren't at all concerned?"

"I'm more concerned one of your boys will set fire to something."

"My children are not—"

"What are you saying, Morgan?"

"You're letting yourself get too attached to a girl who—"

"For once deserves a break."

Morgan paused. "I'm just concerned."

A moment of pregnant silence permeated the kitchen. Roxi pictured the women sitting across from each other at the thick wooden table, sipping from their mismatched coffee cups. Jan was fifty-four but as spry as someone half her age. Her strong hands would be wrapped around her mug. As she took a sip, she was probably warning Morgan with her blue eyes to back off.

Morgan broke the silence. "Why are you doing this?"

"Because she's a good kid." Jan lowered her voice. "And what happened wasn't her fault."

"Really. The judge obviously felt she played an important enough part."

Roxi leaned her head against the wall. It hurt to hear her history spat out like this, but she should've known that's what people were thinking. She might as well wear a sign around her neck with the word "Delinquent" painted in bold red strokes. Jan and Keith had treated her like a daughter, but it was foolish to imagine the rest of their family welcoming her with open arms. She'd spent the last two years at a camp for juvies. She should've known she'd have a lot of proving to do.

"Has she fooled you so much you can't see reality anymore?"

"You know what? You're right. She *is* living in my house." Jan's voice got louder. "Because I want her to. Because she deserves better than the crap life's thrown at her."

A forced laugh came from the kitchen. "Since when is this girl more important than your own family?"

"Morgan, stop this. You know we–"

"First it was Dad's birthday. His *eightieth* birthday. Then Thanksgiving and Christmas. I could go on."

"What were we supposed to do? Her own mother abandoned her."

"And I'm sorry about that, but just this once, think about

how this girl is affecting *your* lives. Look at all you've had to give up. When she ends up in trouble again, is it going to be worth it?"

Jan's tone fell to a whisper. "I would do it again in a heartbeat. And so would Keith."

Silence spread through the kitchen for so long Roxi almost peeked around the corner to see if the women were still there. She wanted to hug Jan for saying that.

"I'll have to talk to Denny," Morgan finally said in a monotone.

Chairs slid across the linoleum, and Roxi let go of Selah. The dog's nails half scraped, half clacked on the wood as she shot into the kitchen barking. Roxi followed as if she hadn't heard a word. She didn't move to silence her dog, either.

"Hey there, sleepyhead," Jan said, grabbing Selah by the collar and sending her outside to do her business. In her dusty jeans and denim shirt rolled up to the elbows, Jan looked like she'd come straight in from rounding up cattle or working with one of her horses.

"This is Morgan, Keith's sister."

Roxi sent a half-hearted wave in Morgan's direction. Their eyes met, and a little of her resolve withered at the woman's stare. In her maroon, tailored leather blazer and slacks that were stylishly snug in all the right places, she completely contrasted Jan. And made Roxi's old Goodwill clothes feel like rags.

A watch sparkled on Morgan's wrist as she extended a manicured hand in her direction. Roxi shook it extra hard and didn't miss Morgan's glance at the scar on her arm.

"I've heard a lot about you," Morgan said.

"I'm sure you have," Roxi said with a smile, and another firm squeeze of Morgan's fingers. "I kinda shook things up around here, didn't I?"

Jan pursed her lips like she was trying to hold in a smile.

For one moment Morgan seemed taken aback, but she

quickly recovered. Roxi decided breakfast with Morgan wasn't an option, so after grabbing two bread slices from the fridge, she followed Selah out the back door. They headed to the barn to start the day's chores.

⁓

May Williams guided the pickup in like an air traffic controller. It slowly backed up toward the round pen, the stock trailer it towed inching closer to the open gate.

"You're good, Craig!" she called to the driver when the trailer was flush.

The truck stopped, its engine cutting off.

May stood on tiptoe, trying to get a better look inside the trailer at the five-year-old Appaloosa named Doc. Craig didn't tie a horse if it was by itself in the stock trailer, so she could clearly see Doc moving around. The Triple Cross Ranch was his last chance.

"Sure you want him in here?" Craig exited the pickup and stared at the trailer with his arms crossed. Middle-aged with a crazy mop of gray hair, he was the area's top Appaloosa breeder, but he looked like Albert Einstein.

"Yeah, let's go for it." May climbed up one of the round pen panels and dropped inside.

"Be careful," Craig said.

She nodded. Doc was here because he'd almost killed another horse. With rare blood lines, Craig had hoped the stallion would become a prized stud, but when Doc started showing aggressive tendencies, he knew he had a problem. Then someone accidentally put another horse in Doc's pasture with him.

May reached for the trailer latch, took a deep breath, and opened it. She swung the gate wide as fast as she could, keeping it between herself and the horse.

Doc leapt from the trailer, his hooves banging on the metal, and took off into the round pen. May slammed the trailer closed and clambered up and over the railing to stand with Craig and watch. A black leopard Appaloosa, Doc reminded May of a huge Dalmatian.

"When did you geld him?" May asked.

"Three weeks ago."

"Has he calmed down at all?"

Craig shrugged. "Some, but not enough."

May watched Doc canter around the pen. Gelding an aggressive stallion could often cause a complete turn around in behavior, and it usually only took a few weeks to start noticing improvement.

She turned toward Craig. "So what have you been doing with him before this?"

"Doing?"

"Exercising, training, that sort of thing."

Craig shook his head at the horse. "Not much, and nothing without a stud chain."

She tried not to wince. She'd seen too many good horses ruined by the practice of running a chain through their halter and over their nose for better control. The chain did nothing but inflict pain.

"Has he been under saddle?"

"Used to ride him all over the place last year. Until he turned four, he was fine."

That was good. At least Doc had some basic training.

Craig handed her his deposit check and headed for the truck. "Hope you can do something with him."

"Me too."

As Craig's truck rumbled back down the ranch's gravel drive, Doc flew past her in the pen, sending a kick in her direction that hit one of the metal bars.

"Wow, boy. You're full of it," May said, stepping back.

With cattle ranching in a slump, she and her elderly ranching partner Ruth Santos had recently hung up their shingle as horse trainers. All it took was the turnaround May had managed with a neighbor's Percheron to get word of mouth going. People had dubbed them both horse whisperers, and the calls were rolling in from people with problem horses like Doc.

She smiled as the Appaloosa slowed down to a trot, then a walk. She was looking forward to this challenge.

4

All Brynn knew about Elk Valley was what she'd read on the tourist brochure at the gas station. It wasn't much. Surrounded by the Spanish Peaks to the southeast and the Sangre de Cristo Mountains to the northwest, there was no shortage of nature to attract tourists and wildlife enthusiasts. Probably the only thing going for the town. It was too far away from Denver or Colorado Springs to make it convenient for commuting, but the surrounding ranch country and the Cuchara ski resort managed to keep it alive.

Brynn threw another log on her campfire, thankful to rest her weary legs. Her second bus ride had only brought her as far as Walsenburg. From there, she'd hitched a ride with an old man who'd talked her ear off even more than Gladys had.

The Twin Peaks campground lay on the outskirts of Elk Valley. More an RV park than a campground, at least it was a safe place to set up her tent. Since she had no pots or pans, she ate steaming baked beans straight out of the metal cup she'd heated them in, using a sock to hold the cup's blistering handle.

The fire crackled and popped, and as the sun set, Brynn rested her elbows on her knees, remembering Mom. In a matter of six months she'd watched her healthy, vibrant mother morph into a walking skeleton with gray skin and a body so weak she couldn't feed herself.

It was more than a seventeen-year-old could bear, but she'd determined to stay strong until the end. Mom never saw the plummeting grades or the nights she begged for sleep but couldn't find it.

Her mother needed all her strength to stay alive, and finally that failed her. That last night in the hospital, Brynn had been sitting in a chair by the window trying to hold herself together when her mother's whisper called to her. She was by the bed in seconds.

Brynn carefully held her mother's hand, afraid to squeeze too hard. Tubes and IVs stuck from Mom like guy wires. Cut them, and she knew her mother would float away.

"I'm here, Mom."

A slight smile crept onto her mother's lips. "My little girl."

Grief washed over her. How could the one who'd given her life no longer give life to herself? How could this be the end? Mom was supposed to watch her graduate, cheer her on, and be the rock she leaned on.

"I'm so sorry," her mother whispered. "You . . . you shouldn't have to see me like this."

"We're gonna get through it. You'll see."

Mom closed her eyes, then slowly opened them again. "No, sweet Brynn." She shifted in the bed, winced, but still managed to wrap both her clammy hands around Brynn's. "You need to think about what you're going to do without me."

"Mom . . ."

"You're so talented and smart. And your art . . . I want to hear all about it up there in heaven."

Brynn tried to smile, but couldn't. She hadn't told her mother she'd thrown her paints away. And her canvases. Mom was the one who'd believed in her, encouraged her, kept her from giving up on the days when inspiration flew the coop. What was the point of art if she wasn't here to admire it?

Mom looked straight into her tear-filled eyes, which gave away her thoughts, as always.

"God didn't do this," Mom whispered.

It was all Brynn could do to hold her gaze. She'd thrown away her Bible, too.

"He didn't, honey."

Brynn was shaking her head. What did it matter? The end result was still the same.

"Base your faith on Him, sweetheart. Not me." Mom squeezed her hand. "I would hate to see you turn your back on what's held us together."

Brynn lowered her head to the sheets and cried for the years they wouldn't spend as a family, the moments they wouldn't share.

"I just wanted you to get better," she sobbed.

Mom stroked her hair. "That's all I wanted, too."

Brynn clenched her teeth and forced herself to hold back the curses she felt like screaming, only because she didn't want them to be the last words she spoke to her mother. She didn't know for sure how long she stayed with her head buried, but it was long enough to hear a Code Blue somewhere over the intercom.

She slowly lifted her face, wiping her eyes with the back of her sleeve. She took in the full picture of her mother's chest rising and falling erratically, her forehead and upper lip dotted with sweat.

Mom's smile was gone. She still held Brynn's hand, and she squeezed it again, harder than before.

"I want you to find your father."

Brynn stared at her. She still clearly remembered being eight and hearing for the first time how her father had abandoned them. That's all Mom had said, and it was clear she wanted to leave it at that. She wanted to forget the man who broke her heart. But Brynn never forgot.

Mom took a shallow breath, and tears Brynn didn't know she had left to cry filled her eyes. She leaned in close. Her voice was almost inaudible, and it caught on the lump in her throat. "But he left us."

Mom shifted in the bed, trying to hide her pain. Brynn started to say more, but her words were cut off by Mom's coughing. She knew each one sent spasms through her mother's body.

Tears built up again. Brynn leaned close, kissing her mother's cold hand. "Please don't leave me, Mom. I can't do this without you."

"Give him a chance. Will you do that for me?"

"Mom, I–"

"That's all I ask."

Brynn met her mother's gaze, then looked away. If she'd asked her to climb Mt. Everest it would've been easier, and Brynn would've found some way to make it happen. But this?

"Promise me you'll find him."

In that lonely hospital room six years ago, she'd promised her mother she would, and then Mom slowly sunk into a coma.

Brynn stared into the fire. Mom never woke up, and she never kept her promise. It was as simple, and as complicated, as that. At seventeen, the state pretty much left her alone, and she'd moved in with some college-aged girlfriends who tried to help her. She couldn't blame them for what happened after that.

In a way, she was glad her mother wasn't here. At least then she couldn't see the mess Brynn had made of things.

"I'm sorry, Mom," Brynn whispered as she adjusted a log in the campfire. She needed to stop this brooding and focus on the here and now. She was finally keeping her promise.

5

May always enjoyed meeting her older sister Christy at The
Perfect Blend coffee shop. Sitting at a table by the
window, Christy closed her laptop and stood up to give her a
hug.

"You forgot the books, didn't you?"

May hit her forehead with the palm of her hand. "They're
sitting on my desk. I promise I'll show you tonight. Beth called
me, by the way. An emergency came up so she won't be able
to meet us."

Beth Eckert, her best friend and the ranch's veterinarian,
often joined them for their coffee chats when her busy sched-
ule allowed.

"That's too bad," Christy said.

They went up to the counter together and placed their
orders. Both of them asked for medium house blends. May got
hers with half and half. Christy took hers black. Back at the
table, her sister eyed her as they sipped their drinks.

"How are things?" Christy asked.

"Got in a new horse. Not sure what to think of him yet."

"Oh?"

The bell above the coffee shop door jingled as May started

to explain Doc's story, but then she glanced up and saw Shane Newman walk in. She tried not to groan.

"We can leave," Christy whispered.

"That'd only make things worse."

"He might not see you."

May had her back to the counter but could already feel Shane's eyes on her. She heard him pay for something, and then he was at their table. He wore a straw cowboy hat, and his white muscle shirt exposed tan arms and tattooed biceps.

"How you doing?" Shane cracked open a can of Red Bull and took a swig.

May let an uncomfortable moment pass before responding. Shane wasn't over here just to chat. "We're fine," she said. "How 'bout you?"

"Still ticked."

She'd thought as much. "I know you are."

"It was pretty crappy what you did."

"Three calves died on your watch." She focused on the deep brown color of her coffee. "That shouldn't have happened."

"I admitted I made a mistake."

May shook her head and took a sip. It wasn't the only time either. A few mess ups here and there she could deal with, but he'd been given two rules when he came to work for her—no drugs and no girls. Those calves died because he'd been getting high in the Airstream with his girlfriend and then slept through two checks on the herd.

"We've been through this, okay?"

Shane took another swig from his Red Bull. "I was a good worker. I did a better job than that guy you've got over there now."

Christy raised an eyebrow. "I think maybe it's best if you move along."

May held her hand up to her sister. She understood Christy bristling at the jab toward her ranch hand, Jim Parker. He and

Christy had become close friends, and maybe even more than that, in the past few months, but she wasn't looking to push Shane's buttons. He was like a young bull ready to charge, and it would be stupid to provoke him.

"What do you want, Shane?"

"An apology."

May felt her blood heating and forced herself not to react. That's what he was looking for, and she wasn't giving it to him. "I have nothing to apologize for."

"How 'bout the mess you made between me and my father."

She tried to feel some sympathy for Shane. Being the sheriff's son couldn't be easy. The reason she'd hired him in the first place was to cut him the break no one else would. He'd gotten in trouble as a teen and spent several stints in rehab, but he seemed to have gotten his act together in the last year or two. She'd seen the difference even if no one else had. She and Ruth hired him during calving season to help with the extra work when Jim had to leave temporarily to help his ailing mother. There'd been several warnings, but losing the calves had been the last straw.

"Shane, come on." She caught the barista glancing at them. Lowering her tone she leaned across the table. "I wish it had worked out. I really do. But I couldn't afford to lose those animals."

"I said I was sorry. I thought Christians were supposed to forgive."

May sent up a prayer for wisdom. "Let's just forget it."

Shane's jaw muscle twitched. He guzzled down the rest of his Red Bull and slammed the empty can down on their table. Then he left, and she and Christy watched out the window as he got into his blue Toyota and zoomed off down the street.

"That went well," she muttered.

"You did what you had to, May."

"Why doesn't that make me feel any better?"

Christy stared out the window for a moment. "We should pray for him."

"Yeah, that God would knock some sense into that head of his."

May sipped at her lukewarm coffee. Something needed to happen before that boy got into serious trouble. She was just glad to have him off her property.

Across the table, Christy gave her a look.

"Well He should," May said.

"I guess."

A half hour later, May reluctantly rose to head out on her next errand. She still needed to hit the bank, post office, and Walker's Feed Store before she could head back to the ranch.

"See you tonight?" Christy asked.

"You bet."

6

As Brynn walked down the Elk Valley sidewalk, she tried not to stare at every man she passed. What if one of these guys was her father? He could be living in this town.

She shook her head. It was foolish to think she'd have an immediate, magical bond. When she met her father she'd be meeting a stranger. The only thing connecting them was their blood, and that hadn't meant anything to him. This wasn't a Hallmark movie. She couldn't expect open arms and reconciliation. She had absolutely no idea who her father was.

Brynn shifted the backpack to her other shoulder, her neck aching from the strain. Her plan was to get a feel for this place and then find the address she'd gotten for May on the campground's public computer terminal. She hoped the woman still lived there.

Outside a coffee shop called The Perfect Blend, Brynn slumped into a cast iron chair and tried to get her bearings. She knew she was dehydrated, and her thoughts were coming slow and mushy. Nothing was going as planned.

Resting her arms on the table, she lay her head on top of them. After all this time, she still longed for Mom to hold her and tell her everything would be alright. Nothing could separate them. They'd always have each other. Those were the types of things Mom had always said growing up. Nothing had prepared either of them for the horror of those last six months.

She'd never truly admitted to herself she'd felt like Mom abandoned her. The cancer hadn't been her fault, but not making plans beyond asking her daughter to find a ghost of a father was. Mom focused so much on getting better, never allowing Brynn to even speak of her death except for that last night, that by the time she died Brynn didn't have a clue what to do.

She still remembered the first time she took one of Mom's OxyContin pills. Sleep came, and finally she'd felt a semblance of peace. Her mother never knew she got to sleep that way every night for the last few weeks they had together. Then when Mom died, there was nowhere for Brynn to go but down.

Reluctantly, she lifted her weary head. She needed water. And food. Passing out before she reached her destination wasn't an option. She turned in her seat and peered in the window of the coffee shop, spotting the rows of chilled drinks by the counter. If only she had extra cash.

Inside, a woman leaned into the crash bar of the door, a slim laptop case slung on her shoulder. She held a coffee cup in one hand and a bottle of water in the other. Their eyes met, and the woman smiled at her. Before Brynn could look away, the woman was out the door and placed the water bottle on the table in front of her.

"You gotta drink a lot in this dry weather," she said.

It took a moment for the gesture to register. "Um, thanks."

"No problem." A pencil stuck out from behind the woman's ear, and her jeans were worn at the knees. "Mind if I sit here for a minute?"

Brynn shrugged. She twisted off the water bottle lid and downed the first half in one shot, relishing every gulp.

The woman sat down, sipping from her cup. "No matter

how much I try, my stuff never tastes this good. And I even use the same beans."

It had been a long time since Brynn had made small talk. She wiped her mouth with the back of her hand. "Do I look that bad?"

"Pardon?"

"I figure I look pretty bad to warrant a free water."

The woman smiled. "Just a little tired."

"Water never tasted so good," Brynn said, holding up the bottle.

Extending her hand over the table, the gal gave Brynn a handshake. "My name's Christy. I own the bookshop a block up."

Brynn introduced herself and glanced down the street. "I haven't read a good book in ages." Most of the novels in the prison library were over thirty years old and falling apart.

"I can recommend a whole truck full," Christy said.

"Where exactly is your shop?"

"Just up there." Christy pointed in the direction Brynn had come.

"Maybe I'll take a look." Brynn finished off her water and stowed the empty bottle in her pack, reminding herself to refill it somewhere later.

Christy was right. She was tired, and a little break at a bookstore could be just the recharge she needed. Not that she had enough money to buy anything that wasn't a necessity, but she needed something to occupy her thoughts. Otherwise, she'd drive herself crazy.

"What do you like to read?" Christy tried to sip her coffee as they began walking in the direction of her shop.

"I used to read mysteries."

Christy broke into a big grin. "Really? My absolute favorite author is Agatha Christie, and not because of her name, either. The woman was a genius."

"And ancient," Brynn said.

"Are you kidding? She's classic."

For a brief moment, Brynn felt like she was actually a normal person living a normal life. She could just walk down the street and have a conversation about something trivial without watching her back.

If only for a moment, she was the girl she used to be, the one with big dreams, ready to make her mark and live grand adventures.

When they got to the shop, Brynn saw the words The Book Corral stenciled in white paint on the front window. Someone had also painted colorful book ends beside the words, as if to hold the name together. The "Jump into a Mystery" window display featured over twenty Nancy Drew and Hardy Boys books scattered and stacked with a magnifying glass, flashlight, and Sherlock Holmes style hat.

"I just opened up six months ago." Christy waved her inside.

The smell of old paper and dust met them. Glancing around the room, Brynn was surprised to see many of the shelves were empty. She slipped out of her pack and stretched her arms.

"I'm still trying to stock the place," Christy said. "Guy who sold it to me had a lot of junk I had to clear out."

"It's just you?"

"Yeah, just me." Christy shook her head. "I'm gonna make a go of it though. I live upstairs, so I can devote every spare minute to building up the place. So anyway, you like mysteries, but not the best mystery author ever."

Brynn hesitated, and Christy winked at her.

"What about Nancy Drew?"

Christy reached into the display window and pulled out a copy of *The Secret In the Old Clock.* It didn't look like the one Brynn had read as a girl with a picture cover and yellow spine. The cover was plain blue.

"They first published this in 1930, and it's still in print,"

Christy said, handing it to her. "Nancy Drew transcends time and age."

Brynn opened it. A neat price of three-hundred-fifty was penciled on the first page. "This is worth that much?"

"It's a first edition."

"Sorta beat up."

"I found it at a garage sale. It's very collectible, even without its dust jacket."

At her blank look, Christy explained. "That's the paper cover publishers often put over their hardcovers. A first edition of that book with a dust jacket could be worth thousands."

"But how do you know it's a first edition?" Brynn thought of the Jane Austen in her pack and almost pulled it out to show the woman.

Christy's face seemed to light up at the question. "How much do you know about Nancy Drew?"

"I read a few as a kid." She decided not to mention she was way too old at twenty-four to pick them back up again since Christy seemed to enjoy sharing the information about the series.

Christy pointed at the author's name printed in orange on the front of the book. "Carolyn Keene was actually a pseudonym. In fact, it was a lady named Mildred Wirt Benson who wrote most of them, though a few were actually written by a man."

Brynn stared down at the book. She'd always pictured the author as a stylish old lady hunched over a typewriter.

"Open it up again," Christy said.

She did, and was once more slapped in the face with that crazy price.

"These are called the endpapers." Christy tapped the piece of paper glued to the front cover and then the page adjacent to that, the one where the price was written. "In later editions they were illustrated with little scenes from other books in the series. Collectors call them the multi-scene endpapers. Some earlier ones had only a silhouette of Nancy. But notice how these are just plain white. That's one way to tell you have a first edition. The other thing we look for is whether the illustrations are printed on plain or glossy paper."

Brynn paged through the book and found one. She ran her finger across it.

"These are glossy," Christy said. "They're more expensive to produce, but first editions of the first three books in the series had them. We call them glossies."

Brynn gave the book back to her. "I hope you sell it."

"Me too. I've got it listed online, so maybe someone out of state will want it."

"Had no idea running a bookstore was this complicated," Brynn said.

That got a laugh out of Christy. "So . . . first edition lesson over. Let's find you something to read."

"I probably should get going."

"Tell you what." Christy tapped Brynn's arm with her knuckles. "You're new in town, right?"

Brynn nodded. No sense in denying it.

"Anything you find under twenty bucks is on me."

"So first the water, and now a book?"

"Consider it a welcome gift."

"Okay, I'll take a look. And thanks."

Walking to the nearest shelf labeled "New Acquisitions", she pretended to browse, but she was watching Christy out of the corner of her eye. This was a small town and all, but Brynn wasn't used to kindness.

She wondered what type of a woman ran a bookshop all by herself. Had Christy always been the girl with her nose in a book who'd never fit in? Brynn had never fit in either. The only place where she'd felt accepted and understood was in art class where all the other creative misfits finally had a safe haven and her imagination was encouraged.

That's why what caught her attention more than any of the books in the store was the painting on the wall by the checkout counter. Brynn studied the hauntingly life-like portrait, probably oil on canvas, of a young, bearded man looking straight at the viewer. She knew who it depicted without looking, but still she stepped closer to read the small card sticking from the frame.

"Jesus". Artist: Ruth Santos. $300.

Brynn stared at the piece.

"What do you think?" Christy asked.

"She's good."

"I had to beg her to let me put this one up."

Which made perfect sense. A painting was a piece of an artist's heart, not easy to bare to the world. She remembered Mom having to talk her into her first exhibition at the local art store. It wasn't fancy, and no big-wig dealers or critics attended, but it still hadn't been easy to present her creations to the public for the first time. It felt like nailing her soul up on the wall for everyone to see.

Christy set a tower of books on the counter. "If I could paint like that I wouldn't want to hide it."

"Maybe she doesn't realize how good she is."

Brynn took in the painting again. There was something about the man's face, his eyes especially. It wasn't easy to paint eyes like that. To capture their life on canvas took a special touch, but Ruth Santos had managed to present the eyes of this Jesus in a way that made it seem like He was looking through her.

"I think I've got a book for you."

Brynn was glad to turn away from the painting.

Handing her a green and brown softcover, Christy quickly went back to her sorting. *The Rivers Run Dry* by Sibella Giorello.

"Have you read it?"

"It's a great mystery."

"How much would you normally sell it for?"

Christy waved the comment away. "Oh, don't worry about it."

She decided protesting further would only make things uncomfortable. "Thanks," she said and headed toward the door. "Again. For this and the water. I really appreciate it."

"See you around?"

"Maybe," Brynn said.

She moved toward the door, then stepped back as a brown-haired, teenage girl walked in. The girl smiled at her. Brynn gave her a slight nod and walked out.

7

Brynn lucked out again when a passing hay truck stopped and gave her a ride to May's ranch. The grizzled old farmer didn't say much as the magnificent Spanish Peaks filled the windshield, and with each mile, Brynn became more uneasy. This felt like a wild goose chase. Even though her father and May shared a last name, she couldn't count on May actually knowing him.

The truck slowed, and on the right Brynn saw logs forming a canopy at the beginning of a long dirt drive. Three black metal crosses, the middle one slightly taller than the rest, poked up from the top log, and hanging beneath them by a rusted chain was a wooden sign.

Triple Cross Ranch.

She checked the mailbox number and re-checked her scrap of paper. This was Pronghorn Drive, and the number matched the one she'd scribbled off the computer.

"I'll get out here," she said, thanking the farmer for the ride. He drove away, leaving her staring down the lane. She swung her backpack onto her shoulder.

A twenty-minute walk later and the simple, one-story ranch house came into view. Beside it and off to the side was a small trailer home and an old Airstream. Brynn straightened her back and headed for the main house. May Williams was a stepping stone to her destination, and every lead she followed could bring her closer to her father. For now, she just needed to put one foot in front of the other.

Brynn approached the less intimidating and more accessible back door of the house where a lone white pickup sat a few feet away. She hesitated, then made herself knock. It was time to keep her word to Mom.

After a moment of silence, she knocked again and heard footsteps. The door cracked open, and she was met by an aging Hispanic woman with a salt and pepper braid. The woman's eyes crinkled as she smiled and greeted Brynn with a warm "hello".

"Is May Williams home?" Brynn asked.

The woman brightened, her gaze drifting briefly to Brynn's pack. "She went into town, but she should be back by four."

Brynn sighed, glancing at the truck.

"Can I help you with something?"

"Um . . ."

Opening the door wide, the woman gestured inside. "You're welcome to come in."

Brynn decided she hadn't come all this way to stammer an excuse and leave empty-handed. She stepped into the kitchen.

"I was about to sit down to some coffee. Would you like some?" The older woman closed the door and walked over to the counter. Were all small-town people this friendly?

"Yeah, sure," Brynn said. The room was petite, with a wood stove sitting in the corner. Was this woman May's mother? Grandmother?

"Sit, sit," the woman said with a wave toward the kitchen table. It didn't sound like an order but was a request to make herself at home. She dropped into one of the chairs, slipping her pack to the floor by her feet. She wished she'd left it outside. The tent and sleeping bag strapped to it screamed of desperation.

Bringing two steaming cups to the table, followed by a small jug of milk and a sugar bowl, the older woman sat across from her.

"Now, tell me your name, chica."

"Brynn."

"I'm Ruth Santos. May and I own this ranch."

She blinked, recognizing the name. "There was a painting at the bookstore in town. Was that . . . "

Ruth's self-conscious smile was answer enough, and Brynn found herself awed again that the woman who'd painted that piece could be so unaware of her own talent. But isn't that the way she'd felt after winning the art competition in school? Accolades could be showered on an artist and they could still be blind to their skill. Mom had always said that was a good thing, because it would keep her from getting a big head.

Brynn pictured the painting again and how it had unsettled her. She wondered if Jesus had really looked like that. The painting made him seem so . . . human.

"I used to be an artist," Brynn said.

"Really?"

She remembered staying up late at night as a teenager, wondering what her future would hold. Wondering the plan for her life. Back then, she'd even prayed, asking God to show her. She'd thought her future was art. She ate it, drank it, slept it. She could spend an hour trying to get just the right shade of pink mixed up for the petals of a rose bush. The brilliant color of a sunrise might inspire her to paint all weekend. She would still be painting if life hadn't given her a crash course in reality. Art was in her past now, just like Mom.

"What kind of art?" Ruth asked.

"Painting, drawing. Anything I could get my hands on." She pulled up the sleeve of her t-shirt, unveiling a tattoo of the Phoenix on her shoulder. "I designed this."

She'd had it inked the day before Mom found out she was

sick. Brynn let the fabric go and it re-covered the bird. At the time she'd seen the image as a symbol of rising above adversity and becoming the artist she yearned to be. When Mom died, she almost had it removed.

"You're talented," Ruth said.

"I'm not an artist anymore."

Ruth fingered her coffee mug. "I don't really think of myself as an artist. I'm just a rancher who likes to paint when she can. And that's not very often with all the work we've got around here."

Seeing her chance to bring up the reason for her visit, Brynn gathered the nerve to change the subject. "I'm trying to find my father," she said. "I think May might be able to help me."

"Really."

"Her great-aunt, Edna Williams, probably knew him."

Ruth gave her a sympathetic look. "You do know Edna died several years ago."

"That's why I'm here. I'm hoping May knew him, too. His name's Peter Williams, and I think they could be related."

Something changed in Ruth's face. "What makes you think that?"

Brynn reached down and unzipped the inner pocket of her backpack, pulling out *Sense and Sensibility*. She opened to the blank page she thought Christy had called the flyleaf and pointed at the inscription.

"My father gave this to me."

Ruth stood up and retrieved a pair of reading glasses from the counter. Slipping them on, she bent over the book and slowly read the words Brynn's father had penned twenty years ago.

When she was finished, Brynn showed her the address in the back. "I figured since they have the same last name . . ."

Taking off her glasses, Ruth held them in her hand and sat back down. "How old are you, chica?"

"Twenty-four."

Ruth was silent for a moment.

"Has she ever mentioned him?" Brynn asked.

"Why are you trying to find your father?"

Brynn closed the book, not sure how much she wanted to share or why this woman seemed coy all the sudden. "What difference does that make?"

"Would you recognize him in a photo?"

Her insides jumped. "You have one?"

"I think so," Ruth said softly.

She couldn't help the huge smile that came to her face. "Can I see it?"

Without a word, Ruth got up again, leaving Brynn alone. All the years of wondering, all the struggle to even get here. She could hardly believe her questions might finally be answered. Then a new wave of apprehension crashed over her. What was she going to say to him when they met?

Ruth returned, holding a framed picture. She gave it to Brynn. Taking it gingerly in both hands, she stared at the photo of a smiling man and woman standing in front of an RV. A lake was visible in the background, and in front of the couple were two small children, neither older than ten.

"Is this him?" she asked in a whisper.

Ruth nodded.

Brynn stared at the man who's blood she shared. His wavy blond hair was mussed in a boyish way, and some stubble dotted his face. She finally realized where she'd gotten her long nose and the small gap between her front teeth. She couldn't tell the color of his eyes, but she wondered if they were blue like hers.

"You look alike," Ruth said.

She glanced up from the photo. "I . . . I never met him."

"I figured."

"But who are these other people?" Brynn focused on the woman beside her father, noticing how he wrapped his arm around her waist in such a familiar way. And the kids, they had his nose, too. Both also had their father's dimples when they smiled.

"The woman's name was Ellen," Ruth said. "His wife."

Brynn's gaze suddenly shot up to Ruth. *Wife?*

"The girl on the left is Christy. The girl on the right . . ." Ruth touched the glass with her finger. "That's May."

It felt like there was no more oxygen left in the room. Brynn's pulse pounded as she realized what this woman was saying.

Ruth gently rested her hand on Brynn's arm. "Peter Williams was May's father, too."

8

Brynn couldn't take her eyes off the photo. For six years she'd imagined this moment, but she still wasn't prepared for it.

Suddenly she realized Ruth had used the past tense. Brynn glanced into the older woman's compassionate face. Ruth sat down. She folded her hands, and that's when Brynn knew.

"You would've been four or five when he died," Ruth said. "He and Ellen were both killed in a car accident."

Tears she hadn't intended rushed to her eyes. He was dead? She'd come all this way for *nothing*? It hit like a load of cement.

She glanced down at the photograph still clutched between her fingers. The two girls—

Brynn stared at *Sense and Sensibility* sitting on the table before her. There would be no reconciliation, no explanations from the man she'd dreamed about since she was a child.

Ruth reached over and wrapped her fingers around Brynn's. It was a kind, maternal gesture.

"You do look like them," Ruth said.

Brynn took in a deep breath and tried to face this head-on. If this really were true, she had two half sisters who didn't know she existed.

"You mentioned visiting the bookstore in town," Ruth said. "Did you meet Christy?"

Brynn nodded.

"She's May's sister."

Brynn slumped back into her chair.

"And yours too, I suppose." Ruth returned to her coffee, the hint of a smile creeping to her features, though Brynn had no idea why. There was nothing amusing about this.

"How old are they?" she asked.

"May's thirty-four. Christy's three years older."

Brynn held her hand to the back of her neck. Great. So she was the illegitimate child of a jerk. She should've guessed. Maybe that's why Mom would never talk about him.

"I've never even met him," Brynn whispered.

"It sounds like you and May are going to have a lot to talk about."

"And what am I going to say?"

"The truth?"

Sisters were not in her plans. Neither was Dad being dead.

Brynn abruptly stood up. She asked for directions to the bathroom, and excusing herself, she just about ran up the hall toward the first doorway on the left.

Closing herself inside, she locked the door with a curse. How could Mom have done this to her? She had to have known, right? Or had Peter Williams hidden his wife and kids?

For a moment Brynn thought about turning around and walking back down the driveway and out of this family's life. She wasn't here to be a whistleblower on her father's infidelity. She was here to fulfill a promise to her mother, and now she had. But she was her father's flesh and blood. That had to count for something.

She couldn't help that she was instinctively drawn to the medicine cabinet. Brynn quickly opened it, staring at the bottles and silently reading off the labels. Buffered Aspirin. Extra

Strength Tylenol. Band Aids, gauze, iodine, Neosporin. A bottle of rubbing alcohol.

She slammed the cabinet shut and turned the sink on full blast, splashing her flushed cheeks with cold water, hoping it would help her get a grip. She'd come all this way for answers, but her father was dead. She'd never meet him. Never get to ask him why.

It took several minutes before she returned to the kitchen, but when she did, Ruth was rinsing out the coffee pot in the sink, her back to the doorway.

Brynn took a deep breath and crossed the threshold. That was when she decided her next move.

Brynn knelt on the floor and stuffed *Sense and Sensibility* back into her backpack.

"Please don't tell them who I am."

Ruth gave her a questioning look.

"I'm serious."

"I can see that." Opening the dishwasher, Ruth placed her mug inside. "I'm just wondering why."

There were a million reasons, but she couldn't tell any one of them to this Ruth lady. She couldn't explain how much it would hurt to be rejected. These women might actually hate her if they knew who she was. Why wouldn't they?

Brynn felt her shoulders sag. "Do you really think they're my . . . sisters?"

Ruth stared out the window for a moment, then turned back to Brynn. Her eyes were soft. "The pieces do fit."

Before she could say anymore, Brynn heard an engine outside, and the crunching of tires on gravel.

Ruth glanced out the door. "It's May."

"Promise you won't tell her. Not yet."

Ruth answered with a small nod, and Brynn braced herself, knowing one way or another her life was about to change.

When May Williams walked through the kitchen doorway

it was all Brynn could do not to stare, and she suddenly wished she'd cleaned herself up before coming. She needed a shower, washed clothes. Did she look as homeless and pathetic as she felt?

A black-and-white terrier bounded toward Brynn with a bark as May set several plastic bags on the floor. One of them clattered like there was glass in it.

"Scribbles, hush!" May's dark blonde hair was pulled back in a loose ponytail, and several unruly strands had escaped and hung in her face. She smiled, then looked to Ruth, and Brynn saw the question in her eyes about the stranger in the kitchen.

Thankfully, Ruth filled the awkward moment and introduced them to each other.

"Brynn's looking for work," Ruth said, giving her a slight grin.

May stared at her. "What kind of work?"

She thought fast. "Anything, really."

"We're not hiring right now," May said. "But—"

"I'm sure we can find something." Ruth sat down at the table, her focus on May. Would the older woman really keep her word?

"At least for a week or two," Ruth added, waving at the door. "Why don't you let May and I talk for a minute?"

Brynn pleaded with her eyes for the older woman to keep her secret, but Ruth didn't respond either way. Stepping outside with the dog who took off into the nearest corral, Brynn walked toward the green pickup, which hadn't been there when she arrived. This was crazy. She'd lived with hardened criminals for five years and she couldn't deal with two unknown sisters?

Peering inside the pickup, she searched for clues about May. There wasn't much to see. The floorboards were missing mats. The carpet was worn down to the metal and decorated with chunks of dirt and a few ratty strands of hay. A long crack in the windshield spread across most of the passenger's view.

She walked toward the corral where the dog had disappeared. A horse lumbered toward her, swishing its tail against the flies. The whole thing was hard to wrap her mind around. Brynn glanced back at the house, wondering what Ruth was saying. Why not just tell May everything? What was the worst that could happen?

But she couldn't. Not yet. She needed to think this through. If things went poorly, she might never forgive herself for giving up the chance to make a good impression. She had enough going against her.

A door slammed, and she swung around to see May coming toward her.

"Looks like Ruth's set on hiring you whether we need help or not." May headed for the driver's side of the truck. "Like we can afford it," she said under her breath waving at the truck. "Get in."

Brynn hesitated, then obeyed, thankful the old woman had apparently kept her secret. She slammed the door closed. "Where are we going?"

May started the engine and backed the truck up so fast its tires spit gravel. "Got a call from a neighbor. He was up in his ultralight and thought he saw a dead cow in our top pasture."

"Why would there be a—"

"I have no idea. That's why I gotta check it out."

They drove through two gates without another word, and Brynn started to feel uneasy. The truck rattled and bumped through the pastures, May jumping out to open and close gates, some a little more forcefully than needed.

Back in the cab, May glanced her way. "I'm sorry, but I'm really riled up about this."

"Maybe it's not dead."

"We're not the only ones. Last week a guy on the other side of town lost one, too."

"Are they sick?"

"Hardly."

The pickup climbed the ridge. At the top, May stopped and scanned the pasture. A breeze blew through the window bringing the scent of pine . . . and something else. Brynn couldn't help wrinkling her nose.

May grimaced, apparently smelling it herself. She spotted something on the edge of the field and turned the truck in that direction. When they reached the area, Brynn saw what.

A cow-sized mound of brown hide.

Switching off the engine, May got out and marched over to it. Brynn followed, holding her nose at the pungent, dead animal smell.

"It wasn't sick?"

May crouched down beside the carcass and Brynn watched over her shoulder. "No." May pointed at the maggot infested hole in the cow's head. "It was shot."

9

"Shot?"

Brynn's gaze was glued to the carcass. Maggots wriggled where the cow's eyes should've been.

May frowned as she stood and looked around. They were on the edge of a forest of pines. A few feet from the carcass, May picked up a beer can. She squatted again and motioned for Brynn to see. A pile of half-burned logs were surrounded by trampled grass, and another crumpled beer can sat in the midst of the wood.

"Looks like they've been back here more than once," May said. "The road's not that far, and they can hike in."

Brynn wandered around the area, poking at the ground with the toe of her shoe. "You know who it is?"

"Not by name, but we've been having trouble in these parts for a couple months, and now the cattle aren't even safe." May let out a long breath. "Kids partying where they think no one will see . . . . I think some of it's drug related, really. The kids get high 'cause there's nothing better to do, and then things like this happen."

Brynn turned her back on May, wondering what she'd think if she knew Brynn herself could've been one of these trouble-makers a few short years ago. No one ever knew how bad her addiction had gotten. By the time she was hooked, she'd lost any friends who could've helped.

A silvery glint caught her eye in the bushes, and Brynn bent down to see a discarded needle and syringe. "What were they doing? Meth?"

May came and stood beside her. Brynn pointed out the paraphernalia.

"I guess whatever they can get their hands on," May said.

If these kids were doing meth, that could explain their violent behavior. Oxy was a downer and had always had a calming, if not depressing, effect on her, but she'd seen people crazy on meth. "They can make that stuff pretty easy," Brynn said.

May gave her a probing look, and she wished she'd kept her mouth shut.

"What's going on with you, Brynn?" May carefully picked up the syringe. "You don't just land on a doorstep for no reason."

It would be so easy to tell her the truth like Ruth had suggested, but it would also open her up to questions she wasn't ready to answer. May could not find out she'd been in prison.

Brynn glanced over at the woman who could be her older sister and felt something tighten inside. May had lost both of her parents at a younger age than Brynn had lost Mom, yet she'd still made something of herself.

"My Mom died," Brynn said softly.

May stepped closer. The look she gave Brynn in that moment was kind. "Recently?"

"Recent enough." She couldn't look May in the eyes. She knew this wasn't really what May wanted to know, but perhaps it would satisfy her.

May stood over the dead cow one last time, shaking her head. "No matter which way you slice it, death stinks."

Grabbing a plastic bag from the back of her truck, May and Brynn slowly gathered the trash. A few minutes later, they were back in the cab heading for the house.

"We can't offer you much here," May said. "I hope you know that."

"I'm not looking for much."

"And frankly, I don't see the need to hire anyone, but lucky for you, Ruth disagrees. It's two-fifty a week with full room and board. Sound okay?"

"Yeah, that's great actually."

Brynn watched the forest amble by as they slowly drove back. A far cry from their mad dash earlier. "How long have you lived here?"

"Sixteen years."

Which would've made her about eighteen when she started?

"I always dreamed of doing something with horses." A smile crept onto May's face, and Brynn got a good look at her. Her nose and cheeks were tan, but her forehead was three shades lighter, like she wore a hat more often than not. Her fingers had dirt under the nails, and there was a long, faint scar on her cheekbone. Brynn leaned back in her seat and realized she wouldn't mind facing a crisis with May in charge.

They spent the next minute or two lost in their own thoughts, but as they drove through the last gate and May instructed her on how to make sure it was latched properly, the reality of what could be happening hit Brynn again.

"I think I met your sister today at her bookstore."

May drove them into the yard. "Well, then you'll see her again soon. She's coming for dinner tonight."

"She seemed nice."

May chuckled. "Just don't get between her and her books."

Pulling the truck up by the house next to a third pickup, May got out. Brynn did the same. She stood for a moment and took in the whole picture of May and the Triple Cross Ranch. She hadn't been given a choice in knowing her father, but she was being given a choice here.

"Come on," May said, tapping Brynn's shoulder and heading toward the weathered barn. She disappeared inside and returned with a pitchfork. She handed it to Brynn, pointing out a large, round corral.

"So I just . . ."

"Clean out the crap. We've got a manure pile behind the barn. Dump your loads there. I'll be in the house."

Without waiting to hear if she had any questions, May left her alone with nothing but a pitchfork to talk to. It was probably for the best. Maybe the work would help her sort through her thoughts.

Mom obviously hadn't known Peter Williams had died, or she wouldn't have asked Brynn to find him, but Brynn wished Mom had told her more about how she'd been born. What had Mom really known about the man?

Scooping a pile of manure into the wheelbarrow, Brynn paused and stared at the heap. What right did she have to barge in here and expect these two sisters to accept her? They had their own lives, their own troubles. She would only be adding more by tarnishing their father's image.

Brynn sighed, for some reason thinking of the painting in Christy's bookstore. She hadn't given God the time of day since Mom got sick. A god who stood by and let one of his children suffer the way Mom had didn't deserve it. At least that's the way she'd felt back then. Now she wasn't sure what she felt, but it was too late anyway. She could never go back to the closeness she'd felt to God before. He wouldn't want her, and she wasn't a hundred percent convinced she wanted Him.

She dumped another load in the wheelbarrow, and when she glanced up she saw a towering man with a handlebar moustache watching her from the fence. He raised a hand and smiled. Graying, sandy hair stuck out from under his cowboy hat. His black t-shirt sported a faded American flag, and his jeans were faded, too.

"You must be Brynn. I'm Jim. May and Ruth's ranch hand."

They had a ranch hand? Brynn didn't know what to say, realizing this guy might not appreciate someone encroaching on his territory. "I . . . if you don't want me to—"

Jim laughed, thumbing at the pen. "Be my guest."

"Ruth she . . . she thought I could be useful." Even as she said the words they sounded stupid. It was probably obvious to someone like him she wasn't ranch hand material. Jim had to be wondering at the sanity of his boss right about now.

"So she told me."

She couldn't tell if he was laughing at her under that moustache or not. Brynn marched to the corner of the corral and shoved her pitchfork under the nearest pile of manure. She needed a little time to adjust and discover who these women were before she thought about telling them anything.

"So why are you really here?"

She dumped her load in the wheelbarrow and went back for more. "I need a job."

"No car?"

"Hitchhiked."

Another load went in the wheelbarrow. It shook from the force.

"Why this ranch? There are bigger ones than ours."

She risked a glance at his face. She saw no malice, but he was definitely picking up on her desperation. Same as everyone else, apparently.

She hated to lie, but she didn't have a choice here. Brynn rested on her pitchfork. "I just picked a ranch and came out. If you hadn't needed anyone, I would've picked another."

"We *didn't* need anyone."

"Ruth hired me."

Next pile.

Jim stepped into the corral with her, an oversized shovel in hand. "Ruth's a kind soul."

They didn't speak for several moments, both of them working. When the corral was clean, Jim took the wheelbarrow behind the barn for her. The manure pile wasn't as disgusting as she'd pictured. It had begun to dry out, and the breeze took most of the smell away.

"How many horses do you have here?" she asked, trying to direct the conversation away from herself.

"Ten of our own, but May and Ruth have several in for training right now." Jim led her over to a bunch of pens made with movable pole panels on the other side of the barn. As they approached, the horses lifted their heads, and she imagined them wondering who the stranger was.

"We keep 'em separate from our herd, but they can all still see each other."

They came up to a pen where a spotted horse stood in the corner, chewing on a mound of hay.

"This guy's Doc. He just got here."

"What's wrong with him?"

"Almost killed a horse."

She watched the animal carefully. "He doesn't look dangerous."

"We think he'll come around. Owner just gelded him, and that usually makes a big difference."

It took Brynn a moment to figure out what "gelded" meant.

"How well do you know May's sister, Christy?" she asked.

"Pretty well, I guess." Jim parked the wheelbarrow outside the barn's huge sliding door.

"Does she come out here often?"

"Every weekend, and some evenings, too. Like tonight."

She decided she'd quizzed Jim enough and headed toward the house to ask May for her next chore. She'd be meeting Christy again soon enough.

10

Ruth roped Brynn into helping her make dinner that night while May and Jim were outside working on the corral gate.

"Why don't you want them to know?" Ruth asked, checking on the chicken roasting in the oven.

Brynn was cutting up lettuce for the salad at the table, her back turned away. "I just don't. Not yet."

"They would welcome you."

"You don't know that."

Ruth closed the oven door and came over to her. She wore a frayed checkerboard apron over her pudgy torso. "I know those girls. I think you're the one who doesn't know, chica."

"You're going to tell them."

"I promised not to." Ruth sighed. "But I can't say I like it."

She chopped into two carrots at once. What if Ruth was right? She tried to imagine how she would feel if she were May or Christy, but she couldn't even begin to place herself in the Williams sisters' shoes.

"I didn't say I wouldn't tell them ever."

Ruth patted her shoulder. "Just don't wait too long."

A few minutes later, Brynn jumped when the back door opened and she was face to face with Christy. She still wore her short sleeve polo shirt, jeans, and sneakers from earlier today at the bookstore.

Ruth pulled the woman into a big hug. Over her shoulder, Christy caught Brynn's eyes.

"Hey, didn't we . . . " Christy let Ruth go, dropped her purse on a kitchen chair, and pointed from herself to Brynn then back to herself.

"Yeah, small world," Brynn said.

Christy sat down. She definitely looked like an older version of May. "Wow, isn't it? What are you doing here?"

"I . . ."

"She just started working for us," Ruth said, lifting the lid on a pot of rice.

Brynn felt like mouthing "thank you" to Ruth, but instead started chopping up the spring onions. This was too weird. Maybe Ruth was right, and she should tell them tonight.

"Cool." Christy stood up again. "What can I do to help?"

"Go tell your sister and that boyfriend of yours it's time to eat."

Christy smacked Ruth playfully on the shoulder. "He's not my boyfriend."

"Mm-hmm."

Even from here Brynn could see Christy blushing as she walked out the door.

"You're talking about Jim?"

Ruth rested her hands on her hips. "She comes alive whenever she sees him. And after what that woman's been through, it's good to see her smile again."

Brynn dumped the onions into the salad bowl, hoping her next question wouldn't sound too nosy. "What's she been through?"

Pulling a loaf of French bread from a paper bag on the counter, Ruth began wrapping it in foil. "She was engaged to the manager of the bookstore where she used to work. Up in

Longmont. They were good together, and he was a kind man. But about two years ago he was murdered in a robbery at the store."

"You're kidding."

"It hit her hard. She and Jim were friends before she was engaged, but a couple months after Hunter's death, their friendship started to become something more."

Smiling, Ruth slipped the bread into the oven and removed the chicken. "I don't think either of them have quite admitted it to themselves, but I can see."

Brynn popped a carrot slice into her mouth and chewed for a few seconds. "What about you? Were you ever married?"

The older woman looked off into space, a smile on her lips. "My Luis and I shared many wonderful years together on this ranch. We began it with our bare hands and our sweat, but I finished it with my tears. He died doing what he loved a couple years before May arrived."

They worked quietly until May, Jim, and Christy barged through the back door and the heaviness instantly lifted. One glance at Christy's face, and Brynn knew Ruth was right about her and Jim. She wondered how May felt about her ranch hand falling in love with her sister.

"Something smells g-o-o-o-d," Jim said, reaching for the chicken still in the roasting pan.

Ruth batted his hand away with a hot pad. "Sit, sit. You'll eat it soon enough."

A few minutes later, they were all at the table, Brynn and May on one side, Christy and Jim across from them with Ruth at the head. The older woman folded her hands, and everyone else followed suit. Brynn resisted, but finally decided she wanted to fit in here.

"Lord, thank you for this food," Ruth said. "We appreciate the opportunity to share it together and ask that you bless it. Thank you for everything You've given us. Amen."

The others echoed her amen and dove into the spread. Besides the roast chicken, salad, bread and Spanish rice, Ruth had prepared a delicious looking dish of black beans, garlic and onions.

Brynn filled her plate with as much as she could without looking like a pig. It had been years since she'd had a home cooked meal like this.

For a little while, everyone just ate. The only sounds were the clink of silverware and chewing, but then Christy gave her a nod. "So what brings you to Elk Valley?"

Brynn glanced at Ruth who just smiled at her.

"I'm kinda in between things," Brynn said. "And I needed a job."

"Ruth hired her," May said, pointing with her knife. The frustration she'd exhibited earlier in the truck seemed to have diminished. Brynn was relieved that her irritation must have been directed at the trespassers than at having a new ranch hand.

To Christy's credit, she didn't ask Brynn to elaborate, but she knew everyone was wondering about her. She'd come with next to nothing. No car, nowhere to stay. There were only so many conclusions you could draw.

"So, Ruth tells me you're an artist," May said.

"Was."

Another smile from Ruth. "That kind of talent doesn't just go away."

It does if your cheerleader dies.

Brynn shrugged. "It was a phase."

"Show them your tattoo," Ruth said, buttering a piece of French bread.

She shot a look at the older woman, but Ruth either didn't get it or was ignoring it. Ruth couldn't understand what the drawing symbolized for her. With a sigh, Brynn pulled up her sleeve and quickly showed them the Phoenix. She just as quickly covered it back up.

"She designed it," Ruth said.

"You might not believe this." May elbowed Brynn. "But I was really close to getting one myself back when I was a teen."

Christy laughed. "You almost got a tattoo?"

"Had it all picked out and everything."

"Of what?"

"A horse. What else?"

Everyone laughed, but Brynn focused on eating. If she told them who she was now, what would happen? How would they react? She almost did it again, blurted out the truth and waited for them to respond, but then they started talking about Christy's bookstore and the challenges she faced, barely making ends meet.

"I wish I could hire someone to help me." Christy took a sip from her water glass. "If my sister here ever gets annoying, look me up, Brynn."

Jim sent a wink her way. "Because we all know how May runs her help into the ground."

"Hey, watch it," May said.

"Seriously." Christy wiped her mouth. "I've got a big book sale coming up, and I really need extra hands."

Brynn cut a piece of chicken and popped it into her mouth. "Book sale?"

"Yeah, they're a trip," May muttered.

"This one's up in Pueblo," Christy said. "It's one of the largest around. I'm hoping it'll be a good shot in the arm for my inventory."

May leaned toward Brynn and whispered loud enough for everyone to hear, "In case you didn't notice, she's a little cuckoo about books."

Brynn let herself smile.

"Speaking of," Christy nodded at her sister. "You promised you'd show me those books you found."

"Okay, okay. I'll get them now."

Jim waved a chicken wing at May's retreating back. "What books?"

"They're from our father. May's had them packed away." Christy raised her voice loud enough for May to hear. "Apparently she didn't think to mention it to me until last week."

Brynn could barely chew the piece of lettuce she'd just put in her mouth. What was Christy talking about? When May returned, she placed two books on the table in front of Christy.

"I forgot I had them," May said, then explained how after their parents died she'd pretty much just packed up everything that reminded her of them in boxes, sealed them up, and left them alone. When she'd moved out to the ranch, she'd brought the boxes with her and stuck them in the attic. Last week, she'd rediscovered them when Ruth asked her to bring down an old kitchen chair after one of the new ones broke.

"How can you *forget* something like that?" Christy teased.

"Hey, I'm not a bibliophile like you."

Christy sighed, but she was grinning at her sister.

The food that only minutes earlier had made her stomach growl held no interest for Brynn now. Her eyes were fastened to the books with the blue/gray covers. Those faded pink labels. The black lettering . . .

Brynn didn't have to read them to know what they said. *Sense and Sensibility.* Only instead of the number "3" as appeared on hers, these were 1 and 2.

"You didn't find them until after they died?" Christy asked.

May talked with her mouth full, gesturing with her fork. "Aunt Edna and I were going through Dad's desk. We found them in a drawer."

Aunt Edna. Edna Williams?

Brynn threw a worried glance at Ruth, but the woman was focused on Christy, who picked up the first book and opened it.

Christy started to read something. When she finished, she was teary. "Wow," she said, looking across the table at May, who blinked fast a couple times, too. "Why didn't he give them to us?"

"Maybe he was going to."

"What do they say?" Brynn asked in as casual a voice as she could.

Christy turned the book toward her and held it out. Leaning across the table, Brynn saw an inscription like the one in her own.

To my daughter Christy,
You are my prima donna, my first born. I will hold you in my heart forever. I love you very much, even if I've made mistakes. Your Great-Aunt Edna thought you especially would appreciate this book. I think so, too.
Love, Dad

"There's also one in mine," May said, picking up the other book and paging through it. Brynn could just see it over her arm.

To my daughter May,
You've grown up so much and have such a bright future! I hope you know I have always loved you. And no matter what happens, I always will. I hope you'll like this little gift. Your Great-Aunt Edna thought it was perfect, and I agree.
Love, Dad

With weak fingers, Brynn lifted her spoon. The handwriting was exactly the same. She'd read her father's words enough times in the past week alone to spot it instantly.

Brynn tried to focus on the meal again in the hopes that the Williams sisters wouldn't see how shaken she was. These women really were her sisters, weren't they?

She watched Christy turning the pages of her book, examining the volume with the care and precision of a museum curator, flipping through a few pages, then turning the book around first one way, then the other. Brynn calculated that Christy would've been eleven when she was born.

"Do you know what this is?" Christy asked. She and May exchanged books, and Christy began examining May's volume the same way she had hers.

"Jane Austen," May said. "I'm not a complete idiot."

"But not just any Austen. It was her first published novel." Christy turned the book out and pointed at the date. "1811. That's the year of the first edition, which is what I think these are."

May pushed aside her own plate and reached for the other volume again. "Are they rare?"

Brynn took a bite of rice and tried not to look at May. A longing hit Brynn for what she'd missed. She'd spent so much time alone. If she'd had sisters to look out for her and teach her things when Mom couldn't, what would her life have been like?

"Um, yeah." Christy stacked the books on top of each other. "Too bad we're missing the third volume."

Ruth caught Brynn's eye, but she looked away.

"Maybe Aunt Edna never had it," May said.

Christy shrugged, unable to take her focus off the books. She kept paging through them, even sniffing the pages. May laughed when she did.

"There's nothing like that smell," Christy said.

Jim and Ruth laughed too, and Brynn tried to echo them, but nothing came to her lips. They had no idea. She could sense it. Somehow their father had kept his illegitimate child a secret, and if Brynn told them now, she'd be changing their lives forever.

11

The futon in the office was comfortable, but Brynn still woke up at two-thirty. She was just starting to drift off again when someone shuffled down the hall to the kitchen. Ruth?

Brynn had left the office door open a crack. Since the house was small and the office was near the kitchen she was able to hear the sounds of a cabinet opening and a mug tapping the counter. Water ran, and another cabinet opened. She lifted herself up on an elbow. Was Ruth making coffee at this hour? In a moment the telltale dripping and gurgling confirmed it.

Falling back onto her pillow, she listened until it crescendoed, then stopped. The cabinet opened again and something popped. At first Brynn couldn't place the familiar sound, but then she recognized the muted clattering noise as someone popping off the lid and then tapping pills from a bottle.

Brynn listened as the cabinet closed and Ruth poured a cup of the freshly brewed coffee. Then the back door clicked open and all was silent again.

She tossed away her blankets, slipped on her sneakers without socks, and tiptoed into the kitchen. Just as she thought, it was empty.

Curiosity got the better of her, and she was about to follow Ruth out the door when her gaze drifted to the cabinets. As she passed them, she quickly opened the nearest and peeked in. Staring back at her on the first shelf were two orange prescription bottles next to the dinner plates. She examined the labels in the dim light. The first bottle contained Losartan, a common blood pressure medicine. The second was a nearly full bottle of Percocet. Brynn quickly closed the cabinet and went out the door.

Ruth hadn't turned on the porch light. Brynn took a few steps into the darkness and then stood still and listened. The light from the barn illuminated the yard, and she caught sight of Ruth's form slowly walking around the back of the huge structure. Brynn followed her.

It didn't take long for her to wish she'd thrown a long sleeve shirt over her t-shirt and sweatpants. The chilly air brushed her bare arms, quickly erasing the memory of the afternoon's heat.

Brynn lifted her gaze to the startling display overhead, wishing she knew more constellations than the Big Dipper. But not knowing their names didn't detract from their magnificence. Even with the half moon, they shone titanium white on a black velvet background. She paused at the end of the yard, wondering what it would be like to pull out a set of paints and try to capture them.

Her sneakers crunched in the dirt as she peeked around the corner of the barn.

"Have a seat, if you'd like."

Even at a whisper, Ruth's voice from the shadows startled her. With effort, she could barely see the woman sitting on something, she couldn't tell what from here, up against the side of the barn. Brynn took a few hesitant steps. "If you want to be alone . . ."

"I wouldn't have invited you if I did."

She walked over to the old woman, and Ruth patted a

bucket beside her. Carefully sitting down, Brynn rested her elbows on her knees.

"I couldn't sleep," Ruth said. "My back's been acting up."

Which explained the pain pills.

The moon painted everything a bluish hue, its light illuminating the forms of several still horses in the corral, and beyond that . . . beyond that was a sight Brynn wouldn't soon forget. The mountains, in all their splendor, stretched up into that black velvet. Moonlight reflected off every crag in the rocks that still held a few handfuls of snow.

"How long does the snow stay up there?" She kept her voice low. To speak any louder seemed irreverent.

"Usually gone by now." Ruth brought a mug to her lips, and steam drifted up around her face.

They both sat in silence. Should she have spoken up tonight? She wasn't sure. That could've broken the friendship she'd barely begun to forge with the Williams sisters.

"What's holding you back?" Ruth whispered.

"I'm not sure."

"I think they'll surprise you."

"Their lives are already complicated."

"They need to know."

"I don't want to ruin their memory of their dad." Brynn wrapped her arms around herself, trying to ward off more than the cold air. She couldn't shake the feeling she'd be nothing but a burden here. And that was without them knowing she'd been in jail.

Ruth set down her coffee cup and slipped off her sweater. Before Brynn could stop her, she draped it over her back.

"I'm plenty warm, chica."

It was a kind gesture from a sweet, old woman who was cutting her a break she didn't deserve. Brynn felt her throat tighten.

"My mother didn't tell me he had another family."

"Does she know you're here?"

"She's been dead for years." And before she knew it, she was telling Ruth about that last night in the hospital. "She asked me to find him. It was the last thing she said to me."

Ruth gently rested her hand on Brynn's shoulder.

"I promised her I would." Brynn hated to cry in front of a stranger, but just like they'd fallen in that hospital room, the tears came spilling from her eyes without her permission. Her next words came out low and broken. "But I didn't. If only I had."

"You were just a child."

"I was old enough." Brynn stared up at the mountains, swiping at her eyes.

"And now you don't have anywhere else to go."

"Yeah."

"What happened?"

She could easily lie. It was a familiar habit, but for some reason she didn't want to lie to Ruth. She'd been to enough prison-sponsored counseling sessions to realize she had major trust issues, and she knew if she couldn't break down that barrier and start trusting people again, she'd never live a normal life. If anyone deserved to know the truth it was Ruth, but she just couldn't bring herself to tell the old woman she was a girl with a record. She might pass it on to May or Christy, and Brynn would immediately be labeled, always having to prove she wasn't the same person who'd landed in the back of that police car six years ago.

"It's complicated," Brynn finally said, leaning against the barn. She'd never thought herself capable of any of the stupid things she'd done after mom died. She was a good Christian girl who'd grown up in a stable, single parent home. Mom had tried her best, and somehow they'd always had enough. Sure, there weren't fancy vacations or designer clothes. Brynn hadn't cared about those sort of things, anyway. She'd been as happy to shop in the thrift store for a vintage look and save her allowance money to buy new canvases. She never expected to get hooked on those pills.

Ruth stared off at the moonlit mountains. "You know something? The past is the past. It's best kept there. Give the girls a chance."

"Yeah, and how do you think that'll go? Oh, by the way, your dad knocked up my mom, and here I am."

The old woman smiled. "Brynn, I'm seventy-four years old. I've seen just about everything you can imagine. Good and bad. Christy and May are part of the good."

But I'm not.

"They've been through their own troubles," Ruth said. "They can handle your story. They know their father wasn't perfect, and I don't imagine this'll surprise them as much as you think."

"You haven't heard everything," Brynn said softly.

Ruth lifted her mug to her lips, taking a long sip. "If you want to tell me more, I'll listen."

Shame held her tongue. This old woman may think she'd seen everything, but she had no idea what it felt like to steal from your friends to feed your habit or to face the demon of withdrawal in a prison cell.

"I should probably go inside," Brynn said, climbing to her feet.

"Chica, you haven't done anything God can't forgive."

Brynn didn't say what she thought about that. Forgiveness was for people like the woman she'd met in lock-up who'd accidentally punched the gas rather than the brake in a grocery store parking lot and hit a man. Not for someone who repeatedly chose the wrong path. She'd walked away from God and never looked back. No one could forgive that.

Ruth reached up and took her hand, squeezing it. She said nothing more. Brynn left her sitting behind the barn. Later, after Ruth came back inside and shuffled again down the hall to her bedroom, Brynn lay wide awake, unable to forget the image of those prescription bottles in the cabinet.

12

Roxi woke with a jolt. The only light came from the moon outside her window, painting everything in the bedroom an eerie blue.

Her room. It still seemed strange to call it that.

She rested her hand on Selah, sound asleep under the covers. Rolling onto her side, Roxi tried to drift off again. The nightmares didn't come as often as they used to, but they still came, and it was usually an hour-long struggle for her to get back to sleep. Tonight she decided not to bother.

Pulling a hoodie over her pajamas, Roxi opened her bedroom door and tiptoed out into the hall. Selah leapt out of bed and followed her. They crept down the stairs, and she carefully let them both out the front door. Outside on the porch swing, she sat with her knees to her chest and Selah at her feet. She'd tried once to get Selah to cuddle up with her on the seat, but the swinging movement had scared the dog silly and Selah would have none of it now.

It was colder out here than Roxi expected, but she didn't move to get a coat. She stared up at the stars and felt like a speck of dirt. In the whole universe, that's what she really was, right?

She wasn't sure how long she sat there before she heard movement inside the house. The porch light flicked on, and Roxi squinted at the sudden brightness. Then it flipped off, and the door creaked open.

"What are you doing out here?" Jan stepped onto the porch, tying off her flannel bathrobe.

"I tried to be quiet."

Jan sat down on the porch swing beside her, wrapping her arm around Roxi. She smelled faintly of peppermint soap, and Roxi leaned into her.

"It's so good to have you back," Jan whispered.

Roxi hung onto her words. Jan's calm presence always made her feel safe and loved. She'd missed her so much the two years she'd been at camp, and she'd lived for her and Keith's weekly visits. Back then, she used to wonder if Jan and Keith ever regretted taking her in and giving her the first real home she'd ever had.

"What're you thinking about?" Jan rocked the swing with her foot, the rusty chains scratching out a steady rhythm.

"Nothing really."

"That's why you're sitting out here by yourself in the middle of the night?"

She managed a smile. Jan always saw through her, just like a mother would.

"I bet when Trae was my age he had dreams. He knew who he wanted to be."

Jan pulled her bathrobe tighter around herself. Trae was the son they'd lost in a tragic accident seven years ago. He'd only been seventeen, but even at that age, he had grand plans to start an outfitter business on the ranch property.

"I've never had any dreams," Roxi said.

"You love books."

"I used to."

"Not anymore?"

Roxi stood up from the swing and leaned against one of the porch supports. "Christy asked me to help her at a book sale, but I said no. It didn't feel right. Not after what happened to Hunter. Except that means I have no idea what to do with myself."

Jan got up and stood with her. "Sweetheart, look at me."

She did, and in the moonlight, the woman's face was full of love and acceptance.

"You're still so young," Jan said. "God totally has a plan for you. But he doesn't always give you the whole picture all at once. There's plenty of time to figure this out, but there are only so many hours in the night."

Which reminded Roxi just how tired she was.

"Come on," Jan whispered, guiding her inside. Upstairs and in her bedroom again, Roxi climbed under the covers with Selah. Jan pulled them to Roxi's chin as if she were a little girl, and Roxi didn't mind letting her.

"I'll be right back."

She listened to Jan walk down the hallway toward her own bedroom and open the door. It squeaked, and then there was nothing. Like there should be at two in the morning. When Jan returned, she brought a book and a flashlight.

"Close your eyes," Jan said, shutting the bedroom door and pulling a chair up to her bedside.

"But you're tired too, and—"

"I'm fine, honey. Just rest."

The flashlight clicked on, and pages rustled. She knew the book was Jan's Bible. She and Keith read from it every day around the breakfast table.

Her voice soft, Jan began to read. "For God so loved the world that he gave his one and only Son, that whoever believes in him shall not perish but have eternal life."

The words hung in the air for a moment. "For God did not send his Son into the world to condemn the world, but to save the world through him. Whoever believes in him is not condemned."

Roxi felt the muscles in her back loosen. She never minded when Jan read from the Bible, and for some reason, it always intrigued her. She'd never even owned a Bible before Jan and Keith, much less read one. But there was something about the verses. Or maybe it was the way they rolled off Jan's tongue— sacred, yet familiar. Much loved. The reverence Jan had for the Bible made Roxi want to listen. She didn't understand half of it, but it always seemed to calm her worries.

Jan turned a few pages and continued, "You see, at just the right time, when we were still powerless, Christ died for the ungodly. Very rarely will anyone die for a righteous man, though for a good man someone might possibly dare to die. But God demonstrates his own love for us in this: While we were still sinners, Christ died for us."

Roxi kept her eyes closed and listened. Before she knew it, her senses dulled and Jan's voice came from the other end of a tunnel. But even as her mind screen went black and she vaguely realized her body was falling asleep, she still drank in Jan's voice calmly reading the words she wanted so much to be true.

13

It seemed like she'd just fallen asleep again when Brynn heard more movement down the hall. Through the gap in the office door she saw a slim figure creep toward the kitchen, holding boots in her hands. The hints of dawn in the sky out the window told her that May wasn't battling insomnia or pain like Ruth, but she was actually getting up to start her day.

Brynn groaned and draped her arm over her eyes. She knew trying to get back to sleep this time would be futile. She was wide awake. Waiting until she heard the coffee maker gurgling for the second time in the past four hours, she stumbled into the kitchen, still in her sweat pants.

Already fully dressed in her work clothes, May was pulling a box of cereal from the cupboard. When she saw Brynn she sighed. "I didn't wake you, did I?"

"I was up anyway."

May held out a box of Raisin Bran. "I'm not much of a cook."

"Neither am I." The last meal she'd made was a ramen noodle goulash using hot water from her cell's sink.

Together they sat at the kitchen table and poured flakes into their bowls, then doused them with milk. She wondered what it would've been like to grow up with May. Would they have sat at a kitchen table like this as kids?

"I know you weren't planning on hiring anyone," Brynn said softly.

"Yeah . . ." May pulled up a mound of flakes with her spoon. "I gotta say I don't know how long we'll be able to afford another ranch hand. But Ruth thinks we should make a go of it."

"And you don't."

May shrugged. "We're better off now than we were a couple years ago, but I guess I'm still nervous about over spending. I mean, we almost lost this place to the bank twice."

"Really?"

Crunching her cereal, May nodded. "When I first started working for Ruth I was younger than you, and I didn't realize how much she was struggling financially. My parents' life insurance money rescued us. That's how I became a partner. Then four years ago it happened again. We got so behind on the payments we were just weeks away from foreclosure. If it weren't for my great-aunt Edna's inheritance we would've gone under for sure."

Edna Williams. Brynn could see the name emblazoned on the inside back cover of *Sense and Sensibility.* Edna would've been her great-aunt, too.

"She died around that time and left Chris and me everything," May said. "My share wasn't enough, but Chris gave me hers, too, so I could save this place. And now she's barely making ends meet herself."

"She wasn't kidding then about things being tight?"

"No she wasn't, and I hate that I can't do a thing to help her."

Brynn went back to munching her breakfast. May was being nice, but her presence here was clearly an inconvenience. Telling the truth about their blood ties wouldn't help that. They'd think she was a mooch. What if May thought she was here to claim part of her father's, or even Aunt Edna's, already-spent inheritance?

"Did Christy live with your great-aunt too?"

Setting down her spoon, May didn't answer immediately, and Brynn hoped it wasn't too personal a question.

"You know, I think Chris would be better at telling that story, but no. She was eighteen and really hurting when Mom and Dad died. She basically ran away at that time, and I couldn't find her for years." May gave Brynn a slight smile. "It's water under the bridge now, but there were a lot of hurt feelings on both our parts. What matters these days is we're making up for lost time."

. . .*eighteen and really hurting* . . . What did that mean?

"How 'bout you? Any siblings?" May asked.

Something inside Brynn jumped at the question. This was the opening she'd hoped for last night. It was just the two of them here in the quiet of the kitchen.

But as she looked into May's face, she saw it was just a friendly question, something May would've asked anyone. If Brynn told the truth, May would only have something else to deal with.

She shook her head. "I've been alone ever since Mom died."

"What kind of jobs have you had before this?"

"I used to work at an art gallery."

"Right. I forgot you're an artist."

"Was."

"Ever thought about picking it up again?"

"Sometimes."

"Why wouldn't you?"

"It would never be the same."

"Maybe it doesn't have to be."

"My mom. She was my cheerleader."

"And she would've wanted you to give it up?"

Brynn stared into her cereal bowl. "It doesn't matter what she'd want anymore."

"You think? I still ask myself what my parents would think of me now," May said.

"I bet they'd be proud."

May shrugged, drinking the last of her milk straight from the cereal bowl. "Dad was pretty set on both his girls going to college, and neither of us did."

The mention of her dad–their dad–caught in Brynn's throat. He would've been ashamed of her.

"I never knew my dad," Brynn said. "I wish I had."

"Yeah, there's something in every girl that needs a daddy."

"What was yours like?" She asked the question as casually as she could, but she felt like she'd screamed it. She pictured Peter Williams in the photo Ruth showed her.

May smiled. "When I was little, we had some fun times. I remember him playing outside with me in the dirt and teaching me how to ride a bike. The stories he told me about growing up on a farm are probably where I got the dream to have horses."

"He didn't grow up out here?"

"Back east, actually. He lived on a farm in Pennsylvania and went to college in Denver where he met Mom."

More questions were on the tip of her tongue. How did they meet? Was it love at first sight? How long after that did Christy come along? What caused him to become unfaithful?

"Dad went into the Marines after college," May added. "Later he was an engineer, but I don't think he was very happy. He went to college on a basketball scholarship, then blew out his knee." May snapped her fingers. "In one instant, his dreams were torn away from him and he had to work nights to get himself through school."

May stood and took her bowl to the sink. "When they died, I felt like the floor was jerked out from under me. How old were you when your mom passed?"

"Seventeen." Brynn got up and set her bowl in the sink beside May's.

"No other family?"

"I went to live with some girlfriends."

Those same friends were the ones who later kicked her out when they discovered she'd stolen money from them. With nowhere to go, she'd ended up living at a campground. Then she'd lost her job at the art gallery.

"One thing about Dad I'll never forget," May said. "If he said he'd do something, he would. Never once did I hear him lie. Even if it hurt, he told the truth. If I could take one thing from him, it would be that."

Brynn couldn't look at May as the woman gulped down her mug of coffee.

May nodded at the door. "Ready to work?"

"That's why I'm here."

"Hurry and get dressed," May said. "We've got a full day."

A few minutes later, the pair headed out to the barn, Brynn still rubbing the sleep out of her eyes and trying not to think about May's belief in her father's honesty. Her very existence proved otherwise, but how could she possibly tell that to May? She glanced over at her. They were both about the same height with similar dark blonde hair. In prison, Brynn had kept hers cut short to make it more manageable, but she'd recently let it grow longer, and now it fell to her shoulders like May's.

May set her to work in the tack room cleaning five different saddles, then headed outside with a halter and lead. Soon Brynn heard hooves clopping on the barn's wooden floor.

Brynn leaned out into the aisle of the barn to see May leading that spotted horse she'd seen watched Jim. The horse turned his head to look at Brynn as she stepped closer, his ears erect and listening.

"Wow," Brynn said.

"His name's Doc." May rubbed him on his neck, the lead rope draped across her arm.

Brynn hesitated to approach, remembering what Jim had said about him, but May waved her over. Brynn reached out and touched his warm, spotted side.

"Do you ride?" May asked.

She shook her head. Another check mark against hiring the new girl.

"We'll get you on one soon."

May tied the lead rope to a hook in the wall and pulled a rubber circular brush from a box near her feet. She began currying Doc's coat in a circular motion.

"Did he really try to kill another horse?"

"That's what I hear."

"What happened?"

"He was a stallion until just a short time ago. All those hormones can make a horse do crazy things." May gave a little smirk. "People, too, for that matter, but anyway, he got moved to a pasture where he could see some mares, and someone put a gelding in with him. Apparently, Doc didn't feel like sharing. He would've run him to death if Craig hadn't managed to separate them."

May kept brushing, a cloud of dust rising from the horse. "Brynn, I'm guessing there's more going on with you than you're telling."

She tried to laugh off the comment. "A girl's gotta have some secrets."

May worked her brush down Doc's neck. She reached a spot underneath his mane that caused him to lean into her touch, his lips flapping, and May chuckled at him. The only sound was the rhythmic scratching of the brush against horseflesh. Brynn considered telling May something to satisfy her curiosity.

"I don't have anywhere to live right now," she said.

"Why's that?"

"Does it matter?"

May straightened and faced Brynn, the brush at her side. "As of yesterday, you're living under my roof. I think it does."

Before Brynn could answer, they heard tires in the gravel outside. Doc's ears immediately turned toward the door, but he remained still.

"You expecting someone?"

"Nope," May said.

Brynn peeked out the barn door. It was Christy. She waved when she saw Brynn. "Good morning!"

Christy walked into the barn sipping from an insulated mug.

"Everything okay?" May started her brushing routine again, this time on the other side of Doc.

Christy sighed. "Sort of."

"Uh-oh."

"Right, so last night after I left here I decided to head up and check on that book sale I was telling you about, and they'd already put out numbers."

May frowned. "But it doesn't start until tomorrow."

"I know." Christy sighed again and ran her fingers through her hair. "It's gotten worse even since you came with me. Now they're lining up days ahead of time."

Brynn stepped toward the sisters. "For a book sale?"

"Crazy, I know." Christy reached into her pocket and pulled out two small pieces of paper with the numbers 4 and 5 written on them in black marker. "I don't know which dealer put these out."

Christy explained how dealers often set out a stack of numbers at a sale to determine the order of the line. "But it still doesn't always ensure your place," she said. "Which is what kills me at a lot of these sales. I can't possibly keep my store open *and* line up two days in advance. But if I don't buy new stock, I can't stay in business."

"So why aren't you up there now?" May finished brushing Doc's rump, dumped the curry into the box and grabbed a different brush with bristles.

"I'm here to beg."

May laughed.

Brynn knew what she was hinting. "You need help."

"Totally."

"Jim could go," May suggested, with a wry smile. "It would give you some nice quality time."

"He's helping out at church and can't get out of it."

"I can go," Brynn said. "If May doesn't need me."

May kept brushing.

"I was hoping," Christy said.

With an upraised hand, May gave her approval. "Just don't expect to get any rest tonight. Last time she dragged me along to one of those things we had to sleep in the car."

"When do I need to be ready?"

"Now," Christy said.

14

May mounted Doc, opening and closing the gate on horse-back. She was pleased at how responsive he was, moving with the slightest leg pressure and next to nothing from her reins. She wished she'd asked Craig how much training he'd had.

Once they were out in the pasture away from the other horses, Doc let out a whinny, and she felt his body tense.

"Easy, boy." May urged him into a trot with a squeeze of her thighs and a click of her tongue. He immediately moved right into a faster gait than she wanted, but she let him go with it. There was no better way to get his attention than a little work. Trotting him in circles for the next ten minutes, she finally asked him for a stop when she knew he was listening to her.

"There you go." May scratched him on the withers and stroked his neck. Praise was an important and often neglected part of horse training. She didn't use many words, but her hands told him he'd done well.

Breathing faster from the exertion, Doc stood still.

"Bet you haven't worked like that in a long time, huh?"

They rode at a walk for about a half mile before she urged him into a slow trot again with a slight squeeze of her legs.

Riding the fence was one of her favorite ranch chores. It gave her lots of time to think, and she often took horses she was training out with her. They usually responded well when they knew they had a job to do.

Spotting a gap in the fencing, she dismounted and undid the lead rope she'd tied loosely around Doc's neck. He seemed content to just stand still after his workout, and she pulled out her pliers and gloves to fix the break. Craig would've probably had a cow if he knew she'd foregone the harsh bit and tie-down he'd given her for Doc and instead bridled him with a simple snaffle.

May spliced the wires together again, her mind wandering to Brynn. What was Ruth thinking hiring that girl? They'd seen what a mistake that was with Shane, and now they were taking on a novice who was barely capable of cleaning the corrals.

Job finished, she mounted Doc again and kept her eyes on the fence. There just wasn't enough work to support four of them indefinitely, but she had to admit there was something about Brynn that intrigued her. Maybe Christy would get to the bottom of it. She was so tuned to the fence, she didn't see the horse approaching from the trees. But Doc did. His ears immediately perked, and the whinny he sent through the air made her jump. She followed his gaze and saw a young woman on horseback approaching at a bumpy trot.

May waved, and the rider waved back. Hands resting on her saddle horn, May watched them approach. As they got closer, she recognized the rider as Roxi Gold, the girl the Mercers had taken in two years ago. She was bouncing all over the place, but she was beaming.

"Hey there," May said.

Roxi waved again and brought her horse to an awkward stop across from May on the other side of the fence. She was still relying too heavily on her reins, but she seemed relaxed in the saddle.

And that's when the calm horse May had been riding earlier turned into the just-gelded-stallion Craig had brought for rehabilitation. Doc raised his head and neck, staring at the new horse. He snorted and leapt sideways.

"Let me guess?" May called to Roxi. "A mare?"

"Um . . . yeah. Her name's Sally."

Luckily, Sally was unfazed by Doc's outburst and stood like a statue on the other side of the fence, even lowering her head and eyes like she was falling asleep.

"Want me to leave?" Roxi asked.

"Nope. Stay right there. This guy's gotta learn."

May quickly sunk in her saddle, and cued Doc to back up with her reins and legs. He flung his head up to avoid the small amount of pressure, but she didn't release until he took a step back. By backing him, he'd have to start thinking again, and hopefully thinking would calm him down.

"What brings you way out here?" May asked, giving Doc a chance to stand still. When he carried on again, she backed him up once more, this time asking for several extra steps.

"Needed to clear my head," Roxi said.

"Riding's great for that." May noted how much Roxi had grown up. The last time she'd seen her was at the courthouse as a broken sixteen-year-old. The teen had become entwined in all of their lives when she'd witnessed the accidental shooting of Christy's fiancé.

Some would say two years in a camp for troubled youth was cutting Roxi too much slack. After all, she'd been breaking into the bookstore when it happened. But May and Christy both knew Roxi had just been caught up in something way bigger than she could handle. None of it was really her fault. As hard as it was, Chris had forgiven her, and May had, too.

"What are you doing?" Roxi asked when May brought Doc up closer to Roxi's mare again. This time he stood without reacting for a good ten seconds before she had to start backing him.

She explained her methods and thought she saw Roxi's mouth gape a little in awe.

"Doesn't Jan train?" May let Doc rest for a moment.

Roxi shrugged. "Not since Trae died. But wow, you're good."

Chuckling, May glanced down the fence line. "I don't know about that."

"Could I come watch you sometime?"

May hesitated for a second, not sure how Christy would feel if Roxi started hanging around the property. "Sure. Stop in anytime."

❧

"You should've told me you had donuts." Brynn took a huge bite of a cream-filled delicacy, then washed it down with a swish of the coffee Christy had poured her from the thermos, now rolling around on the Honda's floorboards.

Christy laughed. "If I'd known you liked them this much I would have."

"Haven't had one in years."

"Eat as many as you like."

She took a second from the bag, setting the box on the back seat to keep from being tempted. Bulking up on sugar and carbs probably wasn't a good idea, but she hadn't remembered a donut ever tasting so good.

Brynn wiped her mouth, hoping powdered sugar wasn't sticking to her lips. "So, what's the deal with this book sale thing?"

"Thanks again for coming, by the way." Christy turned onto the freeway. "I can pay you fifty bucks and as many donuts as you can eat. I know that's not much, but–"

"Throw in a pizza and I'm set." She was only half joking.

Christy laughed again. "Deal."

For the next few miles, Christy explained that this sale was one of the largest in the area. "Over a hundred thousand books," Christy said. "There are gonna be a ton of dealers."

"Like you."

"Even crazier than me."

When they pulled into the Ag arena parking lot, the sun was beating down on them, and Brynn peeled off her sweatshirt. She walked with Christy to the front doors. Several cardboard boxes and beat up lawn chairs lined the sidewalk.

She pointed at them. "What are these for?"

"To mark places."

"But I thought you had numbers."

Christy smirked. "Sometimes someone will decide to challenge the numbers."

Brynn eyed the boxes and chairs while Christy checked inside a small Maxwell House coffee can sitting on the pavement by the doors.

"They're already up to 42 here," Christy said.

"What about people who arrive tomorrow?"

"By then all the dealers will be here. They'll have to go to the back of the line." Christy pointed at a Postal Service bin at the front of the line. "This guy is my biggest competitor."

"Number four and five isn't too shabby."

"If the wrong person's ahead of you, and gets to your section first, they can clean out, which is why I try to be as far up the line as possible."

"All this . . ." Brynn waved at the building. "For a bunch of old books?"

"I know."

Tapping at the Postal bin, Brynn remembered the empty shelves in Christy's shop and May's words about her barely making it. "Does he own a bookstore, too?"

"No, he's online."

"Aren't you?"

"Some." Christy took a deep breath and walked down the

queue. Places were marked with bags, some with boxes, one with chairs chained together. "It's the way everyone seems to go eventually, but I've dreamed about having my own real, bricks and mortar store for years now."

The inscription in Christy's copy of *Sense and Sensibility* about her being the one who could especially appreciate the book was starting to make a little more sense. Brynn walked over to the arena doors. Peering inside, she saw people bustling with hand carts and boxes in a huge room full of tables. One of the workers glanced up and saw her standing at the door, and his look made her wonder if somebody had drunk their prune juice.

Christy materialized beside her. "They don't really like us lining up this early."

"Why not?"

"Sometimes they'd rather sell to the community than to book dealers. We're kind of the bane of their existence, but we're the ones who buy lots of books, so it's a catch-22." Christy crossed her arms, and Brynn wondered if she looked at all like her, too. Christy's hair was darker than May's, and her face a tad rounder. She was a few inches shorter as well, with more age lines around her mouth and plenty of crow's feet crinkles. But there was a gentleness in her face. When she looked at Brynn, it was as if she understood her.

Another car pulled into the parking lot, and they both looked up. Christy's eyes widened slightly as the driver got out and came toward them. She wore a sleeveless shirt, jeans and sunglasses, and her dark hair blew in the breeze. She smiled, taking off her sunglasses and resting them on the top of her head.

"I didn't expect you down here," Christy said.

"We should've known this would happen sooner or later," the woman responded. She gave Christy a quick hug, glancing at Brynn over Christy's shoulder.

"This is Brynn," Christy said. "She's helping me."

The woman stuck out her hand. "Abby Dawson."

Brynn shook it, noting the firmness of the woman's grip. "Are you a book dealer, too?"

That made Abby laugh.

"You might as well get used to it, Ab," Christy said, then explained how Abby was the owner of Dawson's Book Barn, the most renowned used bookstore in the state. "I used to work there."

Abby slipped on her sunglasses again. "Actually, she used to manage it for me."

That's when Brynn remembered what Ruth told her about Christy's fiancé being the manager of a store up in Longmont. Is that where he'd been killed? She wondered if that was why Christy had decided to make the break and start her own business.

"So where are you staying?" Christy finally said.

"Probably in my car." Abby pulled out a piece of paper from her pocket and held it up for Christy to see. "We're 6, 7, and 8."

"Right behind us."

"Who else is here?" Abby walked toward the line up of boxes and chairs.

"The usuals."

"Isn't this a little early for numbers?"

"We're up to 42."

Abby seemed to gather everything in with one glance. With her military-like posture, she looked as if she was ready to take charge at any moment.

"Just so you know, I'm not out to compete with you," Abby said to Christy.

Christy smiled. "You should be."

"Well, you know I wouldn't recognize a rare book if it bit me. Ted and Susan do most of the picking."

"I'd like to think I taught you a few things."

Five minutes of small talk later, they parted ways and Christy headed toward her car, waving for Brynn to follow. A blue van pulled up beside the Honda before they reached it. The driver, a half-bald guy with a graying ponytail and bushy beard, made eye contact with Brynn. He got out, wearing shorts and sandals. Stick legs contrasted a large belly over which his t-shirt stretched. He walked right up to Christy, and Brynn closely watched the woman's response. She seemed familiar enough with him, but a guard went up. She stood a little taller, and her expression hardened. Was there bad blood here, or was it just competition?

"When'd you get here?" Christy asked.

"Wouldn't you like to know," the guy said with a bigger laugh than necessary.

Christy continued to her car, and the man breezed past her. When they were out of earshot, Brynn asked who he was.

"Tom Oberman, but everyone just calls him Oberman. He's the competitor I was telling you about."

Shaking her head, Brynn watched Oberman head to the front of the building. He walked right past Abby. "So what's the plan?"

Opening the car, Christy grabbed her travel mug of coffee and took a few sips. "I was hoping you could hold down the fort here while I open the shop for the rest of the afternoon."

"And that means . . ."

"For now, all I need is for you to stay with the boxes. Whatever you do, don't leave. Keep your eye on our place in line. You okay with that?"

Brynn nodded. She knew all about watching her back.

"I'll be back by seven," Christy said, pulling out her keys. "If you run into any trouble, Abby's a good gal to have around. You can trust her."

Brynn gave her a salute. "Got it."

As Christy drove away, Brynn thought about the odd dynamics here. She returned to the front of the line and set her grocery bag lunch of a turkey sub, potato chips and a bottle of water Christy had given her in one of the boxes. Would someone really try to move them?

Abby and Oberman were talking up at the arena doors, or more accurately Oberman was doing the talking. Abby had her arms crossed and occasionally nodded her head. Brynn caught Abby's gaze drifting to her as she walked up and peered inside the doors again. The floor of the room, which could've hosted a rodeo last week, had been covered with some sort of tarp or plastic material. Rows of large, mostly empty tables marked with signs like "History", "Science & Nature", and "Cookbooks" filled the entire space.

"Where are the books?" Brynn asked.

"They're still unpacking them," Abby said.

Like bustling ants, a group of predominantly gray-haired workers scurried about the room. Some carried boxes, others appeared to be unloading them. Christy and May's worlds were as different as their fingerprints, but they were both passionate about their professions. Brynn rested her hand on the glass door. It had been years since she'd cared about anything like they did. Seeing her sisters carving out places for themselves in their fields of expertise made her remember feeling the same way about art. She'd known it was never going to make her rich, and Christy and May seemed to know the same thing about their jobs. But passion drove them and kept them going, despite hard times.

For a moment, Brynn pictured herself staying here in Elk Valley and working alongside these women. Ruth was right. She had the chance to start over. Why not right here?

"Christy leave you high and dry?"

Brynn turned around. Abby stood behind her, and she hadn't heard Oberman leave.

"She went to open her shop."

"Know much about books?"

"Not really."

"Christy's a good teacher."

"She used to work for you?"

Abby nodded. She still wore those sunglasses, which made it hard to get a reading on her.

"I understand why she left," Abby said. "But it's just not the same without her."

Brynn sat down with her back up against the building just as angry shouts came from the parking lot.

"That doesn't sound good." Abby walked toward the parked cars.

Brynn jumped to her feet and followed the woman's determined steps. She didn't seem to lack in the assertive department, and Brynn wondered if that was why Christy had said it would be good to have her around.

"You had no right!" an accented male voice said.

A second male voice swore.

"Oh, boy." Abby stopped in her tracks.

Brynn came up behind her. "What?"

"It's Oberman and Kamil."

"Kamil?"

"They're arch enemies. This is gonna be interesting."

Brynn caught sight of the pair over by Oberman's van. The man named Kamil, with his olive skin and dark hair, looked like he could've been born in India. Wearing sunglasses like Abby, he was pressing in on Oberman's personal space. Suddenly, he lifted an exasperated hand and turned his back on Oberman.

"Why are they enemies?"

Abby had the hint of a smile on her face. "Story goes they used to be friends, worked together even. But Oberman made a deal with one of their competitors to save a space for him at a sale if the guy would return the favor, and Kamil felt like he was betrayed."

Brynn couldn't help shaking her head. She'd never seen anything like this.

"Course, that's according to Oberman." Abby lowered her voice as Kamil approached. She tilted her head in his direction. "According to him, Oberman lied and broke his word."

Kamil marched past them and scooped up the can holding the numbers. He tucked it under his arm and headed back toward the cars.

"What do you think you're doing?" Abby called after him.

He stopped and came back toward her. "No one has ever put out numbers this early."

"They have now."

Brynn wanted to withdraw from the whole scene, sensing a confrontation about to happen. That's how she'd survived in lockup. If someone got rowdy, she withdrew. A girl even shoved her into a wall once, but she hadn't retaliated.

Taking a step toward Kamil, Abby's voice was even.

Kamil pointed toward Oberman's van. "He has no right."

"There's no law against putting out numbers," Abby said.

"These aren't official numbers!"

"Kamil, do you really want to do this?"

"It's not fair to anyone who comes tonight or tomorrow morning."

"That's not up to us," Abby said.

"And you! Getting into that sale early and taking all the good books." Kamil took his sunglasses off. His eyes were on fire.

"I didn't do anything wrong."

"No one has ever gotten in early."

Abby kept her feet glued to the pavement, spread wide. "I don't have to explain to you or anyone else, Kamil, but I will. I am running a *business*. It's not personal, and I never implied to those people I was anything but a bookstore owner. They invited me in."

"That doesn't make it right," Kamil said.

"You would've done the same thing."

A sneer flicked on Kamil's face at the statement, and with the can of numbers still under his arm, he walked to the dumpster beside the building. He opened the black plastic top and dumped the can inside. It clattered against the metal bottom.

Abby shook her head. "Like I said. This is gonna be interesting."

"What's he talking about?"

Rolling her eyes, Abby watched Kamil as he strode back to his car without giving her one glance. She finally turned toward Brynn. "Last week there was a sale up near Denver. I went earlier than normal and started chatting with the people running it. They let me in early, and I bought a lot. Straightforward. They knew who I was and were just happy to get rid of the stuff. When the sale officially started the next day there was more than one very unhappy dealer, and word got out that our store was the one who'd cleaned up."

"What a bunch of weirdos," Brynn whispered. "But you're not too bad," she quickly added.

That got a laugh out of the woman. "Luckily, in my former life, I worked with weirdoes every day. I was a cop for almost twenty years."

Brynn feigned a nonchalant attitude, but was suddenly more nervous than she should've been with Abby. It wasn't that she thought all cops were bad, but the last time the police showed up in her life, they'd brought her nothing but heartache. She wondered what would've happened if they hadn't arrested her that night. Would she still be alive?

15

By sunset Brynn was questioning the sanity of book dealers. All day they arrived, set down a box or chair, and then left again. Abby told her some of them would be back later that night to sleep in their cars. Like she and Christy would be doing. When Oberman discovered his numbers were missing, his face turned a shade darker, but that was it. They could only hope it stayed that way.

Abby had retired to her car and its air conditioning, and except for the occasional arrival of a worker who knocked on the doors of the building until they were seen by someone inside and let in, Brynn was alone sitting with her back against the building.

She took a sip from her water bottle and thought about the Jane Austen books. Why had her father given her the third volume? If he'd truly cared about her, wouldn't he have found a way to be in her life? How long had his relationship with her mother lasted? It hurt to think that Mom had hidden the book from her for so long, but she had to admit she didn't have all the pieces.

Christy returned at seven-fifteen with two steaming pizzas and a 2-liter bottle of icy Coke. They ate off the hood of her car, and Abby joined them. For a minute or two everyone seemed to relax a little. Jokes were cracked, and Brynn enjoyed laughing with them.

She kept a close watch on Christy, unable to quit comparing herself. Christy had a quiet confidence which made her easy to like. She wasn't as bold as Abby, yet the two seemed to get along well.

"So how did you get started in books?" Brynn asked Christy, finishing off her pizza crust.

Christy wiped her mouth with a napkin and took a swig of Coke from her plastic cup. "I've always loved books. When I got hired at the Barn, I knew I'd found my niche. That was, oh . . . almost eight years ago."

"What did you do before that?"

"A little bit of everything. I've been a waitress, hotel maid, a cashier at a gas station."

She was trying to piece together the story of her sisters' lives, and Christy's was still full of holes. Brynn kept wondering about those years of estrangement May had talked about.

"What's the rarest book you've ever found?"

Christy paused and exchanged glances with Abby. "A first edition of *The Great Gatsby*."

"How much was it worth?"

"We sold it for thirty grand," Abby answered for Christy.

Brynn whistled.

"So tell me more about you," Christy said.

"Not much to tell."

"You're from Denver?"

"Denver area."

Christy pulled another pizza slice from the box on the hood. "Why'd you come to Elk Valley?"

Brynn considered her next words carefully, just like she had yesterday, finally deciding a little truth might fit well here.

"I came looking for my father."

Christy raised her eyebrows and made a sound that could've passed for "Really?" if her mouth hadn't been full.

"Did you find him?" Abby asked.

Brynn slowly nodded. "Found out he's dead."

The duo offered their sympathies. Brynn knew her story was full of holes too, and sooner or later May was going to corner her again. But for now it felt good to share something that wasn't a lie. She'd missed friendships that didn't involve manipulation and second guessing. In jail, her guard was up constantly. She could never allow herself to get close to anyone. At nineteen she'd been the youngest inmate in her pod, which made her a target for some of the older con artists.

Isolation had its consequences, and one of them was that Brynn wasn't sure she knew how to make friends anymore. She was suspicious of most people she met. What were their motives? Why were they treating her however they were treating her? Like Christy, for example. Why had she even asked her to come along to this book sale?

"Listen," Abby said, her back against the Honda's front door. "There's no point in all of us staying here tonight. If you want to get a couple hours sleep I'll be happy to watch your place."

Christy closed up the pizza boxes and stacked them on top of each other. They'd eaten all but three slices. "I can't ask you to do that."

"You didn't." Abby smiled. "I'm offering."

Christy considered the offer for a moment. "You're staying all night?"

"I'll catch a few in my car, but I'll definitely stay."

"I can bring breakfast," Christy said.

The decision was made surprisingly fast, and they all agreed to meet tomorrow morning before the sun. Christy and Brynn piled back into her car and headed south on I-25.

⤸

Roxi got back to the house at dusk. She hadn't intended to be gone so long, but at least she had a flashlight in her saddle bag. She'd called Jan on Keith's cell phone so she wouldn't worry. That was the last thing Roxi wanted. They'd worried enough over her for a lifetime.

She untacked Sally and led her to the pasture gate illuminated by the yard light. They turned out all their horses year round in fields with run-ins, only bringing animals into the barn if there was a major storm or they needed easy access to them for work.

"There you go, girl." Roxi led Sally through the gate, making sure to turn her around so she faced the gate again before unbuckling her halter. Jan had ingrained the safety tip in her from the beginning. It was dangerous to lead a horse into a pasture and let them run alongside you out to their field. The animal might get excited to have their freedom and take off kicking or bucking. Jan knew of someone who'd been kicked in the head that way.

She let Sally loose and backed toward the gate to give her space. The mare headed off at a slow trot to greet her equine friends already grazing. Roxi tried to make out their silhouettes in the darkness. She'd spent most of her ride thinking about when she could take May up on her offer. Something about horse training intrigued her. She'd love to be able to communicate with these huge, majestic creatures. She hung Sally's halter on the gate with the others and headed up to the house.

Before she got to the back door she noticed all the cars. At least half a dozen. As she walked into the kitchen, she remembered why they were here. Every other week Jan had a ladies Bible study meeting at the ranch, something Roxi had managed to avoid attending thus far. It wasn't that she minded talking about God and the Bible. She'd gotten used to that with Jan and Keith, but the prospect of being scrutinized by a bunch of strange Christian women was less than appealing. They all would've heard about her and probably drawn plenty of conclusions like Morgan had.

She closed the door as quietly as she could. Selah bolted up from her horse blanket bed in the corner and greeted her like she'd been gone a year rather than an afternoon.

"Shhh," Roxi said, scratching the dog's ears and accepting her joyous licks to her face. On the counter was a plateful of macaroni and cheese with fresh cut tomatoes Jan had set out for her. She grabbed a fork from the dishwasher and was about to head quietly up to her bedroom when Morgan walked into the room.

"Hello again," Morgan said. Tonight she wore a starched, white sleeveless blouse that made Roxi's dusty shirt with the Walker's Feed Store logo look like the hand-me-down it was. She suddenly realized she'd forgotten to wash her hands.

"I'm just getting dinner," Roxi said. Selah was sitting at her side staring up at the plate of food.

"You're not joining us?"

"Um . . ." She glanced at the living room doorway. She knew she'd have to walk through there to get upstairs. Now it would be harder to slip by unnoticed.

"We'd love to have you."

Roxi wasn't sure if it was a genuine invitation or not, but she decided to pretend it was. "Thanks, but I just got in and I haven't showered or anything."

"That's okay."

She glanced down at her food again, then back at Morgan. Maybe it would earn her some points to do what this woman wanted. Setting the food back on the counter, she followed Morgan into the living room.

Ten pairs of eyes instantly locked on her, and she wanted

to turn on her heels. Instead, she squared her shoulders and gave them all a smile. She might not feel like being here, but she was determined to stop running from everything.

Jan stood up from the sofa and waved for her to come sit beside her. "Ladies, this is Roxi, my foster daughter."

She tried not to beam at Jan's use of the word "daughter". She'd aged out of the foster care system when she turned eighteen, but she still considered the Mercers her foster parents, even though it had only been legal temporarily. But even with Jan beside her on the sofa, she still felt uncomfortable. She held her arms close and locked her ankles. Morgan sat down on her other side, making it worse. Especially when Roxi realized a big chunk of manure was stuck to the bottom of her boot.

Jan leaned over. "Have a good ride?"

"Sally was great."

"She always is."

An older Hispanic woman sitting across the room gave her a kind smile, and Roxi focused on her.

"Good to have you here," the woman said. "I'm Ruth, and just to get you up to speed, we've been reading and talking about the book of Matthew."

Keith had given her a Bible months ago, but she hadn't read much past the first few pages of Genesis. Jan had a Bible open on her lap and Roxi surreptitiously glanced at it. A big "18" stood out on the page.

"Morgan, why don't you read verse twelve through fourteen," Ruth said.

Morgan's Bible was bound in pink leather. She picked it up with her manicured hands. "If a man has a hundred sheep and one of them wanders away, what will he do?" Morgan cleared her throat. "Won't he leave the ninety-nine others on the hills and go out to search for the one that is lost? And if he finds it, I tell you the truth, he will rejoice over it more than over the ninety-nine that didn't wander away! In the same way, it is not my heavenly Father's will that even one of these little ones should perish."

Ruth looked around the room. "Have any of you experienced something like this?"

Jan nodded. "Last spring, Keith and I were moving some cattle. It began snowing really badly. I saw this calf break away from the bunch and dart out into the snow. I turned around and went after it, but I couldn't find it right away. Took me over an hour, but when I did, I definitely rejoiced."

A woman with reading glasses perched on her nose sitting beside Ruth nodded, and Roxi listened more intently than she'd planned. The general consensus was that sheep symbolized people, and the man was God. She had to admit it was interesting.

"But why would God do that?" she blurted before she realized what she was saying. When everyone turned toward her again, she swallowed and resisted the urge to sink further into the sofa.

Morgan turned toward her. "What do you mean?"

"I mean, why would he bother leaving all those others just for one? Wouldn't it make more sense to stay with the rest of the flock?"

"Good question," Ruth said.

The room was quiet for a moment, and she wondered if she'd just asked the most stupid question in the world and was too ignorant of this Bible stuff to realize it.

Jan glanced her way. "Because He loves that one sheep."

There were several "amens" and more affirmative nods. Roxi glanced down at her hands knowing Jan had meant the words for her in more than one way.

⌒

Christy unlocked the rear door of the dark bookstore, flicked on a light and ushered Brynn inside. There was an outside entrance to her apartment, but she'd wanted to check her e-mails on the store computer before they hit the sack.

Between the boxes of unsorted books stacked almost to the ceiling in the corner and the cluttered computer table, there wasn't an inch of free space in the small back room.

"Not much to speak of," Christy said. "But it's home."

"Weren't you scared to leave your other job?"

Christy rolled a chair toward Brynn and sat down by the computer. "Can't say it was easy. But having my own shop was a great opportunity."

Brynn slumped into the squeaky chair. After not sleeping well last night and the drama this afternoon, she could barely keep her eyes open. But she was determined to figure this woman out.

"It must be weird having your former boss at the sale."

Facing the computer, Christy jiggled her mouse and the desktop wallpaper appeared, a photo of fuzzy kittens curled up in a basket. "Abby and I parted on good terms. I didn't leave because of her."

"Ruth told me about your fiancé."

Christy paused. Her voice got softer. "Hunter was all over that place."

Which was the same reason why Brynn could never have stayed in the apartment she and Mom had shared during the months she was sick. Every corner of it not only reminded her of Mom, but of her sickness and death, too.

"The Barn was doing well," Christy said. "It was a good time to leave, and as I said, it's always been my dream to have my own store." She logged onto the internet. "You're welcome to look around if you want while I do this. The light switch is on the wall. I won't be long."

Brynn took that as a hint, so she pulled herself out of the chair and walked out into the store. She ended up in front of Ruth's painting again.

What if Jesus had really looked like that? It made him seem more real than she'd ever pictured, and in a way she'd rather think of him like the Sunday school posters portrayed—weak and far removed from her world. Maybe if he was someone like that she could sneak under his radar, and God wouldn't be as disappointed in her.

She was about to head back to Christy when a loud rap pounded on the front door. Brynn jumped, and she realized the curtain over the window was up and anyone on the street could see her clearly.

The banging came again, now more like a fist on the glass. "Hey! Open up!"

Standing inches from the door was the shadowy figure of a man. He pressed his face into the glass, distorting it in a grotesque, horror flick kind of way. He glared right at her.

"Don't make me break down the door!"

Before Brynn could react, the lights went out and someone grabbed her arm, pulling her back toward the storeroom.

"Go home, Shane!" Christy yelled.

The door rattled and shook violently.

"You *know* him?"

"He's the sheriff's son."

"What in the world does he want?"

Thud. It could've been a boot hitting the door.

"I have no idea, but he's probably high and looking for trouble." Christy picked up her cell phone. "One more kick and I'm calling 911."

They waited for a tense minute, but the kick never came, and Shane's dark form melted back into the night.

"Maybe you should call anyway," Brynn said.

"He'll be long gone before they get here."

When a full minute passed and all was quiet, Brynn finally felt free to breathe.

"He's done this to me and other shop owners before," Christy said.

"And gotten away with it?"

Christy flipped her cell phone closed. "When your father's the law, apparently you can. He actually used to work for May, so I'm his favorite target."

She blinked. "He worked for May?"

"Not for long. She fired him."

Brynn followed Christy back into the storeroom. "Won't he just come back?"

"Let's hope not, but I'll make sure to set the alarm." Christy waved at the computer. "I'll do this later. Let's get some sleep."

They climbed the steep flight of steps up to the second floor. It dumped them in the kitchen, and Brynn took in everything she could. A few stray mugs and a plate waited to be washed. A window over the sink had a view of the back parking lot.

"Something to drink?" Christy opened the fridge and pulled out a Sprite.

"After today?" Brynn smirked. "Got any beer?"

Smiling, Christy pulled out a can of Barge's Root Beer. "Best I can do."

She took the chilled can, cracked it open and took a long swallow. "I don't know how you do it. If I had to face what you do every day I'd probably be a drunk."

"Yeah, well I actually was." Christy took a sip from her can and set it on the counter. She started scrounging in the fridge. "It wasn't pretty."

Brynn tried to take the comment in stride, but she hadn't

seen that one coming. Another piece of the sister puzzle slipped into place. She'd meant her comment as a joke, but it suddenly seemed like a stupid thing to say.

"I'm sorry, I–"

Christy held up her hand. "Don't be. You had no idea." She emerged with an enormous green apple. She took a big, crunchy bite and pointed in the direction of the window. "I'm four years sober."

Brynn focused on her root beer. So they'd both had an addiction. That ran in families, didn't it? She finished her drink while Christy ate her apple, and Brynn wondered if she was making a huge mistake not to tell them who she was. Every time she got close to doing it, she folded. Christy actually seemed to like her, and that felt good. If she knew the truth, would it crumble their budding friendship?

She yawned, and Christy noticed.

"Come on." Christy guided her by the arm toward the other rooms. "Got a busy day tomorrow."

Christy set her up in her quasi guest room, half of which was full of bookshelves and boxes of books. It took Brynn forever to get to sleep. She kept thinking about the Williams sisters and how they'd known her dad better than she ever would. She'd dreamed of meeting him, but now that had been snuffed out like every other dream she had.

It felt like she'd just drifted off when Christy's knock came at her door. Brynn groaned, but told her to come in. The light from the doorway fell on her face, and she covered her eyes with her hand.

"Time already?"

Christy flicked on the lights. "Abby just called. We have a problem."

16

They were pulling into the parking lot of the Ag arena by five-thirty. Brynn was barely awake, but Christy seemed to be running on adrenaline.

"I can't believe they did this," she muttered under her breath.

"What's the big deal?" Brynn yawned, nursing a cup of watery gas station coffee and wishing Christy had bought donuts again. "So someone butted in line. You're still in a good spot."

"That's not the point." Jerking on the steering wheel, Christy swung into a parking space. "If one guy does it, someone else will try the same thing. And by the time we get inside all the good books will be taken."

The lot was already starting to fill up, and even from here Brynn saw that the line of boxes, chairs and bags now snaked around the building.

They got out and walked toward the front of the line, and Brynn took it all in like a visitor in a foreign country. There were still only a few people milling around. One conspiratorial cluster of middle-aged men in dirty jeans and flannel shirts surveyed them as they passed. A lady with long gray hair wearing a yellow beret and an oversized sweater sat reading in a beach chair sipping from a thermos.

"This is crazy," Brynn said.

"You've said that five times already."

"Well it is! What book is worth all this?"

"Look, this is how I pay my bills, okay?" Christy said, and Brynn shut up.

When they got to the doors, Abby and two guys were arguing. Brynn couldn't hear what they were saying at first, but Abby was jabbing toward the chest of one of them and then toward the line. He raised his hands, countering something back.

"What's going on here?" Christy approached them, but Brynn held back.

The guy could've been her age and wore a black hoodie, torn jeans, Converse sneakers, and a ski cap. "We showed up and there was no one here," he said with a shrug and a nod to his silent, stringy haired companion. "Seems to me if you wanna keep your place in line ya gotta be here."

Abby swore. "For cryin' out loud, you know how this works."

"Where were you?"

"Asleep in my car!"

Mr. Hoodie gave another shrug.

"Do you have numbers?" Christy pulled out the slips of paper she'd shown Brynn yesterday.

"We don't need numbers."

"Yes, you do," Christy said.

"Not in my book." Hoodie stuck his hands in his pockets and held his ground.

Soon Kamil joined the fray and started his own argument with the men. Apparently, this was about more than a few spaces in line, just like Christy said. It was principle. There were so many unspoken rules to these people Brynn could barely keep them straight.

Something in the parking lot caught her attention, and Brynn turned to see a police cruiser glide up. A flash of apprehension washed over her. Sometimes all it took for her to rush back to a moment in time was a smell or even one word. She'd never be able to smell bologna again without picturing herself eating in the prison cafeteria. Seeing the cruiser brought Brynn right back to the worst moment in her life.

Kamil glared at Abby. "Who called the cops?"

No one 'fessed up, and the police officer emerged from his vehicle. He strolled over to the huddle by the door, but before he could reach it, Abby walked up to him and started talking in a low tone. The officer was chewing gum, both hands on his hips. Brynn wondered what Abby was saying.

Then the cop walked up to Hoodie. "What seems to be the problem here?"

"I'm just standing in line, Officer."

"So nobody was around when you got here?"

"Nope."

"What about these boxes and chairs?"

"No one was here." Hoodie took his hands out of his pockets. "It's not fair that these dealers come days ahead of time and then don't stay with their stuff. You should have to be here. If you're not, there's nothing saying I can't stand where I want to."

He was bold; Brynn had to give him that, but one glance at Christy and she felt less sympathetic toward the guy. The woman's forehead was creased with concern, and Brynn realized this really was about her survival. Christy's bread and butter depended on sales like this. What drove a woman to make her living this way, with so much stress? It took guts, that was for sure.

The cop spoke to Abby and then to Hoodie again. Brynn could make out some of the words, but not all. Through it the cop was a stoic negotiator, letting each side explain. Something had to give.

"Did you bring any boxes with you?" he asked the men.

"Yeah, we've got stuff," Hoodie said.

"Where?"

Hoodie hesitated. "Back there."

One glance at where he pointed, and the cop's whole attitude changed. "You set your stuff down in the line?"

With a glance at each other, Hoodie and his silent friend must've realized their mistake. "It doesn't make it right that–"

The cop pointed at their boxes.

They tried to protest again, but he pointed with finality. With a glare at Abby, they slunk to the back of the line. Brynn wondered if they'd stay put after the cop left.

It was too early in the morning for this kind of drama.

Abby and the cop talked quietly for a minute or two more, and then he left. By then, more people had emerged from their cars, bleary eyed and hair askew to see what the excitement was about. Christy brought out her coffee thermos and shared it with Abby and Brynn.

By eight, the sun was starting to bake the cement, and most of the boxes had found their owners. This was the most rag tag group Brynn had ever seen in one place. Oberman and Kamil were completely ignoring each other as well as Abby, even though they stood two feet apart. Abby's college student workers had shown up and were huddled with her discussing their strategy. Christy had pointed out half a dozen dealers who were direct competition to her, and she kept taking deep breaths like she was trying to calm herself down.

"You okay?" Brynn finally asked.

Christy smiled. "These are the days I would pay big bucks to have a smoke again. How 'bout you?"

"Still wishing for that beer."

They both chuckled.

She seemed to be trying to stay calm, but Christy got even more jumpy as nine o'clock approached. Everyone queued in the line when three old ladies came out with the official numbers. They handed them out quickly and without fanfare. This allowed everyone to go back to their cars and rest for a few minutes or drive off and converge on the gas station bathroom down the street.

Christy took this time to explain what she needed. Since Brynn knew nothing about rare books, she was to follow Christy like a dog, lug her full boxes to the safest corner she could find, throw Christy's sheet with "SOLD" written on it several times in black marker, and then race back for the next one. Once they had a pile and the initial crush was over, she was assigned to guard it.

Brynn didn't have to ask from what anymore.

By nine-thirty, the tension in the line was palpable. Lone conversations continued, but there was a lot less laughing and joking. Abby kept glancing at her watch.

"We're going to History first," Abby leaned over and whispered to Christy.

"You go where you need to go," Christy responded.

"We won't be in Children's until later."

"Ab." Christy smiled. "Don't worry about it."

Her hands full with two empty boxes and the sheet, Brynn craned to see inside the building. Workers were milling just inside the door. One of them checked his watch, too.

Twenty minutes to go. Brynn didn't think the tension could get any higher, but it did. Ten minutes before the doors were to open, she watched people pick up their boxes, fold up their chairs, and stash them in their cars. Not everyone was a dealer. By now some families joined the back of the line with their kids in tow.

Brynn took a deep breath, the scent of someone's body odor way too close. Oberman had tied a purple blanket with gold trim around his waist. The postal bin he'd used to mark his spot had been replaced with two handled boxes. He held one in each fist, and with his legs spread apart he looked like he was about to run a race.

Five minutes. Bodies pressed closer together as everyone inched forward.

"You ready?" Christy asked.

Brynn nodded.

Movement on the inside caught Brynn's attention, and the droning chatter of a hundred voices instantly faded. All eyes focused on the doors and the poor worker who'd been designated to unlock them.

17

Brynn heard the click of the door unlocking and watched it swing open. Oberman and Kamil shot through it faster than she thought either of them capable, thrusting their numbers at the old lady waiting inside. Before she could even read them, they were gone. Christy took off too, and for a split second Brynn froze. It took someone knocking into her back for her own feet to start moving.

The only sounds were feet pounding, sneakers shuffling, and books thudding into boxes. Christy dove for the table marked "Children's Literature", her hands grabbing a book here, two there, and five more after that. The colorful volumes were displayed spines up, and Brynn tried to read some of the titles. She caught a glimpse of *The Wizard of Oz* by L. Frank Baum before a hand reached right across her field of vision and snatched it away. Within thirty seconds, she was surrounded by bodies and grabbing hands, and she had to push to stay by Christy's side.

Christy was grabbing just as fast as anyone, scanning the spines, and Brynn wondered if she was even reading the titles or just guessing based on the look. There were thick books and thin books, fiction and nonfiction. She thought she saw an encyclopedia set of some sort sitting in a box under the table.

From early readers to thick novels, these books covered the gamut, though most seemed to be fiction.

In less than a minute Christy shoved a full box in Brynn's arms, and she struggled to grab hold of it.

"Run if you have to," Christy huffed, taking Brynn's empty box and diving back into the stacks.

She had to squeeze and shove to get out of the throng of bodies between the tables, but she finally managed to jog the perimeter of the room, where she found an empty spot on the floor in a corner, like Christy had instructed. Emptying the box, she threw the sheet over the books and tucked it under, as per her instructions, to keep dealers out.

Brynn paused for one moment and stared out into the room crowded with people of all sizes and types—just like the books they were grabbing. It was a mad free-for-all, and she stood by her original impression. Book sales were insane.

By the time she got back to Christy, she'd filled the second box and they exchanged again. A sheen of perspiration glistened on Christy's forehead, her cheeks red. The room was heating up quickly, the AC probably working overtime to keep up with the influx of bodies.

Depositing the second box's contents under the sheet, Brynn took off with the empty box, searching the crowd. It took her longer to find Christy this time, and she only had half her box full.

"Thanks," she said, when Brynn took it from her, but she kept her eyes on the books.

The frenzy had calmed ever so slightly, and Brynn noticed piles like theirs cropping up all along the edge of the arena. There was Kamil depositing an armful of titles, and she passed Oberman's pile with his elaborate purple blanket covering a mound twice the size of Christy's. Several people were already scanning bar codes with their phones.

She made two more trips back to the pile before Christy

was satisfied she'd gotten everything she could in the Children's section. Then it was on to other sections for general stock to fill her bookstore shelves.

On one trip back from the pile, Brynn passed through the Children's table again and rested her hand on a Richard Scarry picture book. She remembered sitting in Mom's lap reading one of these as a kid, back when she didn't think about who her father was or whether her mother was healthy.

She followed behind a gray-haired old woman clutching a paper bag. Her glasses perched on the tip of her nose, she pulled out books one at a time, paging through the leaves of this one, then setting it back and deliberately paging through another before placing it in her bag. Definitely not a dealer, but she could be a collector, Brynn decided. She spotted Oberman hunching over the tables in History, seemingly oblivious to those around him.

Brynn took the time to read the titles she passed. A scuffed copy of *Trixie Belden and the Secret of the Mansion*, a paperback of *Prince Caspian* by C. S. Lewis, another Richard Scarry. Since these hadn't been snatched up in the first thirty minutes, she wondered if it meant these were all truly worthless to a bookseller. Couldn't they sell books like this, or had they been missed?

Pushing aside some old library books, Brynn spotted a copy of *Anne of Green Gables* underneath. This was another one she remembered reading as a girl. Anne's feisty character resonated with her, and the story made her wish she had red hair.

Plucking the spine from the others, Brynn studied it closer. The paper covering over the book–Christy might've called those dust jackets–was worn, but still intact. She decided to bring the book with her and see if Christy could use it. It seemed old enough.

An hour passed before Christy met her at the pile and sat down on the floor. Brynn joined her, sitting Indian style.

"These'll sell." Christy held up three hardcover books with

dust jackets. *The Egyptian Cat Mystery, The Flaming Mountain,* and *The Flying Stingaree.* They were from a series called the Rick Brant Science-Adventure Stories by John Blaine. "I don't know how much these are worth, but they're collectible," Christy said. "A lot of these children's series are."

"Like the Nancy Drew?"

"And the Hardy Boys, and lesser known ones like these."

Brynn observed quietly as Christy sorted through her pile. This woman was her sister. It was still a strange thought, but she'd already decided she didn't mind. She could just sit with Christy and not feel uncomfortable.

As she sorted, Christy cradled the books like baby animals, barely cracking the covers. If the book had a dust jacket, she might gently remove it and check the boards beneath for . . . something. Brynn had no idea what.

"Are you worried they'll break?"

Christy set the book she was holding, a copy of *Rabbit Hill* by Robert Lawson, on the keeper pile she'd started. "What?"

"Why are you so careful?"

"Here. Look at this one." Christy pulled a book from her discard pile and handed it to Brynn. "Open it up at the back."

Brynn did, and found the back cover pulling away from the pages.

"That's called the hinge, and in this case it's almost broken. That can happen from someone opening a book too far, too often. Unless it's a first edition of *Uncle Tom's Cabin* or something, it's not collectible in that condition."

Brynn returned the book with the cracked hinge to the discard pile. "Those books May showed you the other night." She picked up another book and pretended to examine it. "How much would they be worth if you had the third volume?"

"A complete set?" Christy whistled. "I bet close to a hundred grand, maybe more at auction." She reached for another book on the stack in front of her.

"It's weird your dad only gave you two of the books." Brynn was treading on dangerous territory here, but she knew Christy had no idea why she was asking.

"It does seem a little odd. There's still value in the first two, just not as much. May and I have been talking about trying to sell the two we have, if we cut out Dad's inscriptions. She could really use the cash flow, and I sure would love not worrying about paying my rent next month."

Brynn picked up the copy of *Anne of Green Gables*. The cover was green with a picture of Anne on the front. She ran her fingers over the illustration. The artist had rendered a much older girl than the eleven-year-old she knew readers would meet in the book's opening pages.

She handed the book to Christy. "I picked this up and wasn't sure if you'd want it."

Just like with the other books, Christy barely cracked open the volume and peered inside.

"It says first impression," Brynn said.

"I see that." Christy took a moment to examine the rest of the book, checking the back hinge and the covers. "Not in too bad shape. There's some fraying to the spine ends and the hinges are a little weak, but it's still worth getting. I'll have to look it up when I get back. I know first editions of this are pretty valuable." Christy smiled at her. "Good pick. Maybe I should bring you along more often."

Brynn beamed inside. They spent the next hour sorting through the stacks, then she put back the ones Christy didn't want and helped her box up the keepers. After checking the tables one last time, Christy ended up with five full boxes.

As they pulled away in the loaded down Honda, Christy seemed pleased and chatted about their finds, but Brynn couldn't stop thinking about the book burning a hole in her backpack.

18

Ruth was sitting on a feed bucket in the middle of the horse pen, a sketch pad in her lap. Brynn waved goodbye as Christy drove away, then walked over to the fence. Exhaustion was threatening to overwhelm her, but she fought back.

"How'd it go?" Ruth asked.

"Christy got plenty of books." Brynn rested her arms on the pen's gate. Ruth's back was to the horse, a brown and white paint. "Is it safe to be in there?"

The older woman smiled. "Guess we'll see."

"Seriously."

"This is actually part of his training."

"You teaching him how to draw?"

Ruth closed her sketch pad. "He's had some bad experiences, and I think now he's afraid of people. It's a whole different set of rules for the fearful ones, and my goal is to show him that we're not all bad." Ruth sent a quick glance over to the horse. "Gradually I'll get closer, but not until I feel he's accepting me here."

Brynn watched the paint for a moment. He was facing the opposite way, but his eye was on Ruth.

"He's watching you."

"That's good." Ruth hoisted to her feet with a grimace, the sketchbook tucked under her arm. "We'll leave him alone for awhile."

Opening the gate for her, Brynn followed the old woman to the barn. She wanted to see what she'd been drawing, but didn't feel comfortable enough to ask. "Where's May?"

"She had some business up in the Springs."

Brynn was surprised at her disappointment. She'd hoped to spend more time with the younger Williams sister. After her day with Christy, she felt like she at least had a handle on her, but May was still a mystery.

"Can I ask you something?" Ruth had her hand on the door to a room beside the one that held the saddles and bridles.

She shrugged.

"Why did you give up your art?"

Brynn didn't meet her eyes. "I wasn't that great."

"I'm not sure artists are ever good judges of their own work."

"So I've heard."

Ruth opened the door and turned on a light. Instantly the smell of turpentine and oil paint transported Brynn to the best years of her life, when she first discovered the passion of mixing colors. Back then she poured every hard earned dollar she made mowing lawns into new brushes, paint tubes, and canvasses. She spent hours alone with her paints, and her creations became her friends.

The room couldn't have been larger than ten by ten. Off to the side was an easel splotched with a rainbow of pigments waiting for a new canvas. A stained wooden palette lay on a table beside it, and gnarled tubes of primary colors were scattered next to that. Brushes stuck up from a jar on another table. Brynn couldn't help the longing stirring inside her at the familiarity of these objects of creative expression she'd once revered.

"When I was seventeen, my Mom found a lump in her breast," Brynn said softly. "She died six months later. I never painted after that."

Comprehension dawned in Ruth's eyes, and the older woman gave a slight nod. She set her sketch pad on the chair in front of the easel. "Just remember, chica. God doesn't give us gifts without a reason."

Silence lingered between them, and Brynn focused on the jar of brushes. A fan brush stained blue stood up higher than the others. She couldn't deny that something in her wanted to reach for it. What would it feel like to hold a brush in her hands again? Brynn pushed the thought aside. Even if she had all the tools at her fingertips, her inspiration well had long ago run dry.

Ruth tore the plastic wrapper off a new canvas, but as she started to attach it to the easel, something gave in her legs. She grabbed for the table, and if Brynn hadn't rushed to her side to support her, she wasn't sure Ruth would've stayed up.

"Are you okay?"

"Thank you." Ruth patted her arm. "Yes, I'm fine now."

"You look pale."

"Sat too long, I guess."

She watched the older woman carefully, hoping to see color return to her face. "Maybe you should go in and lie down."

Ruth nodded. "Maybe." Shuffling past her, she reached for the door frame, but her hand slipped, and before Brynn could react, she toppled toward the floor.

"Ruth!"

The old woman fell in a heap, clutching her chest as her body hit the floor with a thud. Brynn couldn't get to her fast enough. She dropped to her knees beside Ruth.

"What's wrong?"

Ruth took heavy breaths in and out. Sweat had instantly sprung up on her forehead, and her fingers trembled.

Brynn frantically pulled her into a sitting position on the

floor. Ruth's body was a lead weight in her arms. Her breaths got more labored, and she leaned into Brynn.

"We have to get you up!"

"I . . . can't."

"Yes you can." She took a quick inventory of the woman's pockets searching for a cell phone, but came up empty. Could she carry her to the house? Her pulse zooming, Brynn tried to lift her, but without Ruth's cooperation she wasn't strong enough. She couldn't just leave her, but what other choice did she have? Something was really wrong. Was she having a heart attack?

"I have to go for help," Brynn said, gently laying Ruth back onto the floor.

Ruth grabbed her hand with a strength she didn't expect. "You . . . you have to . . ."

"I know! I–"

Shaking her head, Ruth tried to speak, but nothing came from her mouth.

"You're gonna be okay. I'll get help."

Ruth closed her eyes, slowly releasing Brynn's hand. Her fingernails were turning dark. Just like Mom's had in that hospital room six years ago.

"Oh, please no . . . no, no."

Ruth's hand relaxed, falling to her side.

The old woman smiled as a long, slow breath flowed from her body, and Brynn watched the pain and tension disappear from her face like ripples calming on a lake.

Brynn screamed for help.

19

Jim felt Ruth's neck with his fingers, and Brynn watched moisture silently pool in the cowboy's blue eyes. The back of his t-shirt was soaked with sweat. For the past ten minutes they'd been waiting for the ambulance, and he'd been trying to revive Ruth with CPR.

"She was setting up a canvas," Brynn whispered.

Jim wiped his forehead with a nod, his adam's apple dipping. "Doing what she loved."

"She just fell, and . . ."

Brynn stared down at the peaceful face of the old woman who'd been kinder to her than she deserved. She'd barely known her, and yet something ripped her heart at the thought of Ruth being gone.

Fresh tears dripped down Brynn's cheeks.

Jim shook his head. "Probably a heart attack. She's had trouble for a couple years now. There's nothing we could've done."

"If I'd only . . . I just–"

"Brynn, don't. She's with her Savior now. Happier than we'll ever be here on this earth."

They stayed with Ruth for several more minutes before Jim stood up and went into the tack room. He returned with a decorative red horse blanket and helped Brynn off the floor. Together they placed the blanket over the old woman.

"Rest in peace, dear friend," Jim said.

Brynn wiped at her eyes. "She . . . I never met anyone like her."

"Me neither."

They walked to the house in silence, and Brynn fell into one of the kitchen chairs.

"You gonna be okay?" Jim rested his hand on her shoulder.

"We have to call May."

"I will."

She glanced up at him. "I'm so sorry."

Jim's gaze drifted in the direction of the barn. "She wanted to be buried next to Luis," he said almost as if Brynn wasn't there, then walked outside again. She watched him make his way slowly to the barn, pulling a cell phone from his pocket. He must've been dialing May.

Alone in the house, Ruth's dying words echoed in her ear and Brynn started pacing the kitchen to keep from losing it. She should've done something the moment Ruth had stumbled at the easel. Weren't you supposed to take aspirin if you were having a heart attack? Holding her head, she squeezed back the rush of memories. Mom had died in a coma, but Brynn had heard every one of her last gurgling breaths. She could still see her disease-ravaged body, the way her mouth hung open, and her eyes staring at nothing.

Panic spread through her, and Brynn went to the cabinet. Flinging it open, she pulled out the prescription bottle of Percocet. She didn't give herself time to think and quickly unscrewed the lid, tapping two of the white pills into her palm. She threw them into her mouth, barely tasting their bitter tang. Cupping her fingers under the kitchen faucet, she drank down three handfuls of water. The effect wouldn't be instant, but in twenty minutes the panic would dull.

Staring down into the bottle, she counted at least twenty more pills. Ruth didn't need them now, and it wasn't like a few would hurt anything. How else was she going to get through this? Even as a warning nagged at her conscience, Brynn tipped all but two Percocet into her hand and stuffed them into the front pocket of her jeans. She'd probably never take them, but it felt better knowing they were there.

When the ambulance and police car pulled into the driveway, she slipped out the front door and parked herself in one of the porch's chalky plastic chairs. If they needed to talk to her, they could find her, but she wasn't going in that barn again until the body was gone.

A few minutes later, Jim stuck his head out the door. "The officer wants to talk to you."

"I can't see her like that again, Jim."

"You can stay here. It'll be okay."

Brynn kept tapping the toe of her sneaker on the porch floorboards. She was just starting to feel the Percocet's calming effects, but it was no match for the police car. Especially when she realized her pocket was stuffed with more pills. Would the cop see anything?

"He just needs a statement," Jim whispered to her as the officer walked up the porch steps and introduced himself as Frank Newman. He was inches shorter than Jim, but probably outweighed him by fifty pounds. As she told him what happened, he wrote in a small spiral notebook.

"And you work here?"

"I just started."

"When?"

"Two days ago."

Officer Newman wrote another line, then capped his pen. "I'm real sorry this happened."

When the paramedic lowered the stretcher out of the ambulance, Brynn broke away and walked toward the horses.

She couldn't watch this. At the gate to the pasture, Jim caught up with her.

"Are you okay?"

"No," she said and without waiting for his response she opened the gate, keeping her eyes on the Spanish Peaks. Her vision blurred, but she kept walking. Only when she reached a stand of cottonwood trees, out of sight from the house, did she drop to the ground and sob.

⤸

Brynn didn't return to the ranch house until it was nearly dark, and she had two less Percocet in her pocket.

She found Christy and Jim sitting at the kitchen table holding hands, Scribbles on the floor by their feet. Closing the door behind her, Brynn knew she looked bad by their concerned faces.

"Where's May?" Brynn asked.

"Looking for you," Christy said.

Lowering her head, Brynn stared at her dusty sneakers. "Sorry. I should've told someone."

Christy got up and gently wrapped her arm around Brynn. For a fleeting moment, Brynn almost broke, but quickly steadied herself. "Should I go find her?"

Shaking her head, Christy guided Brynn to a chair. "She's looking for you, but she also needs to be alone for a little while."

"How'd she take it?"

"Hard." Christy glanced out the kitchen window. "She hasn't talked much yet."

The three of them sat at the table together, but Brynn kept catching Christy and Jim eyeing each other, and she was pretty sure they were wondering about her. She'd been the last one to see Ruth alive.

"I'm sorry you had to go through that," Jim finally said.

Brynn nodded. She'd done enough crying, but the genuine loss she felt over the woman's death was still right on the surface. If it hadn't been for the pills, she knew she'd be out of control. As it was, she'd begun to feel like she was floating above the whole thing. She'd need to flush the rest of them soon, because she was enjoying the relief far more than she expected. She finally gathered the nerve to ask about funeral arrangements.

"We don't know yet," Jim said.

"Does she have any children?"

Christy shook her head.

"May was like a daughter to her," Jim added.

"You guys will keep the ranch going, right?" She looked at Jim.

"Their partnership dictates that everything gets transferred to May," Christy said.

With Ruth gone, would she be asked to leave? Where could she go? Ruth was the one who'd hired her. May had only gone along with it because she respected her partner.

They sat quietly for a few minutes, grief pressing down on all of them. When May didn't show up even after the sun dropped below the horizon, Christy set to work preparing a simple dinner of spaghetti. Jim jumped in to help, and Brynn chose then to slip outside again.

She found May walking back from the pasture, a halter and lead slung over her shoulder. Brynn didn't speak, and she fell into step beside her as they made their way into the barn. She tried not to look in the direction of the art studio.

May hung the halter on a hook next to several others, then paused, her fingers still holding the leather strap. "Did she . . . suffer?"

Stepping toward her half-sister, Brynn almost rested a hand on May's arm in a meager attempt to comfort her. "It didn't look like it."

"If I'd have known, I never would've left."

"You couldn't possibly—"

May swung around, and even in the dim light Brynn could see her puffy, red eyes.

"I should've been here!"

She looked so much more vulnerable than when Brynn had first seen her. Her confidence had been torn away, and what was left was a woman who'd been dealt a devastating blow. Brynn saw her own pain in May, and it knit them together.

"I . . ." she cleared her throat. "I know how you feel."

She saw May's involuntary micro expression that blinked "no you don't", but then May's face relaxed. "I guess you do."

Neither of them said anything more, but Brynn felt like they'd talked for hours. As they headed for the house, May's steps slowed. In the middle of the yard she stopped, looking all around. She gave Brynn a desperate look. "How am I possibly going to run this place without her?"

Could May not know the strength she had? From their first meeting, Brynn had seen it. She was living a life others only dreamed about. Her work counted for something. Her *life* counted for something. She hadn't wasted six years she could never get back.

"You'll do fine," Brynn said, knowing it was true. May would never even think of medicating herself. They might be flesh and blood, but May was obviously made of better stock.

That night Brynn took three Percocet before bed.

20

Brynn walked into The Book Corral with Jim on the morning of the memorial service.

"Thanks so much for doing this," Christy said, giving Brynn a quick hug. It had been a no-brainer for Brynn to offer to watch the store during Ruth's funeral. Christy needed to be there for May, and Brynn didn't want to go anyway. After running her through the paces of using the cash register and computer to record each purchase, Christy dashed upstairs to change. She and Jim left a few minutes later.

As soon as they were gone, Brynn walked back into the storeroom and pulled out three Percocet. She swallowed them without water. She must've taken more than she thought, because there were only two left. Was there any way she could refill Ruth's prescription without someone discovering?

Brynn forced herself to focus on the here and now. She had to chill and be on top of her game. Today was her chance to make another good impression on Christy.

She sat down behind the front counter and tried to ignore Ruth's painting. Tourists milled up and down the street. A few stopped and looked at the window display, but no one entered. After a boring hour, one college kid with an iPad tucked under his arm poked his head in searching for computer books, but

Brynn had to tell him Christy didn't carry any. He turned around and left.

She sat down behind the counter, the Percocet's faint reassurance drifting over her like a cool mist. It was a poor substitute for the much stronger oxy, but it still felt good and was helping more than hurting. She could at least think more clearly without all the worry. It just wasn't going to last long.

The bell above the door jingled a few minutes later, and a teenage girl stepped inside. She came over to the counter. "I didn't know Christy was hiring."

"She isn't." Brynn picked up a pen. "I'm just watching the place for a little while."

"Is she at Ruth's funeral?"

"Seems like half the town is."

The girl paused. "It's so sad."

Brynn regarded the teen. She seemed vaguely familiar. "Did you know her?"

The girl's eyes drifted toward the painting. "Not well, but we're neighbors, and she led a Bible study at my house."

That sounded just like Ruth.

"Our ranch is right next to the Triple Cross," the teen said.

Brynn tapped the pen on the counter trying to remember if May had mentioned any of her neighbors. "Then you know May too, I guess."

"A little."

"I actually just started working for her."

The teen extended her hand and introduced herself as Roxi Gold. "Didn't I see you in here a couple days ago?"

So that's why she recognized her. She was the one who'd been entering the store right as Brynn was walking out. "That was me."

"Maybe we'll see each other around then," Roxi said. "Being neighbors and all."

Another customer walked in, an elderly man with a cane

and a pursed expression on his face. He came over to the counter.

"I'm looking for a biography on Kennedy," he said.

Brynn stood up. "Well, sir, I'll be happy to help you."

Except that her mind went blank. Where had Christy said biographies were? Or would something like that be shelved in history? The shelves loomed in front of her, clearly reminding her how little she knew about books.

"I don't have all day, miss."

"I'd suggest looking right over here," Roxi said, guiding the old man to the other side of the room. "We have many biographies, including those of other presidents you might like, as well. I've heard good things about this one . . ." Her voice faded as they disappeared around the shelves. By the time the man was finished he'd purchased five books, including a novel that took place in Massachusetts.

Brynn gave Roxi a high five as soon as he left. "Thanks."

"I used to work with books," Roxi said.

"I can tell."

Roxi turned toward the new acquisition shelf and started browsing.

"Looking for anything in particular?"

The girl didn't seem to hear her for a moment. She glanced up. "Hmm?"

"Trying to find something?"

"Oh, not really." She slipped out a paperback, paged through it, then put it back. "I'll probably get going anyway. I wanted to get a coffee before Jan and Keith pick me up. They're at the funeral."

"Nice to meet you then," Brynn said, meaning it.

"You too."

A bit later another jingle came from the bell, and Brynn immediately recognized who entered.

She felt her body stiffen.

"Hey," Shane Newman said.

This was a completely different guy than the one who'd banged on the door the other night. He actually smiled at her.

She didn't smile back. "What are you doing here?"

One side of Shane's mouth turned up more than the other, like he was amused. He glanced behind himself, then back to her. "Have we met?"

"The other night?"

"I don't . . ."

"You scared us half to death."

He scratched his head. "That was you?"

"What were you *thinking*?"

"Hey." Shane glanced at the floor with a grimace. "I'm really sorry about that. I was kinda strung out."

Brynn hadn't expected him to admit to anything, so his apology took her off guard. She studied him for a moment. He wasn't all that bad to look at, though the dragon tattoos added a hard edge. She thought of the Phoenix tat on her upper arm, wondering if people would think the same of her. That's part of the reason she'd placed it so high. She could easily cover it when she wanted.

"It was stupid," Shane said.

"I heard you've done it before."

"I was just playing around. Didn't mean anything by it." He came over to the counter, and she noticed his eyes were a bluish gray she would've had trouble duplicating on a canvas.

"Think your dad would agree?"

Shane's face flashed anger. "That's none of your business."

She lifted her hands in a noncommittal gesture. She'd made her point. She also understood what it was like to be strung out.

"You don't really strike me as the reading type," Brynn said, nodding toward the shelves.

Shane sat on the edge of the counter. "Picking up something for my grandmother. Got any suggestions?"

"What does she read?"

"Books."

Brynn gave him a tight smile. "Ha ha."

He waved at the shelves. "Her favorites are mysteries."

"Really? Me too."

She took him over to the mystery/thriller section on the side wall.

"What do you recommend?" Shane asked.

Brynn started to shrug, but then remembered Christy telling her about Agatha Christie. There was a whole row of those in stock. She pointed them out, and Shane grabbed two hardcovers and stuck them under his arm.

If Shane was high the other night, maybe he'd . . . Brynn had a thought she wished she could erase. But as she watched Shane check the book prices, she heard herself clear her throat to get Shane's attention.

He barely looked up. "What?"

"Maybe you can help me with something, too."

❧

Keith and Jan picked Roxi up at the curb of The Perfect Blend, and she told them about meeting Brynn as they drove back to the ranch. Then Keith dropped the bomb—Morgan had invited them over for dinner.

Roxi tried not to grimace. "Did you say yes?"

Keith gave her a crooked grin. "Sure. She's a fantastic cook."

Tolerating Morgan at the ranch was one thing. Treading on her turf was going to require a completely different mindset Roxi wasn't sure she could create. She knew Morgan didn't like her or trust her.

"We won't make you go," Jan said. "But I think it would be good for you."

Roxi shrugged.

"You know, Morgan's eight years younger than me," Keith said, stopping the truck at an intersection. "But sometimes *I* feel like the kid brother."

"I'd never know she was your sister."

"We definitely lead different lives. Her husband Denny Elliot's a real estate developer, and they've done real well. I'm happy for her. We didn't have much growing up." Keith smiled. "And as you can see, I still don't."

"Yeah, but she doesn't have a ranch."

Keith laughed. "Sometimes Denny jokes about buying me out and putting in a big development. But you know what?" He glanced back at her in the rearview mirror. "I'd rather die than sell our place."

Roxi leaned into her seat. She'd never had much either, but living at Lonely River Ranch made her feel rich. They didn't drive flashy cars, and they still used a computer that was almost a decade old, but Jan and Keith had given her something money couldn't buy, something she'd never had.

"Maybe I shouldn't come," Roxi said softly. She fingered the stuffing popping out of a crack in the vinyl upholstery.

"Did Morgan say something to you?" Jan asked.

Roxi stared out at the fence they were passing. She couldn't tell them she'd heard what Morgan had told Jan.

"I know my sister, kid."

"She didn't have to."

Keith tapped the steering wheel with the four fingers of his right hand. The fifth, his ring finger, was a stump. He'd lost it to a tangled rope while branding a calf. "You know, I've been called a lot of things by a lot of people. Some say I'm a fool for trying to keep our ranch going in this economy. But I know right here," he patted his chest, "that I'm no fool. That's what counts. Who cares what Morgan or Denny or the guy down at the feed store thinks? What someone says can only hurt you if you start thinking it yourself."

Roxi finally gave them both a smile. She'd never known what it was like to have parents who truly cared, and it felt better than she could've imagined to have Jan and Keith on her side.

～

The wind blew May's hair in her face, but she didn't move to fix it. Standing over Ruth's freshly covered grave, all she could do was stare at the dirt and let her tears mix with the earth.

Everyone always told her she was strong. Growing up without parents from the age of fifteen had forced her to be. It was only God's mercy that kept her from rebelling back then. She *was* strong, but she wasn't hard. At just the right times God had placed Aunt Edna and then Ruth in her life, two pillars of spiritual maturity and maternal wisdom. When she'd lost Aunt Edna, who'd lived a long full life and died peacefully in her sleep, she'd had Ruth to lean on. But with Ruth gone, who could she turn to now?

As Christy, Jim, and Beth Eckert waited quietly at a respectful distance, May closed her eyes and whispered a few words to her friend. She didn't really think Ruth could hear her from heaven, but it comforted her anyway. She wished for one more day, even an hour so she could thank the old woman for giving her a place and a purpose at a time in her life when she needed it most.

Aunt Edna had loved her through Mom and Dad's death, but Ruth had carried May through the transition into womanhood.

May smiled down at the grave. Ruth was with her Luis now. She was happy. She'd lived a long, full life, too. But that didn't do much to comfort May in the here and now. It didn't explain how she was going to run a ranch by herself. She was doing this alone, and she knew it. If she screwed up, Ruth wouldn't be there to show her how to make it right. She didn't have the luxury anymore of someone with experience looking over her shoulder.

She couldn't place that burden on Jim, even though she knew he'd help all he could. What if someday he chose to move on to a bigger ranch that paid better than the meager check she could give him every month? He certainly deserved it.

"Enjoy your eternal home, my dear friend," May whispered. "Say hi to Mom and Dad for me. I . . . I know I didn't say it much, but I love you. Thanks for all you taught me."

The words came from her heart, but she could barely speak them. May raised her face to the sky, where cirrus clouds were turning a deep red. Her gaze came to rest on the Spanish Peaks. She'd never wanted to live anywhere else but under their shadow.

"I lift my eyes to the hills," May said softly. "Where does my help come from?"

She knew where Ruth was, and she knew Ruth had trained her for this very time. "My help comes from the Lord, the Maker of heaven and earth."

She hoped saying the words out loud would help her believe them.

21

By the time they pulled up to Morgan's home, Roxi's stomach was in knots. She stared up at the massive house, and the view was overwhelming. They'd had to drive through a black gate with a security guard to get in, passing five other mansions before reaching this one. It even had a circular drive-way that allowed them to pull right up to the columns of the front porch, which was bigger than the Mercer's living room and dining room combined.

"Pretty impressive, huh?" Keith said.

Roxi nodded. The sinking sun was painting the columns a burnt orange, and she felt as out of place as Keith's rusted truck looked on the cobblestone driveway. Jan and Keith led the way up to the carved front door, and Roxi trailed behind, trying to guess how many bedrooms a place like this would have. She looked down at her sneakers and tried to stomp them a little. The carpets were probably white, and she wasn't about to leave dirty footprints.

On the way over, Keith had told her about Morgan and Denny's kids. Their oldest was seventeen-year-old Skylar, who Keith said looked like she was twenty and reminded him of Morgan when she was that age. Tony was fourteen and all boy, according to Jan. Twelve-year-old Ethan was fascinated with anything that had wheels.

Denny answered the door in khakis and a white Oxford rolled up his muscular forearms. She wondered how many hours he spent at the gym. His welcoming smile seemed nice enough as the three of them stepped into the foyer. The ceiling stretched up to the full height of the house, letting in the sunset through the tall windows. Their voices echoed in the space, and Roxi hung back behind Jan and Keith.

"And this is Roxi," Keith said, turning toward her.

Denny stretched out his hand. "I've heard a lot about you."

Yeah, I bet your wife has filled you in, big time. She returned his handshake trying to muster her confidence. It would definitely have been easier at the ranch.

"Skylar's out back if you want to go find her," Denny said.

She hesitated, but Jan gave her a nod, so she quickly took a guess on which way was out and left the foyer. She had to remind herself these people were Keith and Jan's family. And they had invited her.

It was hard not to gawk as she passed through each room. In the living room, the entertainment system took up an entire wall, its dark cabinets and shelves holding rows of DVDs and a TV that was almost as tall as she was. The two leather sofas with mounds of neatly arranged throw pillows made her want to sit down with a bowl of popcorn. She bet the sound was fantastic.

The dining room table could've sat the whole cast of *Glee*. Keith wasn't kidding when he said Denny did well. She had no idea it was *this* well.

She finally found the back door, made of glass, and gingerly opened it. She stepped out into a lush garden with flowers and strange plants she'd never seen before. The sound of trickling water floated across the patio with lanterns set on a stone wall ready to illuminate when it got dark.

In the distance she saw something familiar. A barn. Only this one looked like it was built in the last ten years, rather than the last hundred like the Mercer's barn. Fashioned out of stained logs with a green roof, the structure was built next to a fenced arena. And that's when Roxi got her first glimpse of Skylar. Riding a sleek, black bay with a white star and blaze, she trotted around the arena in full English riding regalia. Roxi didn't know the names of all the tack, but she'd seen pictures in one of the magazines the Mercers had laying around the living room. Skylar could've been one of the models in *Horse Illustrated*. Her pink helmet, shiny black boots, leather riding gloves, and a lighter pink short-sleeved polo shirt were as impeccable as her parents' house.

Roxi approached the arena slowly, observing the girl and horse. Her reins were so short the horse's nose nearly touched its chest, and as she trotted past, Roxi saw white lather on the upper muscles of the bay's front legs. The pair made a lap around the ring. Roxi still didn't know much about horses, but it was obvious this one was nothing like calm Sally. She could see the whites of its eyes.

She didn't have to wait long to find out why. As Skylar and the horse made another pass, she saw a crop in the girl's hand. She brought it down on the horse's rear with a loud whack, causing the horse to pin her ears back and surge forward. The crop came down hard three more times before the horse moved into a less than graceful canter. They made two circles at this speed, and then Skylar yanked on the reins harder. Mouth open, the horse kept cantering, and Skylar pulled harder, giving it another whack with the crop.

Roxi reached the fence, mesmerized and horrified all at once. The horse was beautiful but clearly as confused as Roxi was as to what Skylar wanted it to do. Without thinking, Roxi blurted out, "You oughta give her some rein!"

Skylar's head jerked around to spot her, and the scowl she

sent in Roxi's direction was enough to make her want to run back to the house. But she'd faced harder girls than Skylar in the past two years. She had to do something. Even if she was a pauper in a princess's palace, she could walk out at any time. This horse could not.

Jerking violently on the reins a few more times finally got the horse back down to a trot, but her eyes were even wilder as Skylar manhandled her over to Roxi. As they approached, Roxi saw sweat on the girl's forehead.

"Who are you?"

She would not hesitate. "Roxi Gold. Your mom invited us to dinner."

"Oh," Skylar said in a tone that confirmed Morgan had most definitely told her family what she thought about the delinquent girl her brother and sister-in-law had living with them.

Dismounting at the fence, Skylar waved at the horse. "This has gotta be the worst horse I've ever owned."

"She's beautiful," Roxi said softly.

That made Skylar laugh. "If you like stubborn."

"What were you trying to get her to do?"

"How about actually obeying me?" Skylar reached for the mare's head, and the horse instantly threw it way up out of the girl's reach, her ears once again pinned. "It took me twenty minutes to get a bridle on her, and look what she did to me."

Skylar held up her arm, showing Roxi an angry pink welt.

"Bit me when I tightened the girth. Man, I let her have it for that."

Roxi studied the mare. "Maybe she was scared?"

Skylar laughed again. "She should be. I've had enough of her stupid antics."

After walking the mare around the arena a few times to cool off, Skylar brought her out and headed toward the barn, crop hanging from her hand. The horse continued to pull on the reins, pushing ahead of Skylar.

"What's her name?" Roxi asked.

"Lacey."

The only dirt in the immaculate barn was in the walkway where it looked like Skylar had picked Lacey's hooves. Attaching cross ties to the horse's bridle, Skylar went to undo the girth, and the mare swung her head around. Only the cross ties kept her from getting close enough to bite Skylar, but the girl still slapped the crop hard across the mare's neck.

Roxi felt herself flinch and hoped the horse wouldn't try to bolt. Jan had told her never to tie a horse using a bridle, both for the sake of the tack and the horse's mouth.

"Shouldn't you have her in a halter?"

Skylar rolled her eyes like she'd asked the dumbest question ever. "You don't know anything about horses, do you?"

"I . . ."

"You gotta show them you're the boss, the alpha mare. Otherwise, they'll walk all over you." Skylar pulled off the girth, saddle, and pad, and handed them to Roxi without hesitating. "Here. Hold these. Think you can handle that?"

She managed to nod. Skylar attempted to sponge the mare down, but Lacey would barely stand still.

"Knock if off!"

Roxi kept her distance from the horse to keep from being blindsided, but she couldn't help wondering how Jan would handle this animal. Roxi didn't think she'd ever seen her hit a horse like this. She didn't have to know much about horses to know Skylar's techniques didn't feel right.

"That's all I'm gonna be able to do," Skylar said. She undid the crossties, and Lacey promptly tried to take off down the aisle. A couple jerks and the mare was locked in her stall. Roxi and Skylar stood outside watching Lacey pace. Roxi was still holding the saddle, but couldn't stop staring at the horse. Lacey shook her mane and gave Roxi one quick glance before she went over and checked her empty feed bucket.

Skylar let out a long sigh, pulling off her helmet. Auburn hair spilled to her shoulders. She was taller than Roxi, like her mom, and Keith was right—even without much makeup she looked older than seventeen. She made no move to take the saddle from Roxi.

"Where do you want this?" Roxi held it up.

"Oh, just bring it in here." Skylar turned on her heels and walked to the other end of the barn. Roxi followed, noticing several other horses in the stalls.

"Are these all yours?"

"Mine and my mom's."

"I didn't know she rode."

"She grew up on a ranch."

Skylar led the way into a well-lit tack room, one whole wall full of saddles perched on neat metal racks. It was probably climate controlled. Skylar pointed out an empty rack, and Roxi deposited Lacey's gear onto it.

"Not the pad and girth," Skylar said in an annoyed tone.

"Oh . . . so where do they go?"

The girl pointed at a wall of towel rack style bars where multicolored pads, most of them pink, dangled. Beside these were several leather girths of different lengths hanging from hooks.

"But you gotta wipe the girth down first."

Roxi got the girth and pad and handed them to Skylar with a smile, making sure the pad was sweaty-side-down on her arm.

"I better head inside," Roxi said.

She didn't wait for a response and walked back the way she'd come, stopping for a second outside Lacey's stall. Resting her hand on the door, it rattled ever so slightly, and at the sound the mare swooshed her tail.

"I'm not gonna hurt you," Roxi whispered, then quickly made her way toward the house before Skylar could order her to sweep the aisle.

Roxi could feel Morgan's eyes on her as she walked into the kitchen. Skylar's mother stood at the stove wearing a dark blue apron and stirring something in a pot, and Jan was at the island grating cheese. Roxi made for the empty bar stool near Jan.

"Where's Skylar?" Morgan asked.

"In the barn."

Morgan rolled her eyes. "She knows it's dinnertime."

"How's the new horse working out for her?" Jan asked, dumping the cheese in a bowl.

"I should never have believed that lady." Morgan waved her wooden spoon in the direction of the barn. "Said she was a good, well trained horse. The vet said she was perfectly sound too, but ever since she got here she's been nothing but trouble."

"She looks stressed," Roxi said. "Maybe she needs . . ."

Morgan's mouth opened slightly as she raised her eyebrows at Roxi. "And what sort of experience do you have with horses?"

Roxi crossed her legs at the ankles and glanced down at her hands. Then she forced herself to look Morgan square in the face. "I'm going to be a horse trainer someday."

"Oh, really?"

Skylar saved Roxi from bumbling any further. The girl breezed through the kitchen, heading straight for the fridge. Still in her riding clothes, her boots clipped on the floor. Keith and Denny came in behind her laughing at something, and Roxi wished she could just go wait in the truck.

While everyone else chatted about moving cattle and which pie to have for dessert, Roxi kept thinking about Lacey. Maybe she didn't have the credentials and experience of Jan, Morgan or even Skylar, but she knew what it felt like to be alone, and she wondered if horses felt that way too sometimes in a world full of cruelty.

Somehow Roxi made it through dinner without having to say much more than "please pass the bread". Dessert was Morgan's cherry or blueberry pie with the richest vanilla ice cream Roxi had ever tasted. Made with real cream, they special ordered it from some gourmet restaurant Roxi couldn't pronounce.

Then Morgan and Denny got started describing their summer vacation in Europe. When they headed in the living room to show Jan and Keith a video of the trip, Roxi's eyes glazed over. She asked Jan to point her to the bathroom and got up before Morgan could object, but not before she gave her an if-you-break-anything-you're-paying-for-it look.

She used the bathroom, but didn't return to the group. Instead, she found herself slipping out the back door and heading toward the barn. It was almost dark now, but she didn't mind. There was something comforting about a barn, even if this one cost more than Keith and Jan probably made in a year.

Like she had with Selah two years ago when she'd found her abandoned behind the Safeway, she felt a connection with the bay horse. If they did get rid of her like they threatened to do, Roxi would never see her again. Would they sell her to another girl like Skylar or ship her off to some auction where someone would buy her based on a pound weight?

Inside, she slowed her steps as she approached the mare's stall, not wanting to startle her. "Hey, there, girl."

A huge head popped up, water dripping from her mouth. Roxi took a deep breath of the sweet horse smell, catching whiffs of hay, manure, and a splash of leather, too. Maybe she was being too hard on Skylar. It's not like the horse wasn't cared for. She had a nicer stall than any of the Mercer's ranch horses, probably ate the best hay and grain, and how hard could it be riding around the ring once in awhile?

She inched closer to the stall, and Lacey plastered her ears back, walking to the opposite side. Skylar would probably say that was a sign of disrespect. And maybe it was in a way. How could Lacey respect someone who hit her if she didn't understand her commands? Roxi knew she really didn't know much about horses, but Skylar's way just felt cruel and confusing.

She reached for the latch. At the sound, Lacey's ears went back again and she faced Roxi, head lowered in a menacing way. Roxi took a chance that it was all posturing and opened the sliding half-door. She wasn't brave enough to step inside, but this way she could get a better look at the animal. In the dim light of the stall, Lacey was a dark ghost with four legs. The mare's ears eventually relaxed to a normal position, and she cocked one back foot, like she was relaxing.

Leaning against the doorway with her shoulder, Roxi let out a long sigh. She had so many questions with no answers. She bet Skylar had the next ten years of her life planned out.

"So what do ya think, girl?" She smiled in the darkness. "Think I could be a horse trainer?"

"What in the world are you doing?"

Roxi spun around as the lights flipped on.

Morgan stood in the aisle, akimbo.

"I . . ."

Without waiting for a reply, Morgan pushed past her and wrenched the stall door closed. It slammed with a bang that made both her and Lacey flinch.

"I wasn't doing anything," Roxi said.

Morgan grabbed her by the arm. "You come in here without permission, in the dark. What are you up to with our horse?"

Roxi twisted out of her grasp. "I was just looking at her."

"You opened the stall! That's hardly looking."

She made herself take a deep breath and count to five. Blowing up over Morgan's assumptions would hardly help her win the woman's trust.

"Really. That's all." Roxi waved toward the stall. "Skylar seemed like she was having trouble with her, and I was just wishing I could help."

"Skylar is an excellent rider." Morgan's voice held pride.

"I could tell. But the horse—"

"Is a mess."

Roxi edged over to Lacey's stall again. She knew what it felt like to be misunderstood. "Our neighbor, May Williams, is a trainer. I think she could help Lacey."

"We're not clueless, Roxi." Morgan joined her at the mare's stall. "I've been around horses my whole life. Skylar, too. What could your neighbor do that we aren't doing already?"

Was it Roxi's imagination or had her tone softened just a little?

"May could help Lacey calm down a little."

Morgan shook her head. "Sometimes you gotta count your losses."

"But . . ."

"She's just too much horse."

Lacey sent out a snort as Roxi studied Morgan's face. For the first time, she felt like she was seeing the real Morgan, a person who fiercely protected what was hers. She knew what she knew and wouldn't let anybody talk her out of it. Maybe she hadn't lost her rancher's blood after all. They were made of tough stock.

"I could talk to May for you," Roxi said.

Morgan sighed and dropped her hands to her sides. "You sound just like Jan."

Whether that was meant as a compliment or not, Roxi didn't care. Morgan couldn't have said anything nicer.

"But if I get a trainer, it's going to be me who does the talking." Morgan pointed her finger toward the house. "Now get inside, young lady."

Roxi reluctantly followed Morgan back to the house, but

as they closed the huge barn door, she could've sworn she
heard Lacey nicker after her.

22

The shrieking phone startled May from her much-needed sleep. She almost let it go since nothing good could come from a call in the middle of the night, but then she reached across Scribbles snoozing beside her on the bed and picked up the cordless.

"Hello?"

"Those kids are back," Jim said. "I see a fire up by the top pasture."

"What?" May threw off her covers, instantly more awake.

"Could be wrong, but—"

"I'll be right out." She tossed the phone on the mattress, and Scribbles thumped his tail. "Sorry, boy, but you're staying in here."

She slipped on her dirty jeans from yesterday, closed the dog in her bedroom, and carefully treaded down the hall to the office. She hesitated to wake Brynn, but they might need help, and it was better the girl realized sooner rather than later the realities of a rancher's life.

May knocked on the office door, but she heard no response. Opening it a crack, the hall light illuminated Brynn still asleep on her stomach, her arm hanging over the edge of the cot.

"Brynn, wake up."

Nothing.

May walked in and stared down at her faintly snoring employee. She shook Brynn's shoulder.

"Come on, Brynn. I need you up."

The girl groaned, then turned over. May shook her again, and Brynn finally opened her eyes.

"Get dressed, quick," May said.

"What . . . what's going on?"

By the light pouring in from the hall, May opened the gun case beside her desk and removed the Remington rifle. She grabbed a box of shells, too.

"Jim spotted a campfire up near where we found that dead cow."

Brynn pushed up on her elbow. "You're going up there?"

"*We're* going."

"But isn't that dangerous?"

May loaded the rifle. "We'll be okay."

"Is Jim coming too?"

"He's waiting for us." May pointed at Brynn's pack and the girl quickly slipped on her clothes.

They were out the door two minutes later, and Jim met them with his truck running.

"Maybe they don't know it's your property," Brynn said, climbing in.

"Then we'll tell them." May got in beside her and slammed the door, carefully holding the rifle between her legs with the business end pointed at the ceiling.

~

As the truck rumbled through the pasture, Brynn felt an element of adventure about the whole thing that stirred her.

Doing something important, something that mattered, felt strangely good.

May jumped out at each gate and quickly opened and closed it for the truck. Slowly, the faint glow Jim had said was a campfire grew bigger in the windshield, and they began to hear music.

When the scene finally came into view, Brynn recognized a party. There must've been almost twenty people her age and younger milling around a bonfire. The flames were jumping four feet into the air, sparks flying dangerously close to the pines along the edge of the forest.

"You've gotta be kidding me," May muttered.

They pulled up with the headlights shining on the group, and most of them lifted their hands to shield their eyes. A pounding dance beat echoed through the forest. At least half of the crowd held beer cans. Their laughter quickly died off as Jim stopped, pulled up the emergency brake, and opened his door.

May reached for the other door, but Brynn caught her arm. "You sure this is a good idea?"

"They're on my land," May said.

"Twenty to three."

"She's right," Jim said, reaching behind them and pulling his own rifle off the rack. "Be careful."

May climbed out.

Brynn didn't want to follow her, but she also didn't want to be left alone in the truck when the people with the guns were outside. She fell into step behind May.

"Hey, who invited you?" A lanky guy with a ball cap stood up from the ground and came toward them.

"This is private property," Jim said loud enough to be heard above the music.

"We aren't hurtin' nobody."

A chorus of complaints came from all around them, and

Brynn noticed several couples entwined on sleeping bags, oblivious to the fact that their party was about to be broken up. She'd been to parties like this where alcohol, drugs and promiscuity flowed together like three streams converging into the ocean of misguided youth. Brynn looked at the kids surrounding that fire and understood them.

May stepped toward the guy with the ball cap. "Not hurting anybody?" Her voice rose. "Just one of these sparks could set the whole forest on fire!"

Two more guys and a girl came and stood beside their friend. All four of them squinted in the headlights, but there was a look in the fourth guy's eyes that sent a shiver up Brynn's spine. They were probably on something, and the wildness in this guy's face told her to tread carefully. Like a ticking bomb, she knew if May and Jim said the wrong things, this whole situation could explode in ways neither of them could imagine.

She touched May on the shoulder, but her half-sister didn't seem to notice.

"I'm giving all of you five minutes to be out of here," May said.

Guy #4 stepped right up to her. "We were just having a little fun."

"Yeah, well it won't be so fun when the cops charge you with underage drinking and trespassing, now will it?"

By then everyone, even the ones still lying by the fire, had turned toward the group and were murmuring curses and groans. Someone turned the music down a few notches. Maybe they were hoping for a show. Nothing like a good fight to get everyone's attention.

"You heard the lady," Jim said. He was holding his rifle casually with one hand. "You all need to clear out now."

"And who are you, pops?"

Brynn's heart pumped faster as Guy #4 approached Jim.

His clothes hung on his bony frame, but he was just as tall. If he had anything like meth running through his veins right now it could give him the upper hand. Jim stepped back and raised his gun ever so slightly.

"Not a good idea, son."

May and Jim didn't seem to realize they were escalating the scene, and as much as Brynn hated to get involved, she knew what these people were feeling. Placing herself right in the middle, she marched up to stand by the fire where everyone could see her.

"Listen up!" She clapped her hands, and all turned in her direction. "We know you're just having some fun. Can't blame you for that. We just need you to move the party somewhere else."

She could feel Jim and May staring at her.

"Why don't you all head over to one of your houses? Someone's parents have gotta be out, right?"

A few laughs came from around the fire.

"Aw, but we don't wanna move!" someone yelled.

"I know, I know. But we'd really appreciate it, and it's getting cold out here anyway."

She wasn't sure if it was going to work. No one moved, and the flames burned on. Finally a girl approached the group facing off Jim and May and whispered something in Guy #4's ear. He seemed to consider her words, then pulled back with her and disappeared into the woods.

One by one others followed suit, flipping on flashlights and gathering up their clothes, blankets and coolers. The music flipped off. Several stumbled around the fire like the drunk kids they were, and Brynn wondered how many times she'd looked that pathetic.

A guy kicked a beer can into the fire and gave them the finger, but joined the others in a procession of weaving and bobbing flashlights heading toward the road over the hill where they'd all probably parked their cars and trucks. She didn't want to think about them on the highway.

When the last light disappeared, Brynn went to the other side of the fire and started picking up empty cans.

May was still standing where she'd started, perhaps wondering if these kids were the same ones who'd killed her cow.

"That was pretty impressive," May said.

Brynn shrugged.

"I guess I was getting a little worked up."

"Understandable," Brynn said.

"What in the world were they thinking?" Jim dropped trash in the back of the truck.

Brynn stared into the fire. Its center glowed white.

"They *weren't* thinking," May said. "That's the thing. I recognized a few of 'em, too."

"Same here," Jim said, his rifle resting in the crook of his arm. "John and Debbie's kid. And Carl's grandson."

May picked up an empty brown bag. "They know better."

"So did I," Jim said. "But I still managed to get in trouble as a kid."

Sending a teasing look in Jim's direction, May rested her rifle against the truck's front fender and grabbed a long stick from the edge of the woods. She began spreading the logs apart. "Oh, really? That doesn't sound like you at all, Jim."

He set his rifle next to hers and pulled a shovel from the bed of the truck. "Bet you did, too."

"Sure I did," May said. "Just not this kind."

"What, you got in trouble for not emptying the trash?"

May pushed the largest log away from the others. "I got grounded once for being out till two a.m."

"Partying, eh?"

"I was watching a meteor shower."

Laughing, Jim dug the shovel into the dirt and started scooping it onto the fire.

"What?" May was trying to hide her own smile, but Brynn saw it, even in the dimming firelight.

"That just fits, is all." Jim chuckled.

"I once went into an abandoned house on a dare." May spread out the coals with her stick. "And my so-called friends called the cops on me while I was still inside."

Jim laughed again.

"It wasn't funny," May said. "I was so scared I almost wet my pants."

"Oh, I can just see you now." Jim threw more dirt on the fire.

Brynn kept picking up cans to give herself something to do. In May, she saw who she could've been, and it caused a deep ache in her heart. There was an innocence about May. She could look back on her years and clearly remember things. She didn't have chunks blacked out by the fog of drugs.

Crouching in the darkness by the quickly smothering fire, Brynn picked up half a joint and flicked it into the flames. This woman, her older sister, when given the choice between right and wrong, had chosen what was right. Perhaps some would've said May had missed out on all the fun, but in that moment, Brynn would've given anything to be her.

23

The next morning Brynn was surprised when May asked her to drive into town for groceries and to pick up some stuff from Walker's Feed Store. It gave her the perfect cover to meet with Shane. They'd debated the best place, finally settling on the church parking lot.

Guilt ate at Brynn as she drove Ruth's truck into Elk Valley with the windows down, the breeze playing with her hair and bringing with it the scent of dry pine and freshly cut hay. It was the first moment since stepping away from those prison gates that her freedom really hit home, but she couldn't enjoy it. She was out of pills.

The only reason she'd taken any in the first place was to get through Ruth's death, and now it was just until she got up the nerve to tell May and Christy who she was. She had to make the best impression possible, and that wasn't happening if she couldn't sleep or was too stressed to think clearly. As soon as everything was out in the open she'd cut drugs out of her life forever again.

Brynn drove right past the Safeway. Pulling into the empty church lot, she slid Ruth's truck into a space on the edge to wait for him.

This was May's church, the same one where Ruth's funeral

had been held, but Brynn tried not to think about that. Instead, she conjured up memories about the churches she and Mom had attended over the years. Mom had always searched out the untraditional ones. They'd even attended an African American church for a couple months, only leaving when they had to move. Brynn had liked that one. The ladies there didn't hesitate to wrap you in a hug.

Those days seemed so far away. Never again would she be that idealistic Christian girl with a head full of dreams, wanting to make a difference. The old ladies who'd smiled and nodded their approval when she shared in Sunday school would surely look down their noses at her now.

Brynn rested her head on the back of the seat. What a disgrace she must be to God, and she would be to her sisters, too, if they knew. May was trusting her, and she was breaking that trust with every step she took.

It wasn't long before Shane pulled up beside her in a blue Toyota, and she reached over to unlock the passenger door. He slipped in, slamming the door with finality.

"Wasn't sure you'd show," he said.

"I wasn't either."

He rested his arm on the seat behind her. "I don't do this for just anyone, you know."

"Did you get them?"

"Yeah, but . . ."

"I've got two-fifty." Brynn took the money, her first week's pay, out of her back pocket and gave it to Shane. This morning, May had pulled an antiquated metal cracker box from her desk drawer and counted it out in ones, fives and tens.

"You're going all out, aren't you?" Shane handed her a baggie containing twelve green 80 mg oxy pills. "That's barely a taste. I can hook you up with a whole lot more than that."

Brynn stared at the baggie in her palm. A doctor would

prescribe more than this. They were hardly enough to get her hooked again. Barely enough to last a week.

"I gotta run," Shane said. "Call me on my cell if you need anything."

She managed a nod, then watched him get back in his car and zoom off. That's when she saw the man walking toward her from across the parking lot. What had he seen?

A shot of adrenaline sent her heart pounding. She stuffed the baggie into her jeans pocket. Should she drive off?

The man had a shaved head and goatee. He smiled at her, and she knew leaving now would look more suspicious than staying. She started the truck and rolled down her window, easing the vehicle over to the guy.

"Hi," she managed.

"I'm Pastor Walt," he said, shaking her hand, his meaty fingers swallowing hers. "Can I help you with something?"

"No, I . . . I was just leaving."

"We keep the doors unlocked, and the sanctuary's a quiet place if you need it."

Brynn did her best to look casual. The pastor didn't seem to notice anything, but he kept his arm resting on her door.

"You sure you don't need anything?" Walt gave her a warm smile. "Most people don't come here in the daytime unless they're searching."

"Thanks. I'm fine."

Walt's expression softened. "I didn't catch your name."

"Brynn."

He waved at the church building. "You're always welcome here, Brynn."

She seriously doubted that. If he had any idea what she'd just done he would've called the police.

"Do you know that young man who just left?"

The question sent a ripple through her conscience. "What man?"

"The one who was sitting in your truck."

Heat crept up the back of her neck. "Not well."

"It might be best if you kept it that way."

Something rose inside her. "So I'm always welcome, but he isn't?"

"Not what I said."

"Because that seems a little two-faced."

Walt's expression didn't change, but he looked right into her. "Shane is just as welcome here as you are. But that boy has broken his grandmother's heart, and I don't want him to hurt anyone else. Including himself."

She decided now would be a good time to leave and released her foot from the brake. Walt didn't try to stop her. She hoped he wouldn't call the cops after she left and report a blonde, twenty-something heading out of the parking lot and looking for trouble.

On the road back to the Safeway, she gripped the steering wheel with slick hands. She'd promised herself she'd never do this again. That was the only good thing that had come out of the last five years. She'd been forced to get clean.

Pulling out the oxy, Brynn tried to tell herself this was just helping her face her sisters. And it's not like she was grinding them up and snorting them like she used to. It would be like a doctor had prescribed them to her for temporary pain relief.

As she popped two in her mouth, she vowed these were the last of anything she'd buy from Shane, or from anyone, ever again.

❧

Brynn knew she was high when she passed The Book Corral. Maybe that's why she pulled up to the curb and boldly walked inside. Expecting to find Christy alone with maybe one or two random customers browsing, instead she saw people milling all over the place. It took her a moment to spot Christy talking with a man in a sportcoat. He held a microphone, and a camera hung from his shoulder by a leather strap.

Christy saw Brynn and waved at her. "Perfect timing," she said to the man. "This is the young lady I was telling you about."

Brynn froze. What was going on here?

Waving at her again, Christy walked toward her. "This is Lloyd Stevens, from the paper. They're doing a story on our *Anne of Green Gables* find. I verified the points, Brynn. It's a first edition, and so is the dust jacket."

Lloyd extended his hand to Brynn. His moustache made him look older than he probably was. The bald spot on the top of his head didn't help either.

"I understand you were the one who actually found this book," he said. "I'd love to take a statement from you, if I could."

Christy's eyes betrayed her excitement over the exposure The Book Corral was going to receive from this coverage. That's the only reason Brynn agreed to talk to the reporter. Christy was trying to survive here, and she could help.

"Did you know it was a first edition when you found it?" Lloyd asked.

Brynn took a deep breath. "I had no idea. Christy here is the expert."

"But something must've drawn you to the book."

"It looked interesting."

Lloyd turned to Christy. "How do you suppose everyone else at the book sale missed a find like this?"

Glancing at Brynn, Christy smiled. "Maybe God was looking out for us."

After a few more questions and several photographs with Brynn and Christy holding the book together, Lloyd checked the spelling of both their names and left with the promise of running something in tomorrow's edition.

"I didn't expect all that," Christy said after he'd gone. She still held *Anne of Green Gables* in her hands.

"How did he find out?"

"I sent an e-mail to the editor, but really, it was a long shot."

"Congratulations." Brynn looked up and stared at the blank spot on the wall. She felt something tug inside.

Ruth's painting was gone.

"Did someone buy it?" She stepped closer to the wall.

"Yesterday," Christy said.

If a painting was a piece of an artist's soul, then a part of Ruth had just been sold for a measly three hundred. "It was worth a lot more than that," Brynn muttered.

A customer appeared for Christy to check out.

"I should get going," Brynn said.

Outside at the truck, she took a moment to glance up at the puffy clouds. She'd always been drawn to landscapes and had laid down blues and whites on a canvas sky so many times she couldn't count them. She glanced down at her arm where the Phoenix tattoo peeked out from under her t-shirt sleeve. Only toward the end of her painting career had she branched out to other subjects like exotic birds and animals, learning the finer points of things like acrylic under paintings and the angles of light. She'd even dabbled in the abstract once or twice. What would it feel like to hold a brush again?

Brynn climbed into the truck and slammed the door. It was a stupid question.

24

Roxi watched Jan tack up her sorrel gelding in the middle of the barn aisle. The older woman hoisted the heavy leather saddle onto the horse, setting it down slowly so it wouldn't thump uncomfortably on his back.

"Now tell me about this idea of yours," Jan said, looping the leather cinch strap through the ring of her saddle, "because I think you'd make a great trainer."

"Really?"

With a deft hand, Jan tied off her cinch. "You connect with animals in a special way. Just look at Selah."

Roxi smiled. She'd found the abandoned dog behind the Safeway back when she first came here to Elk Valley, and there'd never been a doubt in her mind she had to help the pup.

"There are lots of good trainers out there," Jan said. "But not all of them have the heart to be great ones. You've got the heart."

Roxi nudged a chunk of dirt on the floor with the toe of her boot, basking in Jan's words. She couldn't remember a time when her mother had ever praised her, but Jan was always telling her how smart she was and how she was going to do great things. She was even starting to believe it.

"There was something about Skylar's mare, Lacey." Roxi pictured the horse out in the ring. "She seemed so confused and upset. I just wish I knew what she was thinking, how I could help her. Is that even possible?"

"Of course."

"Have you seen her? Do *you* know what's wrong with her?"

Slipping off her horse's halter, Jan reached over his head and eased the bit into his mouth. "I'd have to work with her a little first, but from what I've seen, that mare is pretty stressed. If Skylar could learn to relax, I think things would get better. But it'll take time."

"Are they gonna sell her?"

Jan gave Roxi a smile. "Not every horse fits every rider."

Which meant Jan thought the same thing she did—they'd probably get rid of the mare, and Roxi would never see her again. In some ways, she wished she'd never met the horse. At least then it wouldn't matter when they'd sold her.

"I ran into May while I was riding the other day."

"Oh?"

"She's a trainer."

Jan nodded.

"Is it okay if I go over there sometime?"

"Sure. May knows a lot."

"I was hoping I could learn a few things," Roxi said.

Jan gave her shoulder a quick squeeze. "You're a good kid, you know that?"

"I'm trying," Roxi said, leaning into her and purposely trying to knock her off balance.

With a laugh, Jan faked her out, and she almost toppled. "It's all gonna work out just fine, kiddo. Don't worry."

With people like the Mercers on her side, it was easier to think so.

"So, are you ready for the barbeque?"

Roxi glanced up at Jan.

"Let me guess. You forgot."

She racked her brain but came up blank.

"I told you about it last week."

Oh . . . now she remembered. The annual thing the Mercers had at their house every year. Jan had told her how Morgan and her family always came and stayed over, camping outside.

"*This* weekend?"

"There'll be lots of people here, not just them."

Roxi groaned.

"Don't get too excited."

"I don't think I can stand being around Morgan that long."

She quickly realized how that must sound. "No offense, but she's just—"

Jan elbowed her. "Just what?"

"Just a really, really . . . uh, nice lady."

Both of them laughed.

❧

After paying some bills and helping Jim give an antibiotic to a heifer with scours, May climbed in her truck and headed north toward Colorado Springs. She wished she could've made the trip with Christy the book expert, but in a way it was good to have the thinking time.

She glanced at the passenger seat where she'd safely wrapped the Jane Austens in a towel. She hoped Christy would be proud of how carefully she was treating them.

Three hours later she took the Monument exit and pulled into the Starbucks parking lot. She grabbed the books off the seat and tucked them under her arm. Even before she opened the door she spotted Harvey Kurtz at a corner table, his laptop perched in front of him. He looked up when she entered, sending a warm grin in her direction as he stood.

May walked to his table and returned his fatherly embrace.

"It's been way too long," Harvey said. With a receding hairline and wire rimmed glasses, he'd been the executor of her parents' and Aunt Edna's estates. For years she'd made it a point to visit Harvey and his wife Betty every couple months. They were the only connection to her parents she had left. Harvey and her father had known each other since high school and were in the Marines together.

"It really has," May said. She set her bundle on the table and went up to order her coffee with cream. When she returned, Harvey closed his laptop and slipped it back into its leather case on the chair beside him.

"I'm so sorry about Ruth," he said. "I wish we'd been in town to come to the funeral."

When she'd called to tell them the news, they'd been on vacation in Aruba. If she hadn't made him swear not to, the couple would've jumped on a plane that day to be there for her.

"I still don't know if it's really hit me."

Harvey touched her hand. "Honey, you're gonna be okay. Ruth taught you well."

She unwrapped the books and slid them across the table. "These are the books I told you about."

Harvey examined them almost as carefully as Christy had. She watched him closely, and when he read the first inscription, she thought she saw his eyes widen.

"Dad never gave these to us," she said. "I found them in his desk after he died."

"Perhaps he was waiting for a special time?"

"Maybe." She pointed at the top book. "Actually, they were originally Aunt Edna's. Her address is in the back of each of them. But what we're really wondering is where's the third volume? Chris says this was a set and if we had all three it would be really valuable. I'd be surprised if Auntie, the avid collector, only had two parts of a set. Do you remember seeing it?"

Harvey stirred his coffee with one of those flat wooden sticks, his massive Marine Corps ring catching her eye like it always did. "She had an old book list for insurance purposes, and I think I have a copy at the office."

That sounded like Auntie. She loved to keep detailed records of her acquisitions.

"Want to come back there with me and take a look?"

Thirty minutes later, she was sitting in a cushy leather chair watching Harvey go through Aunt Edna's old file. Mahogany bookshelves surrounded them, housing hundreds of law volumes, many leatherbound.

The carpet was plush, and she hoped her boots didn't leave marks. Harvey's desk was a mighty wooden hulk with decorative loops and carvings that were probably done by hand. But even in her work clothes she didn't feel uncomfortable here. Harvey had looked out for her like a father would, and she felt perfectly at home.

"I sure wish I could've known Dad as an adult." May thought back to when she talked to Brynn about him almost a week ago. Alcoholism had stolen a lot of her father, but there'd still been good times. She just wished he'd been a little more vocal about his thoughts and feelings.

Harvey peered over his glasses. "He would be very proud of you."

"I'd love to show him the ranch and get him on a horse again, like when he was a boy. I think he would've enjoyed it."

"I know he would've."

She smiled, and Harvey continued rooting through the file.

"Ah, here it is." He pulled out copies of ledger sheets, all written in Aunt Edna's neat script with the extra curlicues. He took a moment to read over the list, and she placed the *Sense and Sensibility* books on the desk.

Harvey waved her over, and she came around the desk and read over his shoulder. All Aunt Edna's books were catalogued by author and included notations about their condition, where she'd purchased them, or who gave them to her. Several Jane Austen books were included, and *Sense and Sensibility* was the first one. May read over Harvey's shoulder:

Austen, Jane
Sense and Sensibility
3 volume set. First edition. 1811. Found at church rummage sale. Gave to Peter as gifts for the girls.

"But he never gave them to us," May said.

Harvey studied the page, then leaned back into his chair. It creaked. "And you're sure you found only two?"

"Definitely. Aunt Edna was with me, and we were going through everything."

"What did Edna say?"

"Well, she seemed surprised to see them, but she said she'd given them to Dad for us. She never said anything about a third book, though. I didn't know there was one until Christy told me it was a three volume set."

Harvey pulled off his glasses and set them on the desk. "I do remember these."

"You do?"

He nodded, rubbing his eyes. Then he picked his spectacles up again and slowly began cleaning them with a white handkerchief he pulled from his coat pocket. She'd seen him do it in court when he needed to buy a moment to think.

"Is something wrong?"

"I want you to understand that your Dad was a good man. He made mistakes like all of us, but he always tried. And, ultimately, he did what he thought was best for both you and Christy."

"What does that have to do with these books?"

"A lot, actually." Harvey carefully slipped Aunt Edna's ledger sheets back into the file, then rested his hands on the folder.

"I'm not following, Harv. I'm just trying to figure out where that third book got to." May absentmindedly paged through one of the volumes.

Harvey sighed, started to say something, then stopped himself.

"What?"

She waited for him to continue as the creases in his forehead deepened.

"Harv?"

He glanced at his bookshelves for a second, then turned his gaze back on her. "This isn't an easy thing for me to tell you. Your dad loved you girls, and your mother, very much. I want to make sure you know that."

"I loved him too, but you're starting to worry me."

"There *was* a third volume, May."

"Okay."

Harvey reached for her hand. "Honey, I'm pretty sure your father gave it to his other daughter."

25

It took Roxi a half hour to walk to May Williams's ranch, and that was cutting through the pastures. By the time she reached the house, her shirt was damp with sweat. Roxi knocked at the back door.

"It's unlocked."

She walked in to find Brynn, the girl she'd met at the bookstore, pulling groceries from a plastic Safeway bag. She'd forgotten Brynn worked here.

"Is May around?"

Brynn glanced up. "She's out. I don't know when she'll be back."

Roxi stuffed her hands into her jeans, catching Brynn's glance at the scar on her arm. "I'm just here to see the horses, but if it's not a good time . . ."

"Did you walk?"

She shrugged. "It's not that far."

"Far enough." Brynn opened a cabinet and stuffed a box of Raisin Bran inside. "You really must want to see those horses."

Roxi smiled.

"I can show you around." Brynn wadded up the empty plastic bag, and after opening a few drawers, shoved it inside one.

Following her outside, Roxi took in the corrals. She counted five horses in separate pens by the far side of the barn. They were probably the ones here for training. In a larger pasture, she saw others horses she guessed were the ranch's string of stock horses.

"Do you work with them every day?"

"May does."

"How's she doing, now that Ruth's gone?"

"As good as you'd expect."

They neared a pen where an Appaloosa stood with his butt to the back corner. His head hung low, his eyes were slits. One back hoof was cocked. Roxi rested her hands on the metal fence panel. The horse immediately came to life at their presence, ears pointed at them.

"I saw May riding him the other day. What's he here for?" Roxi asked.

Before Brynn could answer, an engine growled behind them. Roxi turned around to see a silver, newer model truck with huge tires towing a matching trailer. It rumbled down the driveway spitting gravel and dust, finally stopping in the middle of the yard. She could barely see the driver through the windshield, but then she stepped out wearing pink cowboy boots and dark jeans with a stylish, faded wash.

Roxi took a step toward the girl. "Skylar?"

"What are *you* doing here?" Skylar said.

Roxi tried to ignore her tone. "These are my neighbors."

A sharp bang came from inside the trailer, and Roxi spun toward it. If she had a horse in there . . . was she even allowed to tow a trailer at her age? Roxi took quick steps toward the trailer, Skylar right behind her, and peeked into the open window. A dark shadow moved inside, and she could see Lacey's white star and blaze. Had Morgan really been listening when she suggested they bring Lacey here?

Another noise rattled the trailer, and Skylar slapped the side of it. "Hey, cut it out!"

Roxi hoped the mare wasn't hurting herself.

"So . . ." Brynn came to stand beside them. "Someone fill me in here."

"I better get her out," Skylar said.

Brynn's eyebrows knitted. "Maybe you should wait until May comes back."

"She can't stay in the trailer," Roxi said.

"But . . ."

"It's okay." Roxi gave Brynn a confident nod. She had no idea how wound up Lacey was, but she'd heard about some horses being so afraid that by the time they got off trailers they were drenched. She'd rather deal with Lacey out here than have her get injured in the confined space of the trailer.

Skylar went to the back and unlocked the door. She swung it open and before any of them could react, the dark horse backed up so fast Skylar had to jump out of the way to keep from being trampled. Lacey spun around, her lead rope flying in an arc. Luckily, Skylar caught hold of it before the animal took off.

"I know I tied her!"

It didn't matter now. Lacey seemed unscathed, so she hadn't gotten caught on anything inside. Still, she snorted, circling around Skylar with her black tail high and flowing. It looked like Skylar was trying to hold onto a living tornado with a piece of string.

Lacey pranced around the teen, and Roxi decided now was a good time for someone to take charge. She stepped up to Skylar. "I'll take her."

Surprisingly, Skylar didn't protest. She handed her the mare's lead rope, retreating to where Brynn still stood by the truck.

"Easy, girl. Easy." Roxi took a deep breath and mustered every ounce of calm she could, remembering Jan's advice about relaxing around a horse. Still, instinct was overpowering any sense of reason for the mare. She whinnied toward the pens, and several other horses answered.

"Whoa," she said, drawing the word out. Lacey finally came to a stop, and Roxi stepped toward her and stroked her on the neck. "Take it easy," she whispered. "Everything's gonna be alright now. I'll make sure."

Skylar was complaining to Brynn all about Lacey's problems, how she was an untrained brat and had been nothing but trouble, but Roxi tried to tune her out and take in Lacey's beautiful, rich coat. Her white blaze was like a squirt of whipped cream on her dark, almost black body. Intelligence shone deep in those charcoal eyes, and if she wasn't mistaken, they didn't look quite as wild now.

"Did May know you were coming?" Roxi asked, while vigorously scratching the mare on the neck and withers.

Skylar didn't answer.

Roxi turned around. "You didn't ask her?"

Lacey snorted, spraying Roxi's arm with moisture. What if May wasn't taking new clients now that Ruth was gone?

"If you guys can't fix her, my Mom's going to sell her." Skylar crossed her arms, like she was trying to be tough, but Roxi saw the worry in her face.

Spotting an empty pen, Roxi relaxed her shoulders and walked Lacey toward it. At first, she felt resistance on the end of her lead. She remembered one time Sally had balked when she'd gone to lead her out into the field, and Jan showed her how to keep tension in the rope and wait. Pulling and yanking would just make a hard headed horse. She needed to have patience and wait the horse out. Eventually, she'd give to the steady pressure.

Lacey held her ground, then Roxi felt the rope loosen, and she began walking with Lacey in tow. Brynn held the pen's gate open for her as she stepped inside with the mare. Then Roxi undid the halter and slipped it over the mare's ears.

She took one step away from her, and Lacey took off around the small pen snorting and bucking while the spotted Appaloosa in the pen next to her ran up to the fence to check her out.

Safely outside, Roxi stood with Brynn and Skylar watching the show. What would May do with a horse like this?

"That was pretty impressive," Brynn said, elbowing her.

She managed a smile, her adrenaline still pumping. She'd probably done everything wrong, but at least the horse, and she, were unharmed.

They watched Lacey as she trotted around the perimeter of the pen, head high and looking outward. Skylar continued griping to Brynn about all the problems she'd been having, but Roxi didn't really care what she said. There was something about this horse.

As she made her fourth pass around, Roxi watched Lacey's eyes. Every time she passed, she would turn her head ever so slightly and glance right at her.

Roxi went to find a bucket she could fill with water. When she stepped into the barn, she heard Lacey nicker from the pen, and she smiled. Skylar was still blabbing away to Brynn, now about her horse show experience, but Roxi barely heard. Lacey was here. Safe. They weren't selling her. At least not today.

❧

Brynn filled a glass with water at the kitchen sink and watched Roxi and Skylar from the window. Soon Skylar left, taking her fancy horse trailer with her, but Roxi stayed. Brynn enlisted her to help unload the feed bags she'd picked up at Walker's. It didn't take much prodding. The girl seemed genuinely happy to hang around, and Brynn was glad to get her thoughts off the oxys.

Grabbing a bag from the bed of the truck, Brynn threw it over her shoulder. Roxi mirrored her. They unloaded the first few into the empty stall in the barn without conversation, and Brynn's thoughts drifted to her father. Had Mom purposely kept him from her?

"What will May do with Lacey?" Roxi asked as they passed each other in the barn aisle.

Brynn dropped her bag with a thud, shrugging. "You'll have to ask her."

"Is it alright that Skylar didn't call first?"

"Good question."

"But you think it'll be okay?"

One glance at Roxi's sincerely worried face, and any annoyance Brynn might've had over the barrage of questions faded. "Listen, I really don't know. I just started working here."

They unloaded for awhile, but then Roxi started talking again, and this time Brynn just went along with her.

"Have you always wanted to work on a ranch?"

"Nope."

"I never thought I'd live out here, either."

"You out of school?" Brynn asked. She wasn't sure how old this girl actually was.

"Just got my GED."

She shouldered another bag with a grunt. She wished she'd gotten one of those, but "high school drop out" was another label she'd earned.

"That's a cool tattoo," Roxi said.

She glanced down at her arm. Her t-shirt sleeve had ridden up to expose the fiery Phoenix. "Thanks."

"I've thought about getting one to cover this." Roxi twisted her arm for Brynn to better see the thick scar on the underside of her arm.

"That might hurt."

"Which is why I haven't."

"Well, my mom freaked when I got mine," Brynn said, almost smiling at the memory. Mom was the biggest supporter of her art, but only if it stayed on a canvas. In one of her few rebellious acts, she'd secretly designed the bird.

Roxi kept pace with her. "When you were younger, what did you want to do with your life?"

"I wanted to be an artist."

"Really?"

"I actually designed this tattoo myself." Brynn pulled the second-to-last bag from the truck bed, trying not to feel guilty over the look of admiration Roxi gave her. She didn't deserve to be admired by anyone, especially an impressionable teenager.

"That's awesome," Roxi said.

Dropping her load into the stall, Brynn wiped her forehead with the back of her arm. "I'm not an artist anymore though."

Finally done, Brynn dusted her hands on the fronts of her jeans and sat down on the truck's tailgate, glad to be finished. She was ready for another oxy.

"Why aren't you an artist anymore?" Roxi asked quietly, joining her.

"Because," Brynn said.

"So maybe it's time to be something else," the teen said softly.

Brynn had no answer for her.

26

The drive down I-25 was a blur. May had climbed into her truck outside Harvey's law office and started home by rote.

A glance at her cell phone showed she'd missed two calls, but she wasn't up for talking to anyone but Christy right now, and that needed to be in person.

Three hours later, she pulled up to the back entrance of The Book Corral. She found her sister going through a box of books at the front register, pencil between her teeth.

"Hey, stranger." Christy said with a smile. She slipped the pencil behind her ear.

The store was empty for the time being, and May was glad. She'd carried the Jane Austen books in with her and set them on the counter still wrapped in their towel.

"What's wrong?" Christy slid a chair over to her, but May waved it away.

"I just got back from a meeting with Harvey."

Her sister gave her a quizzical look. "Meeting?"

"I showed him the books."

"Good idea."

"No, it's actually not good." She changed her mind and sat down.

"They are first editions, by the way. I checked," Christy said.

"Not talking about that." May told her about the conversation, right up to Harvey's revelation that had rocked everything she'd ever believed about their father. When it was time to say the actual words, she balked.

"What is it?" Christy touched her arm.

She met her sister's eyes, then looked away. "You were right. There was a third volume."

Christy started to smile, then stopped when May didn't return it.

"Dad had another kid."

The words were like a bolt of electricity zapping between them. She saw Christy's jaw drop and wondered if her own face had looked like that when Harvey told her.

"*What?*"

May nodded. She stared at the Austen books that had changed everything.

"But I don't–"

"Harvey thinks Dad gave the third volume to her."

Christy pulled up another chair and sank into it. "We have a *sister?*"

"Dad called him one night when he was drunk and just told him."

"How could . . ."

Waving her hand in the air, May glanced at the ceiling. A water stain spread across the drywall above her head. "Apparently, Dad cheated on Mom."

Christy seemed to sink lower in her chair, and May could only shake her head as Christy bombarded her with all the questions she herself had asked Harvey.

"All he knows is that Dad gave her the book." May could still see the grave look on Harvey's face when he'd told her all he knew.

"So Dad knew her," Christy said.

"And never told us or Mom."

"We don't know if Mom knew."

On the drive back, May had tried to conjure up memories of either of their parents mentioning something, anything, but neither had breathed a word that May could remember.

They sat for a few moments in silence until a customer came in and Christy had to show her where to find the cookbooks.

∽

Brynn stood outside Doc's pen, pitchfork and muck bucket in hand. Roxi had finally gone home, and with Jim off checking the fences on horseback, Brynn decided to clean up every piece of manure she could find on the property. Maybe if May got home and the place was spotless, Brynn wouldn't have to feel guilty about meeting Shane.

She opened the gate, trying to ignore the horse like she'd seen Ruth do with that other one. She set her bucket down and picked up a pile over in the corner. If only Mom had died peacefully like Ruth had. A few moments of suffering instead of months. Even with a heart condition, Ruth had been able to live a full life until the very end.

Brynn focused on her task, but images of Mom in that hospital room kept surfacing. She hated how the bad memories would pop up more often than the good ones. With a curse, Brynn shoved her pitchfork under another pile. The social worker had tried to get her enrolled in a grief recovery support group, and her girlfriends had done their best saying all the right things, but in the end, only the pills gave her relief.

Suddenly, she heard a snort and hooves pounding the dirt. Brynn swung around to see a thousand pounds of horseflesh racing straight toward her.

∽

"How old is she?" Christy whispered when she came back to May, who hadn't moved.

"Harvey thinks twenties maybe, but he's not sure."

"Does she know about *us?*"

The patron came with two books to purchase, and Christy rang her up while May stewed. She'd always held her father up as an example of honesty no matter the cost. Even if he wasn't perfect, she'd respected him for that. That image was nicely shattered now.

"Do we know her name?" Christy sat down across from May once the customer left the store.

She rubbed her eyes. "That would be a no."

They both scoured the Jane Austen books again, seeing them in a whole new light. Christy kept paging to the inscriptions. "This is . . . I never realized . . ."

Maybe if she'd been a kid when she found out it would've been easier. Even exciting. But to have lived her entire life believing something so important about her family, and then to find out it was a lie, was a blow to her identity.

"Of course I'm shocked," Christy said. "But I can't say I'm completely surprised."

She turned toward her sister. "You suspected?"

"No, not really." Tapping the counter with her pencil, Christy shrugged. "Maybe it was just a feeling."

"But Mom and Dad loved each other."

"And they were human."

May groaned. "Where's that leave us?"

Another shrug from Christy.

"Harvey said he would try to find her for us. If we want."

"Do you?"

May stood up, wanting to pace. Not knowing didn't really

seem like an option at this point. Whoever this sister of theirs was, they shared the same blood. If they didn't at least make an effort to find her it would always nag at May, like not knowing where Christy was had nagged her only a few years ago.

When the shop phone rang, Christy didn't move to get it. May waved her to go ahead.

"Hold that thought," Christy said, scooping up the receiver. "The Book Corral, how may I help you?" She paused, then turned toward May. "Don't you have your cell phone?"

"In my truck."

"Yeah, she's here with me, Jim."

May thought of the two missed calls and realized she should've checked to see who they were from.

Christy quickly hung up, grabbing her purse. "It's Brynn."

27

May and Christy drove together to the hospital, where Jim met them in the lobby.

"Where is she?" Christy asked.

Jim waved toward the examining rooms. "They're stitching her up now."

May didn't know what to say. Brynn had apparently gone into Doc's pen to clean out manure, and he'd charged her. She'd managed to sidestep a full frontal hit, but she'd been slammed up against the metal gate, and she had cuts that were deep enough to bring her to the ER.

May ran her fingers through her hair in frustration. She'd made such great progress with Doc, and now *this*? He could've killed Brynn. When Brynn was discharged an hour later, she had bandages on her upper arm and a nasty scrape to her forehead.

"Are you sure you're okay?" Christy said as Jim went to get the truck.

Brynn looked uncomfortable for a moment, then smiled tentatively. "You guys didn't have to come."

"Of course we did."

"It's not that bad," Brynn said. "But couldn't you ask them to give me something for the pain? They wouldn't listen to me."

May led them out the door. "Advil will be fine. I've seen a lot worse, that's for sure. You were lucky."

They dropped Christy off at the bookstore only after Brynn had assured her multiple times she really was fine. Brynn rode with Jim, which left May alone for the drive back. Not only did she now have a sister out there, but Ruth was gone, and May suddenly felt the loss more than ever. This never would've happened if Ruth was still alive. She would've known just what to do with Doc.

"Oh, Ruth . . ." May choked back tears. "I miss you so much."

The two trucks pulled into the ranch, and May noticed Brynn wince when she got out.

"Go inside and take it easy," May said.

"I told you, I'm alright."

"Still, don't overdo it, okay?"

Brynn nodded.

Walking toward Doc's pen, May stopped in her tracks when she saw the dark bay in the enclosure beside him.

"What in the . . ."

Brynn caught up with her. "I was gonna tell you about that."

Glancing back at Jim, May questioned him with a slight cock of her head, but he just shrugged. May watched the mare pacing, her long mane and tail flowing with the movement.

"Well, now would be a good time. Jim, please move that horse ASAP."

"Roxi came by, and then--"

"Roxi was here?"

"To see the horses."

That's right. She'd invited the girl to stop by anytime.

"We were both surprised when the truck pulled in," Brynn said. "Apparently, Roxi knows the owner. Skylar's her name."

"Why didn't you call me?"

Brynn crossed her arms. Red was seeping through the gauze of her bandage. "There wasn't time."

"So she just drops her horse off without even asking me?"

"Pretty much."

"And you let her?"

"What was I supposed to do?"

May realized her tone was harsh. That seemed to be happening a lot these days, and she didn't like it. "I'm sorry. Go on."

"When Skylar brought her out of the trailer, she was wild. Roxi was great with her and got her to settle down."

"I hope you got this Skylar's phone number at least."

Brynn pulled a folded up piece of paper from her pocket. "Sounded like money wasn't an object."

"Well that's good." May pocketed the paper. "Maybe it'll cover your ER bill."

❧

Later that evening, Brynn walked out to the Airstream trailer with May. The stars had come out, brilliant titanium specks, just like that night with Ruth behind the barn.

Brynn couldn't see May's face. "Are you mad?"

"No." Weariness tinged May's voice as she unlocked the camper door and ushered Brynn inside. For a moment they were surrounded by darkness, the only light the green digital numbers of the microwave clock.

May flicked the switch over the kitchen sink, setting the stack of clean sheets and towels on the counter. "You might need to air it out."

"It'll be fine."

"Once I go through Ruth's stuff you can have her room, if you'd rather."

Brynn dumped her backpack on the circular sofa and dropped down beside it. Her head and arm ached. If only the hospital had given her a prescription. Then she wouldn't have to worry about her quickly dwindling oxy supply.

May sat down beside her, seeming in no hurry to leave. "In the future, call me if you don't know what to do. He was aggressive because you put a mare in the pen beside him."

Brynn nodded. She knew better than to make excuses, but there hadn't been time to think, and she thought she'd handled things. Doc's pen needed to be cleaned, and she'd hoped to impress her sister by getting it done. Yeah, that went well.

"I can't believe I'm doing this without Ruth," May said softly.

A trapped fly buzzed and tapped into the window. Brynn let a moment pass, then asked May how she and Ruth had connected in the first place.

Smiling, May leaned back into the sofa. "I had this dream of being a cowgirl ever since I was a kid. When I graduated from high school, I started looking around. I visited a friend around here and fell in love with Elk Valley. Found out Ruth was doing it on her own so I came out, asked her for a job, and she gave it to me, with the condition that I had to prove myself."

Brynn wondered what they must look like, flopped on the sofa. If someone saw them side by side, would they have guessed they were sisters?

"God just seems so far away," May said. "I know He isn't, but . . ."

"How?"

May turned to face her.

"How do you know?" Brynn asked.

"I just do."

"But you can't prove it."

"Not on my own, no. But just look at the stars. Or the mountains."

She sighed, expecting as much. She'd been to Sunday School. She'd heard it all. And they'd prayed over and over for Mom to get better, but she'd still died. Brynn thought back to some of those last words her mother had whispered . . . *God didn't do this.* Fine. He didn't do it. But He didn't keep it from happening, either.

"There are so many wonders of the universe I can't explain," May said. "Those are what speak of God a thousand times better than I ever can."

"Then where was He when my mom died?"

May rested her head onto the back of the sofa. "And my parents."

Brynn was surprised there was no bitterness in May's tone. Even though her parents had died tragically too, there was still an awe in her voice when she spoke about God. Brynn was struck with the fact that May might actually understand. Which made what she had to say mean a little bit more.

"Aunt Edna used to tell me that sometimes we have to choose to trust even when nothing makes sense."

"Easy to say."

"I know."

"Do you believe that?"

May let out a long breath. "I think I really do."

After that, they spent a little while chatting about the work that needed to be done tomorrow, and then May wished Brynn a good night's sleep and left for her own bed.

Brynn turned off all the lights and stared out at the little ranch house with the warm glow coming from the kitchen. She imagined May at the kitchen table sipping a late night cup of tea with Scribbles at her feet.

She was still sitting on the worn sofa long after the lights in the kitchen blinked out.

May tried to sleep, but ended up staring at the ceiling. *Oh, Lord, forgive me.* She'd been so absorbed in her own loss, her own worries and fears, that she hadn't noticed the hurting soul right in front of her.

Ruth had.

Resting her hands behind her head, May remembered how adamantly Ruth had insisted they give Brynn a chance. It defied reason, common sense, and their budget. Was that all May ever saw these days? Had she forgotten there were things much more important than money? She, of all people, ought to know that.

She'd told Brynn the truth—she wasn't feeling God these days. But that didn't mean He wasn't there, even with all the worries of running the ranch pressing down on her now.

The wind drifted through her open window, brushing across her face. Deep inside, her faith was solid. It was time to start living like it.

She reached across the bed stand and turned on her reading lamp. Her Bible lay where she'd left it last, and May realized she hadn't picked it up since before Ruth died.

The ribbon marker lay in the Psalms, so she started reading there.'

When she got to Psalm 116, the words spoke to her heart. "Let my soul be at rest again," she read in a whisper. "I believed in you, so I said, 'I am deeply troubled, Lord.' In my anxiety I cried out to you, 'These people are all liars!' What can I offer the Lord for all he has done for me? I will lift up the cup of salvation and praise the Lord's name for saving me."

May sunk back on her pillow. She couldn't remember the last time she'd thanked the Lord for saving her. She knew where she would be without Him. She could've easily walked down the same path Chris had, searching for love in all the wrong places and ending up with a truckload of regrets. But God had placed people like Aunt Edna and Ruth in her path to guide her and love her. She had never truly been alone.

She thought about Brynn out there in the Airstream. "Father, help her," May prayed.

Looking down at the Bible one more time, May read the next verse in the Psalm, and tears filled her eyes.

The Lord cares deeply when his loved ones die.

28

Someone was banging on the trailer door. Brynn jumped up, barely awake. What in the—

It was barely light outside.

Another rap, this one louder.

She stood in her bare feet. The last thing she remembered was taking three pills and falling into bed, still in her clothes. She glanced down. Her very wrinkled clothes.

Brynn parted the curtains to see Roxi poised to pound on the door again. Brynn opened it before she could get off another round.

The teen smiled up at her, hand in mid air.

"Isn't it a little early?"

Roxi glanced at her watch. "Around here, seven's practically noon."

With a groan, Brynn stepped back to let the girl in. Not that the teen would've waited for an invitation. Somehow, she had a feeling when Roxi got something in her head to do, it happened.

"Rise and shine," Roxi said.

Brynn yawned and tried to clear her head.

"May told me to wake you."

Oh, great. The last thing she wanted now was to disappoint

May. She had better hustle and get to work before her sister could rethink keeping her on.

Roxi pointed at her bandage. "He got ya pretty good, didn't he?"

"It's not that bad." She hadn't felt much pain last night, but there was a dull throbbing starting under the bandages, and the scrape on her head was tender. If Roxi hadn't surprised her like this she could've taken something to help.

"What happened?"

She gave an abbreviated version of her encounter with Doc, and Roxi stared at her wounds. "You sure you're okay?"

"I'm fine."

"Lacey seems to be settling in."

Brynn unzipped her pack and rooted around for a clean t-shirt. The one she was wearing still had dried blood on it. "May wasn't thrilled Skylar didn't call ahead, but she talked to her mom last night on the phone, and it sounds like they arranged something."

A grin spread across Roxi's face.

Brynn pulled her last clean shirt from its Walmart packaging, tossing the empty plastic bag onto the sofa, and changed into it as quickly as she could.

"What's that?" Roxi was staring into her pack. The spine of *Sense and Sensibility* was clearly visible. Brynn quickly stuffed her dirty shirt inside and wrenched the zipper closed. "Nothing."

Roxi didn't press the issue. "That reminds me. We've got something to show you."

Slipping on her shoes, Brynn followed Roxi outside. She'd use the bathroom and wash her face in the house. Right now, she wanted Roxi's attention anywhere but on the book in her bag.

May and Jim were leaning against the kitchen counter nursing coffee mugs.

"Hey, sleepyhead," May said with a smile.

"Sorry."

"You must've needed it."

"How's the arm?" Jim asked.

"I'll live."

Roxi pulled her toward the office with a glance at May. "Can I show her?"

May nodded, following behind them. "I got an e-mail from Christy," she said. "Apparently she made the paper. So did you, Brynn. Check it out."

May pointed at the computer screen in the office.

Brynn leaned over the desk chair to see the homepage of the Pueblo Star newspaper. The photo that reporter took of her and Christy holding the *Anne of Green Gables* was front and center on the page.

"It quotes you," Roxi said.

"You're kidding."

May started reading the article out loud:

Situated on the quaint main street of Elk Valley, The Book Corral is preparing to put the town on the map—at least in the used and rare book world. The store is celebrating twenty-five years in business, but owner Christy Williams has only operated it less than a year. "When I heard the previous owner was looking to sell, I knew I couldn't let the opportunity pass me by," Williams says. "I've always dreamed of owning my own store."

Formerly the manager of renowned Longmont bookstore Dawson's Book Barn, Williams has honed her skills at identifying first editions and rare titles. But it was actually her friend Brynn Taylor who made the discovery Williams is calling the rarest book find of her career.

That find is a first edition of L. M. Montgomery's beloved novel *Anne of Green Gables*. "But it's not just any first edition," Williams says. "That, in and of itself, would've made the book worth at least $10,000. But this copy has its dust jacket, which is extremely rare."

Verified with experts, it's been confirmed that the jacket is indeed the real deal. When pressed for a guess on its value, Williams shakes her head. "No one knows. But some have guessed it could bring the book's value to over $100,000."

The Book Corral has decided to auction off this rare tome soon, and Williams is excited about the interest that's already being shown. Visit the bookstore's website for more details, including photos of the book.

Roxi gave Brynn's good arm a playful slap. "You're famous."

"I didn't know they'd put in my picture."

"That's not all." May clicked out of the article, and brought up a Gmail account. "Christy's e-mail says she's already been contacted by a Denver paper, and the TV station called, too."

"That's good, right?" Brynn said.

"She seems pretty jazzed about it."

Brynn rested her hand on the back of the chair. Seeing her face displayed like that made her uneasy, and she wasn't sure why. Maybe it was because all she could see was the gap in her father's teeth in that old photograph, just like her own. And her long nose looked exactly like Christy's. Would May notice the resemblance?

After a trip to the bathroom, she excused herself to grab something in the trailer she said she forgot, and she pulled out *Sense and Sensibility* and re-read her father's inscription. She was going to have to tell them sometime. And soon.

Brynn had two less oxy pills when she returned to the house.

29

Lacey was trotting around in her enclosure when May threw two flakes of hay over the rail. The restless horse dove right into the food, but nervously threw her head up to look around as she chewed. When May entered the pen, Lacey pinned her ears. It was a clear warning, or a challenge. Often, if a horse was thrust into an unfamiliar environment their behavioral issues escalated, and sometimes new ones cropped up. That's why Ruth always gave them time to adjust before working with them. May decided to let the mare finish her meal before taking her to the round pen.

An hour later, May haltered Lacey. She patted her neck, noticing her tense muscles. Skylar had said she was a mess, and May suspected that was due to not having a good leader to follow. Horses were herd animals, and they were usually happiest following a dependable, fair, alpha mare. A good way to show that to Lacey was to have better control of her feet than she did. And it all started here, before they even left her pasture.

May led her to the gate, and Lacey quickly tried to push past her to freedom. May crouched down a little and with a quick flick of her wrist twirled the lead rope beside the horse to encourage her to back up. When Lacey didn't respond, she starting hitting the ground with the rope end. The snapping sound got the horse's attention, and she took several steps backward out of May's space. May immediately rewarded her by stopping the rope.

"Good girl. That's all I'm asking."

She let the mare stand still for a moment, then reached for the gate, swinging it open. Lacey raised her head, energy rising. May paused, then started to walk through, but the mare rushed past her again. Twirling the rope quickly and firmly, she made sure Lacey backed up again.

It took them fifteen minutes just to get out the gate, but May was pleased that Lacey walked calmly out. The first time she introduced a new concept to a horse usually took the longest, especially with one who'd been allowed to get away with a behavior. Horses were so much smarter than people gave them credit for. Because she was communicating on the horse's level, in her herd language, she knew it wouldn't take Lacey long to get it.

She practiced stopping and backing the horse out of her space the whole way to the round pen. A few times, May had to actually touch her with the end of the rope to show she meant business, but she never used it cruelly. It was just an extension of her arm. Her safety, and the horse's well being, depended on her leadership getting through loud and clear.

In the round pen, she let Lacey loose, half expecting her to tear off bucking and kicking. Instead, she stood still, holding her head high.

"Think you'll be able to help her?"

May turned to see Roxi walking up to the round pen. She'd forgotten the teen was still here.

"I'm sure we will," May said.

Lacey saw Roxi, and May watched her body soften. She let out a nicker staring right at the girl.

"Well, look at that," May said.

"She did the same thing to me when Skylar first brought her."

"Why don't you step in here for a minute."

The girl froze. "You sure?"

May nodded.

As soon as Roxi entered the round pen, Lacey walked up to her and halted. When Roxi reached up to stroke her ears, Lacey lowered her head and let out a long sigh.

"Isn't that something?" May said.

Roxi shrugged. "I really don't know much about horses."

May stood watching the pair for a long moment, marveling at the mare's response.

"It's almost like she's bonded with you," May said.

"How could that be?" Roxi lightly caressed the mare's nose, and Lacey's eyes started to close. "I just met her a few days ago."

"I don't know, but there's got to be more to her story than we understand." May clipped the lead rope back onto Lacey's halter and handed her over to Roxi.

"Aren't you going to work with her?"

"I want to see you lead her."

The teen gave another little shrug and led Lacey across the pen. The mare calmly followed her with lots of float in the rope.

"Now stop there," May said.

When Roxi stopped, Lacey mirrored her exactly, even taking a step backward out of her space.

"Come back to me."

May walked them through a few more maneuvers and watched Lacey follow Roxi like a dog, moving when she moved, stopping when she stopped.

"Are you sure you don't have horse experience?"

Roxi laughed.

May was still pondering Lacey's reaction after Roxi went home. She brought her horse, Spirit, into the barn to tack him up for a round of checking cattle. She'd heard about horses forming inseparable bonds with humans before, but usually it was after a lifetime of interaction or because someone had raised a foal from birth.

As she was brushing Spirit's neck, May's thoughts soon drifted toward her unknown sister, and she was filled with a longing to know what she was doing at this exact moment.

❧

Brynn stood in the Airstream's tiny bathroom, staring into the mirror. In her palm lay her last two oxys, and she clenched her fingers around them. Over the past two days she'd started to think maybe she really could reveal to May and Christy who she was. They were good people. Maybe they would understand.

But with Christy coming for dinner again tonight, somehow it seemed so much harder. Whenever Brynn saw the bond they had, she realized that by telling she would be throwing a wrench into everything they knew.

Brynn swallowed the pills, then splashed water onto her face and finished cleaning up. By the time she walked up to the main house, only one thought was on her mind–she'd have to either tell them tonight or get more oxys.

She looked for opportunities during dinner, but each time she thought about it, her heart would race and her throat clamped up. Soon her head was throbbing. When Jim left for his trailer, she excused herself and headed to bed. Hours later she lay in the darkness of the Airstream and tried to relax by taking in deep breaths. It did nothing.

Sitting up on the edge of the bed, Brynn rubbed her temples. There was no way she'd be able to fall asleep.

Finally she felt her way into the living area and looked out the window. The house was completely dark, and so was Jim's trailer. Christy had decided to spend the weekend, and her

Honda was parked beside May's truck. Would she be sleeping in Ruth's room?

Brynn quickly re-dressed and slipped out the Airstream door, careful to close it without a sound. Her shoes crunched in the gravel, but she pressed on anyway.

At the back door she surveyed the yard to make sure she hadn't woken Jim, then walked inside praying Scribbles was sleeping with May and wouldn't sound the alarm. All was quiet.

She tried once again to ignore her nagging conscience as she crept into May's office. For a moment she stood in the middle of the room, orienting herself to its darkness. The only light was the little green dot on the dormant computer. She would have to do this by feel.

She smoothly pulled out the bottom drawer of May's desk. With trembling fingers Brynn felt for the metal cracker box and lifted the lid. Her other hand probed its contents, wrapping around the wad of bills she'd seen May leave behind when she'd paid her before.

Brynn paused. If she did this, would May suspect she'd taken the money, or would she figure she'd used it to pay a bill without remembering?

Brynn latched onto that idea as she replaced the lid and hurried back into the kitchen. Her heart raced, which intensified the dull pain dancing across her skull. She forced herself to breathe in and out and listened for sounds of May's presence, swearing she would never do this again.

There was only the hum of the refrigerator as Brynn reached for the phone on the wall. Shane picked up on the first ring.

30

Scribbles woke May in the middle of the night with a sharp bark. Seconds later he jumped up on her bed, pawing at her arm. She tried to push him away, but he wouldn't stop.

"What's your problem?" May sat up on the side of the bed.

The dog leapt toward the bedroom door, staring up at the knob, tail wagging. Of all the . . . she'd finally gotten to sleep and now the dog had to go. With a groan, May opened the door and Scribbles zoomed toward the kitchen, his nails clacking on the floor. She groggily followed him down the hall.

While he did his business outside, she rested against the counter with her eyes closed hoping she could get back to sleep. When Scribbles scratched at the door, she let him back inside again. She was about to head back to her warm bed when Christy shuffled into the kitchen.

"Did he wake you?" May whispered.

Christy shook her head, tying off her bathrobe. "I thought I heard someone talking out here."

"Nope. We've just been doing our business, right boy?" May reached down and pat a wiggling Scribbles on the head.

With a yawn, Christy filled a glass with water at the sink.

"Thanks for staying over," May said. Chris often spent the night at the ranch, but May was especially glad for her presence tonight.

When their parents died and Chris disappeared for fifteen long years, there'd always been a void inside May that had longed for her older sister. She'd missed Chris terribly, but when she came back into her life almost four years ago, it took awhile for their relationship to heal. May had often felt like the older one as she counseled Christy through her recovery.

But with Ruth gone she was the kid sister needing comfort, and Chris was now able to give it to her.

"She's really gone," May said softly. "I just can't believe it." Everyone she'd ever loved always seemed to leave her. Her parents, Aunt Edna, Ruth . . . even Chris had abandoned her all those years ago. And now, on top of everything, Harvey dropped the bomb that Dad hadn't been who she thought he'd been.

Christy took a sip of water. "You're gonna see her again."

May remembered something Jim had told her when Aunt Edna died. He'd said her aunt wasn't gone forever. "She's *in* forever now," he'd said. Now Ruth was, too.

She smiled. Jim was a man of few words, but when he did speak it was usually worth listening to him. She wished she was more like that herself.

"If he asks, will you say yes?"

Christy set down her glass. "If who asks what?"

"Oh, come on." May gave her a mischievous poke in the arm. "Jim."

Her sister blushed.

"Don't think I haven't figured it out," May said.

"We're just friends."

"Is that how he feels, too?"

Her sister's eyebrows knit together. "Did he say something?"

"See?"

"He did?"

May laughed. "No. But it's as obvious as his moustache. So, would you?"

"We're nowhere near that."

May eased up on her teasing. She wanted to be sensitive. Hunter died only two years ago, and perhaps seeing Roxi had re-opened the wound for Chris.

"Don't get me wrong," Chris let a smile come to her lips, "I've thought of it more than once. But Jim . . . he and I . . ."

"There's nothing wrong with just being friends, Chris. I didn't mean—"

"I wouldn't mind something more." Her sister's smile broadened. "But I wonder if it would be a good idea for two recovering alcoholics to be anything but good friends."

"I think both of you have proved the answer to that," May said.

"Meaning?"

"You've been sober four years. Jim for like twenty."

"He hasn't even asked me out."

"Would you move out here if you married him?"

Her sister smacked her shoulder. "Oh, stop."

May sunk into a kitchen chair, stroking Scribbles on the ear. He thumped his tail. "Should we try to find her?"

Chris knew exactly who she meant. "Probably."

"I wonder if she looks like us."

The idea of having another sister was still an odd thought, but at least this dilemma would keep her mind off the Ruth-shaped hole in her life.

Chris sat down across from her. "Have you thought about whether she *wants* to be found?"

"What do you mean?"

"She might not know about us. What would we say to her?"

"I have no—"

"Because we should think about that."

She hadn't allowed herself to imagine that far ahead. What if finding this girl only caused trouble? If her mother had been having an affair with their dad, they might be stirring up old wounds.

"I would want to know," May said.

"Why?"

"All my life Dad was . . ." she gestured with her hands up to the ceiling. "This just changes everything I ever thought of him."

Chris gave her a sad smile. "You might've been too young, but . . ."

"I know he wasn't perfect."

"Sis, his drinking was pretty bad. At least towards the end."

With a sigh, May fiddled with the hem of her t-shirt. She remembered some of it, but she'd always suspected Chris had seen much more than her. She was the one who'd get into the arguments with their parents, sometimes storming out of the house and not coming back until after midnight.

"I just had this image of him, you know?"

"I'm glad you did," Chris said.

"But it was a lie."

Chris stood up, yawning again. "Not all of it. He did love us."

"How could he have done this to Mom?"

"All I know is that I'm hardly qualified to point fingers." Chris let out a long sigh. "I just want us to think about this girl before we do anything."

"Believe me, I am."

❧

Brynn breathed easier when she pulled the truck out onto the road. A glance in the rearview showed no headlights. That was good. She hadn't woken anyone. She could be back and snuggled in the Airstream again before her sisters or Jim woke up.

She gave the truck more gas, flipping on the radio to help stay focused on anything but May and Christy. Some country singer belted about beer and babes. She tried to focus on the snappy beat, tapping her fingers on the steering wheel. Shane had said the abandoned house was only a few miles past the four-way.

Anticipating the high that was coming, she could almost feel herself rising above all her fears, finally relaxing. She shifted the truck up, keenly aware of the wad of bills stuffed in her sweatshirt pocket.

A car approached from the other direction, almost blinding her with its high beams, and Brynn squinted to see the road.

She didn't see the stop sign until it was too late.

❧

May marched into the Elk Valley police station where Frank Newman was waiting for her. Just her luck he was on tonight.

"You mind telling me what this is about?" May glanced toward the ratty door which led to the station's two holding cells. Was Brynn in one of them? All they'd said was she'd been taken down here.

Frank Newman pointed to a brown plastic chair in front of the desk. "Have a seat."

May stayed where she was. "Frank, just tell me why Brynn's here."

He'd been Frank to her long before he was ever sheriff, and the habit of calling him by his first name never broke.

He leaned against the edge of the metal desk, tucking his thumbs into his belt. This was his turf, and he was clearly reminding her.

"How much do you know about this girl?" Frank asked.

"What does that—"

He held up his hand. "I'm going somewhere with this."

"I know enough," May said.

"You know she was driving Ruth's truck tonight?"

May decided not to let on that she and Christy hadn't even known Brynn was gone, much less that she'd taken one of the trucks. "She works for me."

"Her driver's license is expired."

She tried not to act surprised. "Okay. Did you ask her why?"

"Yep."

"What'd she say?"

Frank scratched the back of his neck. "It expired two years ago."

May paused. She could understand if Brynn forgot to renew by a few days or even months, but *years?*

"You wanna know why?"

"Frank, I'm tired. Please get to the point."

"It expired while she was incarcerated."

"What?"

"Five years. Just got out."

May sucked in air.

"Possession, breaking and entering, evading arrest. I figured you'd want to know, since you have such high standards for your employees." Frank picked up a stack of papers on the desk. "Drove through a stop sign tonight going fifty. She'll need to be in court soon, and probably pay a fine. I'm gonna be watching her, May. You'd best do that yourself."

All she could do was give him a nod as he walked back into the bowels of the station to collect her ranch hand. Her ex-con ranch hand.

Running her fingers through her hair, May groaned. She'd known hiring her was a stupid idea. Brynn had a *lot* of explaining to do.

Brynn could feel the anger radiating off May as they walked out to the truck. She didn't even try to explain. There was nothing she could say. She couldn't change what May now knew.

"You should've told me," May muttered, starting the engine and pulling away from the street. It was almost two a.m.

Brynn swallowed hard.

"Did Ruth know?"

"I should've told both of you," Brynn said.

"Ya think?" May shook her head, focusing on the road.

"Would you have hired me if I had?"

"That should've been my decision to make."

Their headlights illuminated the deserted streets, and Brynn leaned against the car door. Her head pounded. That cop had swooped in out of nowhere.

"I know it was for drugs, Brynn. I know a lot now, actually. And I would've liked to have heard it from you."

Brynn could only stare at the dashboard. There were some things about the night she was arrested she barely remembered, but she'd never forget the shakes and sweating and nausea that had propelled her to break into that house. She'd grabbed a Blu-ray player and an iPod before the occupants walked in on her. She'd gotten away, but later an undercover cop caught her with the profits trying to buy heroin, a cheap opiate substitute for the oxy she could no longer afford.

"Are you clean now?"

"I had to be in prison."

"Not what I asked."

She'd only taken a couple pills, and she had nothing on her now. That didn't count as using. It was like taking aspirin to get rid of a headache so she could face her sisters.

"Yeah, I'm clean."

May smacked her palm into the steering wheel. "Then what were you *doing*? It's the middle of the night! You can't just take a truck whenever you want!"

"I couldn't sleep."

"Neither could I, but I didn't go gallivanting around in a truck that wasn't mine!"

"I'm sorry."

May came to a stop at the railroad tracks, and Brynn thought she saw a coyote slink through the weeds beside the road. She wanted to slink away with him.

"It won't happen again," she said. But how was she going to get through this without more pills? Brynn rubbed her temples with her thumbs. She hated how they were all she could think about. Just before the cop got to her door, she'd stuffed May's stolen money in the crack of the bench seat. It was probably still there. Would they find it when they went to pick the truck up tomorrow?

"Five years. That's a long time," May said.

She leaned back in the seat, hoping the truck would lull her, but each bump sent new pain through her head. "It was."

"When did you get out?"

"The day before I came here."

May seemed to think on that for a minute. "I don't get it. You got out in Denver. Why come all the way to Elk Valley? We're a blip on the map."

"Why not?"

"It just seems . . ."

"My bus ticket took me to Walsenburg. And it wasn't exactly what I expected."

They spent the rest of the drive in silence. May pulled up outside the dark Airstream, and Brynn reached for the door, wanting to escape into the trailer as fast as she could.

"You didn't do yourself any favors tonight," May said.

"Do I still have a job?"

May pulled out her keys. "I don't know, Brynn."

31

Morgan and her family arrived before everyone else Saturday morning. Roxi was busy taking trips from the kitchen to the tables they'd set up when she heard the car approach. The Elliott SUV pulled into the yard, and all four of its doors blew open at the same time.

"Mom! Ethan hit me!"

"Did not!"

"Did too!"

Roxi dropped her stack of paper plates and utensils onto a table trying not to stare. Skylar's younger siblings had been out at friends' houses when she'd gone over there for dinner, and she wasn't relishing the experience of meeting them today.

"Knock it off, you two," Denny scolded. He emerged from the SUV wearing a straw cowboy hat, denim shirt, black jeans and a huge belt buckle that looked like it was made of real silver. He grinned at her. If it had just been him Roxi might not have been so nervous. He'd been nice enough the other day.

"Need a hand with anything?" Denny asked, hanging his sunglasses on his shirt pocket.

"I'm good," Roxi said.

Morgan stepped out of the SUV, and Roxi felt her glare even though she also wore sunglasses. Skylar emerged after her mom. With her starched, plaid western shirt with mother of pearl buttons and those pink cowboy boots, she looked the part of rodeo queen.

Roxi glanced down at her Wranglers that were hand-me-downs from Jan and worn to threads in all the wrong places. She'd had to cut off the bottom three inches to make them fit, and the fabric was now frayed. She too wore boots, but they were scuffed and dusty, and the ball cap Keith had given her suddenly seemed like a dumb thing to wear. She would never feel comfortable wearing a cowboy hat like Jan and Keith. They'd earned the right to wear them, but she could barely stay on a horse, much less ride one working cattle.

Denny rounded up the boys and introduced them to Roxi.

"This is Ethan." He gave the twelve-year-old a fatherly clap on the back. Ethan looked about as pleased as she was about this barbeque. He gave her a good once over she didn't expect from a kid, then popped his earbuds back in his ears. Skinny with a head of disheveled sandy hair, she wondered if Keith had looked like that as a boy.

"Tony here's gonna be my right-hand man someday," Denny said, and his older son gave him a proud smirk. He was almost as tall as his father but hadn't filled out. He dressed almost the same as his dad too, only his jeans hung low on his hips, and his belt buckle wasn't as flashy.

"Hey," Tony said with a nod in her direction.

Roxi nodded back. "Nice to meet you guys."

Denny popped the rear door of SUV and pulled out a sleeping bag. He threw it at Skylar, and she barely caught it.

"So are you coming up to the cabin with us after the barbeque?" Tony asked. "'Cause that part's usually just for family."

Before Roxi could respond, Morgan appeared beside her son. She pulled off her sunglasses and rested her hand on his shoulder.

"Of course she's coming." Morgan nodded at Roxi. "Right?"

She searched for a hint of sarcasm on Morgan's face. "Um . . . yeah."

"Good."

And then Morgan steered her son in another direction. Roxi stood there wondering if she'd really just witnessed Morgan sticking up for her.

❦

Since May's truck only comfortably fit three in the cab, Brynn elected to sit in the bed for the short ride to the Mercers. They'd only be on the road for a mile or two, and May promised to drive slowly. As the wind blew her hair every which way, Brynn tried to ignore the headache she hadn't been able to shake. She'd spent the afternoon avoiding everyone, especially May, but Christy had insisted she come with them to this stupid barbeque, and Brynn was hardly in a position to argue.

She grabbed onto the side of the truck when they passed through the gate and headed down the Mercer's long, bumpy driveway. The truck rocked through a ditch and made her stomach lurch. When they finally parked, she jumped over the side only to meet Roxi coming toward her with a big smile.

"Hey, you guys! Glad you could come."

She seemed genuinely happy to see them, and Brynn tried to greet her with at least a little enthusiasm. Roxi gestured for Brynn to come over and meet her foster parents.

"Roxi's told me a lot about you," Jan Mercer said with a warm smile, coming over and shaking her hand. Brynn saw the same kindness in the woman's eyes that she'd seen in Ruth. Would she be as friendly if she knew more about her?

Keith reminded her a little bit of Jim, only without the moustache. He was busy at the grill, but gave her a wave with his barbeque sauce-stained tongs and pointed out the cooler full of sodas. He enlisted Roxi's help with serving, which left Brynn standing by herself. Off to the side, she saw May and Christy laughing with a group of cowboys who looked like they belonged at a rodeo.

Brynn grabbed a Coke and found a chair. She pressed the icy can to her forehead.

"Mind if I sit here?"

A woman about May's age holding a burgeoning plate full of food pointed at the chair beside Brynn. Dressed in cargo shorts and hiking boots, she wore her dark hair in a French braid.

"It's all yours," Brynn said.

"The ribs are ready." The woman waved toward Keith's grill.

"I'm not really hungry."

"You're May's new ranch hand, right?"

Had everyone heard about her? Brynn nodded.

"I'm Beth Eckert," the woman said. "I'd offer to shake your hand, but I think you'd rather I keep the ketchup to myself."

Brynn tried to smile, but she wasn't feeling it. She'd barely slept two hours last night, and both exhaustion and pain threatened to overwhelm her. She must've grimaced, because Beth gave her a concerned look.

"You alright?"

"Just a headache."

"I think I've got some Tylenol in my car."

Normally she wouldn't have bothered a stranger, but if there was any chance for relief Brynn decided to take it. "Actually, that would be great. Thanks."

Beth set her plate down on the chair, and Brynn followed her over to a Chevy Blazer with the words "Eckert Veterinary" stenciled on it. She unlocked it and popped the glove compartment. She dug around, pulled out a gnarled bottle with the label half worn off, and poured two gel caps into Brynn's palm.

Brynn tossed them both down her throat, and Beth raised an eyebrow.

"Wow, you're brave. I'd gag without water."

"Thanks," Brynn said. "I should've taken something before we left."

Like two oxy.

"Give it twenty minutes, but it should help."

Brynn glanced at the Blazer's door. "You're a vet?"

"I practice with my dad." Beth nodded toward the picnic tables where most of the people had gathered. "He and Mom are here somewhere."

"Are you May's vet?"

"She was actually one of my first clients." Beth closed the truck door. "Best friend, too."

They walked back to the chairs just in time to catch a lithe, black dog, paws on the seat of the chair, polishing off Beth's food.

"Selah, no!" Beth lunged for the dog, but she was too late. It took off running, licking its chops the whole way. Beth groaned, holding up her empty plate. All that was left was a barbeque smear and a few shreds of cabbage from the coleslaw.

"She did look skinny," Brynn said with a shrug.

"She's a whippet! She's supposed to look like that. Believe me, she's well fed. Isn't that right, Roxi?"

Roxi came running up to them. "I'm so sorry!"

"I should've known better than to leave my food out with Selah on the prowl," Beth said with a laugh and a shake of her head. "I'm just glad that was a burger and not ribs. The bones wouldn't have been good for her."

Brynn turned toward Roxi. "She's yours?"

"Yeah," Roxi said sheepishly. "Can I get you another burger?"

"Don't worry about it." Beth headed with Roxi toward the tables. "It's not the first time a dog ate my lunch."

Taking the opportunity to escape, Brynn walked toward the corrals and away from the others. She had to get a grip and think this whole thing through. Would it be kinder just to leave and let the past stay in the past? She wished she wasn't starting to care about May and Christy. She wanted to stay here now, and if they rejected her it would hurt. But she'd made a complete mess of things.

After a few hours many of the guests had gone, but May, Christy and Jim were still playing volleyball with Beth Eckert, Skylar and her family. Brynn mostly stayed to herself, and no one had seemed to notice she was gone, which only made her feel more alone. Everything seemed hopeless, especially without any oxy.

She sat down on the ground behind the barn and closed her eyes, seeing her mother lying in that hospital bed, minutes away from death. Those horrible months were only a small fragment of her mother's life, but they were all she could remember most of the time. Brynn was tired of trying to overcome the memories. She was tired of being strong. All she wanted was to see Mom again, healthy and vibrant. If what Mom believed about heaven was true, the only way to be with her was if Brynn died, too.

Something brushed her arm, and Brynn jumped.

"Sorry," Roxi said, sitting down beside her. "I thought you saw me coming."

A wave of nausea swirled in her stomach. Maybe she should've eaten something.

"What's wrong?" Roxi asked.

She shook her head. *Everything.*

Roxi pulled her knees to her chest, staring out into the fields. Laughter came from over by the picnic tables, and Brynn's heart ached to share May and Christy's sisterly bond.

Even the veterinarian Beth had more of a relationship with her sisters than she did.

"You should be over there," Roxi finally said.

"They don't need me."

Roxi touched her arm. "Are you okay?"

"I'm just . . ." Brynn looked away and picked up a small rock. "I didn't sleep well last night."

"Don't you wanna come be with everyone?"

"I'm tired, Roxi. And my head hurts." All she wanted was to pop a few and float over this whole mess.

Roxi seemed to struggle with what to say, then finally she climbed to her feet, standing over her. "Should I get May?"

"I'm fine, thanks."

"But we'd love it if you—"

"Please just leave me alone."

A hurt expression flashed across Roxi's face, but Brynn turned away from her. It would've been better for everyone if she'd never been born.

32

Even after all the friends and neighbors left and it was just the Mercers and the Elliots, Roxi couldn't stop thinking about Brynn. When she'd found her behind the barn she looked sick, and she wondered if she should've done something to help her.

"So did you have fun?" Jan asked.

Roxi was helping Jan clean up in the kitchen. The others were still outside putting away the picnic tables and chairs and packing up the trucks in preparation for heading up to the cabin.

"It was okay," Roxi said.

Jan stuck a plate in the dishwasher. "I'm glad you and Skylar are getting along."

Roxi dumped a nearly empty bag of potato chips into the trash can. She hadn't seen Brynn leave with May and Christy. Hopefully she was alright.

She glanced up to see Jan staring at her. "What?"

"Earth to Roxi."

"Sorry." She capped a 2-liter bottle of soda and put it in the fridge. "I was just thinking."

"Did Morgan say something again?"

"No." Scraping a few cold baked beans from a casserole

dish into the trash, she licked the sweet spoon and put both in the dishwasher. "Has May told you anything about Brynn?"

"Like . . . ?"

"Where she's from, that sort of thing."

"Not that I remember." Jan started wiping down the counters.

"What did you think of her?"

"Seemed nice enough."

"Something's bothering her," Roxi said. "She acted upset."

Jan rinsed the sponge in the sink, then tossed it to her, pointing at the kitchen table. "What makes you say that?"

"She was sitting back behind the barn all by herself." Roxi swiped at the tabletop, wiping crumbs into her hand. "There was this look in her eyes."

Gathering up an armful of condiments, Jan stuffed them in the fridge. "Sometimes people just need to be needed."

Just then Skylar burst into the kitchen with her mom. She sent a wave in her aunt's direction, then focused on Roxi. "Aren't you ready? The boys are already heading up."

"Almost," Roxi said, mentally changing gears. She needed to focus on what was in front of her. She could worry about Brynn later.

"Why don't you two go on ahead," Jan said. "Morgan and I'll finish up here, and we'll bring Selah."

"Come on!" Skylar held up a wad of keys, jangling them in front of Roxi's face. "Dad said we could take the SUV."

Skylar ran for the vehicle with a giggle, and Roxi followed on her heels. The sun was starting to drop behind the hills, and as they headed up to the cabin they rolled the windows down and let the cool air flow around the car. At each of the gates, Roxi jumped out and let the vehicle through.

As they made their way across the edge of the pasture, Roxi took in the view. The last time she'd been up here at the cabin was with Jan when she'd first arrived at the ranch over two years ago. Back then, she was barely able to receive the love Jan had shown her. To be able to call this place home now was a dream come true.

Roxi quickly closed and chained the last gate behind the car, but before she could reach the passenger door Skylar shot off across the field.

"Hey!" Roxi sprinted after the SUV, even as she heard Skylar laughing in the cab.

"Last one there's a pile of manure!" Skylar called, then let out a "yee-haw!", her arm waving out the window. She made Roxi run until she was breathless before finally slowing down enough for her to catch up.

The moment she did, Roxi jumped up onto the running board, hanging on to the luggage rack. "Gun it!"

Skylar did, and they both hooted and hollered the rest of the way up to the cabin.

The guys already had a campfire blazing and were working on setting up the tents when they arrived. The grownups would sleep on cots in the one room cabin, but the kids got to sleep in the tents outside. Roxi would be sharing one with Skylar.

Morgan and Jan arrived a few minutes later, and the official fun began. As the stars popped out, Roxi sat down in one of the folding chairs by the fire. The air grew colder by the minute, and she was glad for a thick sweatshirt. She studied each of the faces sitting around the fire. Keith and Morgan sat together, and she saw their sibling resemblances. They both had the same wide smiles and chiseled cheekbones. Denny and the boys were roasting marshmallows and making s'mores. Even Skylar joined in and got her hands dirty throwing wood in the fire.

These people were family. They had a connection, a bond. Was she starting to feel like they were her family, too?

"Hey, you." Jan sat down beside her. "You're awfully quiet. That's quite unlike you these days."

Roxi leaned back in her chair. "Remember when you first brought me up here?"

Even in the dim light she saw Jan smile. "We watched the sunrise."

"I'll never forget that," Roxi said.

"Me either."

They'd sat on the cabin's porch eating the bacon and biscuit breakfast Jan had packed. Roxi could almost taste how the salty meat had melted in her mouth. She still remembered how alone she'd felt. She glanced over at Jan and realized she didn't feel that way anymore.

"Thank you," she whispered.

"For what, sweetheart?"

"You didn't give up on me."

Jan reached over and squeezed her hand. She squeezed back. Neither of them spoke for a moment, but they didn't have to. All her life she'd wanted this. When her own mother didn't want her it felt like no one ever could, but the Mercers had welcomed her into their lives as if she were their own.

Roxi started to speak, but found her voice cracking. When Jan had first told her God loved her, she hadn't really believed it. She thought faith in a loving, caring God was just a crutch for someone who'd lost a son as tragically as the Mercers had. Yet every time Jan or Keith read from their Bibles or told her God had a plan for her life, something stirred in her.

Jan had said God placed her here at Lonely River Ranch for a reason, and Roxi realized she now believed it. She glanced up at the stars twinkling above, knowing what she needed to do.

"Could we talk on the porch for a minute?"

Jan cocked her head for a second as if to ask why, but she didn't hesitate to join her. They walked up the steps, standing in the same place where Jan had first told her God loved her.

"I don't really know how to do this," she finally said to Jan.

"Are you alright?"

Roxi smiled but sniffed back her tears. "I actually am, and that's what's amazing. Things could've ended up really badly for me, you know? I shouldn't be here." She gripped the rustic porch railing with both hands. "I should be in jail or on the streets or something."

Jan nodded.

"I didn't think it was true. I really didn't." Roxi stared down at the fire and watched Keith laughing at something Morgan had said. "But if God is anything like you've been to me, I would be a fool to say no to Him."

The older woman wrapped her arm around Roxi. "He loves you even more than we do."

"I think I believe that now." She swiped at her cheeks with the back of her sleeve. She'd never been religious, never gone to church, didn't know any of the lingo. All she knew was that she'd made a decision, and somehow she needed to tell God about it. She looked up at Jan.

"Will you help me do this right?"

Only the campfire illuminated the smile on Jan's face. "There's nothing I'd like more."

Standing on the porch of the cabin that had been in Jan's family for three generations, Roxi closed her eyes.

Jan took a moment to explain to her again how God had sent Jesus to die for all her screw ups, but that He rose again after three days and was now up in heaven with God. All she had to do was believe that was true and ask Him to forgive her.

"That's it?" she asked.

Jan nodded.

Taking a deep breath, Roxi searched for words. She had no idea what she was doing. How could it be that simple?

"God," Roxi began in a whisper. "I don't really know why You would do that for me, but I believe You did. Thank you. I'm sorry for all the crappy stuff I've done. If you can forgive me, I'd really appreciate it." She cleared her throat. "I don't really know what I'm going to do with my life, but if You can do something with it, You can have it."

She glanced at Jan. "How's that?"

Jan was wiping at her eyes. "Perfect."

33

In the darkness of the Airstream, Brynn waited. Only when all the lights in the house were out did she step from the trailer and creep across the yard toward Ruth's truck. Jim and May had brought it back before the barbeque, and there hadn't been a moment when someone wasn't watching her since.

Brynn grabbed the door handle and squeezed. Nothing happened. She cursed, resisting the urge to kick a tire. Of course May would lock it to keep her from taking it again.

Her mind in overdrive, she spun through her options. She knew she couldn't mend things with May without more drugs. She could quit later, after she told her sisters who she was. Because she had to tell them, even if they sent her away after they knew.

With hurried steps Brynn zoned in on the house. She needed to go in there and find the keys. As she'd done last night, Brynn cautiously stepped inside. She stood in the middle of the kitchen trying to breathe normally. Nothing stirred.

May's cell phone sat charging on the counter, and Brynn snatched it up. Sending the text to Shane took less than a minute. She made sure to delete it from the outbox before powering the phone down again. She found the truck keys in a silver dish on the counter. Careful to keep them from jangling, Brynn walked back outside, heading straight for Ruth's truck. She unlocked it, and the dome light flicked on as she opened the door.

She stuffed her hand into the crack of the bench seat, and Brynn smiled as her fingers wrapped around the wad of bills. She returned the keys to the house without any trouble, and soon met Shane at the end of the ranch drive. He pulled up in his car, and she slipped in. Stale cigarette smoke met her. An old Taco Bell bag crinkled at her feet.

"I was hoping you'd call me again," Shane said with a smile she could barely see in the dark car. He smashed his cigarette into the ashtray.

Brynn handed him May's money, trying not to think about what her sister was saving it for. "That's another two-fifty."

Shane reached into his pocket and pulled out a baggie of pills. He dropped it into her palm. "You sure you want these?"

She glared at him.

He shifted the car into park and flipped off his headlights. By the light of the dashboard Brynn popped three pills and sunk back into the seat knowing she should get back to the trailer before May discovered she was gone. But she couldn't bring herself to move. It would take several minutes for the oxy to work, and she wanted to enjoy it when the moment arrived. Soon all her pain, worry, and guilt would be erased. Shane didn't seem to mind her staying, either.

He tapped the steering wheel, glancing up and down the deserted road. "You wanna go somewhere?"

Brynn wasn't sure what he was implying with that invitation, but at this point she really didn't care. She'd already wrecked everything. May had all but implied she wanted her gone, and Brynn couldn't think of how to fix the mess she'd made.

Shane flicked his headlights on again and glanced over at her. Her shrug was all the answer he needed. He did a quick three point turn.

"Where?" she asked.

"You'll see."

She didn't argue. Soon Shane turned onto a dirt road that wound through the pines, and she was suddenly aware of the darkness. No lights shone through the trees. She hadn't seen any other vehicles, either. The truck rocked through a pot hole, and she steadied herself with the door handle.

By the time Shane pulled the Toyota as far off the road as he could without ending up in a ditch, Brynn felt the familiar buzz.

For a moment they sat in the car, and Brynn knew she would've done anything Shane asked. But he didn't ask anything. He just got out and waited for her to do the same. They met in the middle of the road where he rested his arm on her and guided her into the trees using a small pen light attached to his key chain.

Only then did she see the flames. Far off in the distance they flickered, and human forms came into view, too.

"What is this?" Brynn asked

He laughed. "You need to relax."

She didn't protest as he led her into the trees.

～

Lying in the tent with Skylar, Roxi stared up at the ceiling where the last flames of the dying campfire still danced. Everyone but Jan and Keith had turned in. The couple sat together by the fire talking in whispers every once in awhile. When Roxi had looked out a few minutes ago they were holding hands, and she'd laid back down with a smile on her lips.

"You still awake?" Roxi whispered to Skylar.

"No."

She turned over, spooning Selah who was curled up in the sleeping bag with her. The dog's body radiated warmth, and she thought about how wonderful this moment felt. She was safe, loved, and had started making friends with Skylar and maybe even Morgan.

It was a start anyway.

"How long have you had Lacey?"

"Three months."

"Why'd you get her?"

Skylar's sleeping bag rustled. "I needed a show horse."

Roxi rested her arm across her forehead and realized there was a lot more to Skylar than she knew. "So how did you find her?"

"The daughter of a friend of Mom's was selling her horse, and when we went to see her, she was perfect." Skylar's bag rustled again and her face was illuminated by the screen of her iPhone. She fiddled with it for a minute, then turned it for Roxi to see.

"Here's a picture from that day."

"I thought iPhones were contraband on this trip."

"You gonna tell?"

Roxi took the phone from her to view the photo. Lacey filled the screen, her ears perked but her body relaxed, and Roxi thought again how beautiful the animal really was. She could've easily won ribbons at a show on looks alone. But the horse Roxi had seen at Skylar's was hardly relaxed.

"You didn't notice any problems with her?"

"None." Skylar slid her fingers across the phone and brought up another shot. "Here's one of me riding her when we went to see her there. She was a push-button horse."

It was an action shot with Skylar and Lacey flying over a white jump.

"Wow."

Skylar laughed. "I've been riding since I was five." She fiddled with the phone again and handed it to Roxi. "Here's Lacey with her owner."

Roxi stared at the shot of Lacey beside a young woman with dark hair pulled into a ponytail. Her hand rested on the horse's neck, and Lacey had her head turned so that her nose rested on the woman's shoulder.

"Why was she selling her?"

"She was heading off for college."

Roxi handed the phone back to Skylar. That must've been hard. Pushing up onto her elbows, Skylar kept glancing from the phone to Roxi, then back to the phone.

"What?"

"I didn't notice until now." Skylar handed the phone back to her. "Don't you see it?"

"See what?"

"You look just like her."

Roxi studied the image of Lacey's old owner. Skylar had zoomed in on her. "Maybe a little."

"No, really." Skylar took the phone back. "You could be twins. No wonder Lacey likes you."

Could that really be—

The zipper of their tent opened, and Jan stuck her head in. Skylar doused the iPhone, and Roxi wasn't sure if they should pretend to be asleep or not.

"Listen, guys," Jan said. "Just want you to know that Keith and I have to go check on something up in one of the pastures. We'll be back as soon as we can."

34

Brynn sat in front of the blazing bonfire laughing at a lame joke Shane had just cracked. He smiled and tapped his beer bottle to hers in a toast.

"Was I right?" he asked.

"About?"

"That you needed to relax."

Brynn took a long swig from her bottle. "Yep."

She didn't really know where they were. At the edge of the woods they'd had to step over a fence that looked like it had been cut. She remembered thinking that was uncool, but in the span of an hour that thought drifted away with everything else she'd been worried about.

Rock music beat through the night, and Brynn lay back onto the blanket she and Shane were sharing, almost spilling her beer in the process. She laughed and stared up at the sky. It took a minute for her eyes to adjust, but soon the stars came into focus. She hadn't painted many night scenes, but this was one she would've liked to immortalize on canvas. With the flames licking upward, it made an interesting contrast. Fire and ice. Or were stars fire, too?

Brynn closed her eyes. Being drunk had never felt quite as euphoric as this. The oxy was working nicely with the Coors.

Shane lay down beside her, and she didn't mind. Shoulder to shoulder they both stared up at the brilliance of the stars. After a few minutes Brynn pulled herself up on her elbow, finishing off her beer.

"Want another?" Shane asked.

She shook the bottle so he could see it was empty, then laughed again. "Yeah, but I better wait."

"Oh, come on."

He started to get up, but she grabbed hold of his sleeve. "Later."

Shane sunk back down and Brynn tried to focus on the whole scene around her. The fire with its sparks shooting up into the sky like they wanted to touch those stars.

A cluster of kids younger than she on the other side of the flames were drinking and laughing, too. By the coolers, guys tried to outdo each other with how much beer they could chug in one breath.

On the edge of the woods another group was huddled in the shadows, probably smoking joints. And then there was Shane. He sat close enough that she could smell the cigarette smoke on his clothes and feel warmth radiating off his leg.

"Did you shoot May's cow?"

Shane laughed. "What?"

"We found the carcass."

He rolled his eyes. "Why would I do that?"

"If you didn't, who did?"

"How should I know?" He let out a long sigh, then took a swallow of beer. "Actually, I could take a good guess, but I promise it wasn't me."

Brynn's eyelids drooped, and she lay back down on the blanket wishing she hadn't thought of May. It only reminded her she was never going to have a storybook ending. This was the real world.

"May's my sister."

Shane stared down at her. He started to laugh again, but she shook her head.

"She doesn't know it."

"How the—"

"We had the same father, but he's dead, and I never met him."

For a second Shane was silent. He stared down at his bottle. "That sucks."

"I can't bring myself to tell her."

"Yeah, I wouldn't want to be related to May Williams either." His tone was bitter, but then he chuckled and took another swig of Coors. "It's kinda funny though."

"Funny?"

"You're complete opposites." Shane waved toward the fire. "You think she'd be caught dead having this kind of fun?"

Something inside Brynn cringed at the jab at May, but he was right. She could never be like May. Didn't tonight alone prove it?

May was sound asleep in her bed and would wake up remembering everything she'd done the day before. No matter her struggles, somehow she would end up better for them. She had friends who'd stick by her, and a sister who'd do the same. She didn't need someone like Brynn screwing things up.

"Have you ever thought about, you know . . ." she could feel her mood sinking again. "If I was gone tomorrow no one would care. Would they care about you?"

"I guess."

"Who?"

He shrugged. "Mom. Dad maybe."

"Two more than me."

"Grandma." Shane's beer bottle hung from two fingers.

"See, I've got none of that."

"Sometimes I wish I didn't."

"Why not?"

Shane's jaw muscle twitched. "Will you lay off it? Thought this was about relaxing." He got up and walked over to the coolers. He returned with another beer for each of them. "Here."

She took the chilled bottle. He had a point. For once she just wanted to be a normal twenty-something and enjoy the moment. Who cared about tomorrow?

But then someone spotted headlights coming through the woods, and curses flew. The group who'd been huddling by the trees quickly disappeared. Brynn knew she should be moving along too, but when she tried to stand she couldn't keep her balance, and the fire was looking psychedelic.

Shane jumped to his feet. "Let's go."

The headlights quickly became two trucks, and they pulled right into the camp. Several people got out, slamming their doors. Brynn recognized them all. Jan and Keith Mercer approached first, but then came May, Christy, and Jim. Even from here she could see the rage on May's face. And the gun in her hands.

"Are you coming?" Shane grabbed her arm.

"I . . ."

He tried to pull her up, but she resisted.

"Fine. Have it your way."

Before she could move, he vanished into the woods like the others. Brynn was starting to feel sick and crumpled back onto the blanket wondering if there was a chance May wouldn't recognize her.

Keith Mercer stepped closer to the fire. "I'm gonna ask you one time to leave."

A chorus of groans and complaints responded, but unlike when May and Jim had confronted that group the other night, these people got up and started to leave without a fight. One by one they gathered up their things and wandered away leaving Brynn sitting alone, her shoulders hunched, her head lowered. The world was spinning.

Someone threw a beer bottle into the fire, and sparks shot everywhere. The laughter faded. Footsteps crunched beside her. Someone touched her shoulder, but Brynn couldn't move. She knew she was slipping into the alcohol and drug haze that had ebbed and flowed all night, but she recognized Christy's voice.

Strong arms lifted her onto her feet. Jim was on her other side.

"Come on, kid. Let's get you home."

~

May drove the truck back to the ranch in silence. One glance at the barely conscious young woman sitting between her and Christy, and she knew anything she said tonight wouldn't be remembered anyway.

It was bad enough when the Mercers had called asking for help in confronting another group of troublemakers on their ranch. But when May had knocked on the Airstream's door to ask for Brynn's help and discovered her missing *again*, all bets were off.

When they finally pulled up to the house it was after two. Jim had been riding in the back of the truck and jumped out as soon as she stopped.

"We've got this. Thanks, Jim." May said with a wave toward his trailer. "Get some sleep."

He hesitated, then nodded and left her and Christy to help Brynn into the house. May went around to the passenger door, and each of them supported one arm. Brynn reeked of alcohol and was mumbling barely coherent apologies.

"We'll talk later," was all May said.

In the kitchen, May kicked the door closed with her foot, still holding onto Brynn's right arm. Brynn was stumbling, barely able to stand by herself. How many beers had she had?

"She can have my room," Christy said. "She needs to sleep this off."

They managed to help Brynn into bed and out of her dirty clothes. Christy pulled the covers over her and then just stared down at the young woman who'd already passed out. Her hair spread out on the pillow, mussed and in need of combing.

May clenched her fingers. "How could she do this after last night?"

"You didn't talk to her all day, did you?"

"What was I supposed to say?"

Christy gathered up Brynn's clothes. "I hate seeing her like this."

"I hate it, too."

"I'll help you talk to her tomorrow if you want," Christy said.

"What was she *thinking?*"

"Didn't you notice how quiet she was at the barbeque?"

May replayed the evening but couldn't remember seeing Brynn much after they'd arrived. "Beth said she had a headache."

Christy went to throw Brynn's clothes in the washer while May made some tea. How much did she really know about Brynn? She'd spent five years in prison for crying out loud, and as much as May wanted to give Brynn a chance, she couldn't ignore the statistics about ex-cons often ending up right back in jail. She'd already driven illegally without a license. What was next?

Christy's footsteps slowly came up the basement stairs right as the microwave dinged. May pulled out their mugs and placed a Bigelow Chamomile Mint tea bag in each as Christy came to stand beside her.

Her sister carefully set a small plastic bag on the counter.

May fingered it. "What's that?"

"Something I was hoping I wouldn't find."

She picked it up. A handful of small green pills lay within the plastic.

"Remember those pain meds they gave you after you broke your arm?" Christy sighed. "I think that's what these are. She didn't get a prescription at the hospital, did she?"

May shook her head, realizing what this meant. "No, but she asked for one."

"I'm not—"

"Come on, Chris. She went to jail for drugs. And I saw her with Shane tonight before he bolted. Where do you think she got these?"

Christy's voice lowered. "I was hoping it wasn't him."

"It was."

Picking up the bag, Christy seemed to be thinking. "We should give her a chance to explain."

"So she can lie to me again?" May could hear her voice getting louder.

"Let's deal with this in the morning," Christy said.

May leaned against the counter and pictured the drunk young woman lying in Ruth's bed. She didn't think waiting until morning would change a thing.

35

When Roxi woke up, the hard ground was digging into her back, but at least her sleeping bag was warm. Her eyes focused on the cloth roof of the tent where a small spider was crawling across the mesh outside. Had last night been real?

She reached down to pet Selah, but the dog wasn't there. Roxi hoisted up on an elbow and looked around the small tent. Skylar was still sleeping on the opposite side.

"Skylar, wake up."

The girl moaned.

"Wake up!"

Rolling over onto her back, Skylar batted Roxi's hand away.

"Is Selah in your sleeping bag?"

Skylar opened one eye. "What?"

"Is she in there with you?"

"Are you kidding?"

Crawling over, Roxi felt up and down Skylar's bag. Sometimes the cuddly little dog could get into the smallest spaces without anyone even noticing.

"Hey, cut it out!"

Nope. She wasn't with Skylar. Maybe she'd used her nose to push open the zipper and wiggled out of the tent.

Climbing out of her bag, Roxi shivered as she slipped on her jeans and sweatshirt. Skylar rolled over again with another groan.

Jumping out, Roxi scanned the area. She spotted Keith and Denny over where the campfire had been. Keith had a load of split firewood in his arms. He dumped it by the ring and began stirring up the coals.

"Have you seen Selah?" she asked in a loud whisper, not sure who all was awake or even what time it was.

Keith glanced at her tent. "I thought she was with you."

Roxi crossed her arms and started walking behind the cabin. Could Skylar have accidentally let her out of the tent when she got up to go to the bathroom?

"Selah!" she called.

"I'll help you look," Keith said.

"Me too," Denny added.

They spent the next few minutes calling for her, and Keith even whistled when he realized how panicked she was beginning to feel. She couldn't lose Selah. Together they'd risen above their adversity and together they had to continue. She checked inside the cabin, but found nothing out of place. Jan and Morgan had probably gone back to the ranch house to check on the herd and feed the horses.

"We'll find her," Keith said.

"What if she's gone? What if—"

He squeezed her shoulder. "We'll find her. You know how she is. She probably just took off after a jackrabbit."

Roxi nodded and tried not to think about the cougars and coyotes that roamed these hills. The images sent her closer to panic.

By the time the boys emerged from their tent and Jan and Morgan drove back up, Roxi was nearly in tears. Jan took one look at her and rushed over.

"What's wrong?"

"I don't know where Selah is. She was in my sleeping bag last night." Roxi headed back around the cabin again. She'd checked the woods ten times already, but maybe Selah wandered back by now. She was surprised when she spotted Morgan also combing the woods for her beyond the campfire.

"Selah! Girl, where are you?"

Nothing.

Roxi was crying now, and she didn't care who saw her. She couldn't lose Selah. Not when things were finally turning around.

Selah was still gone an hour later.

Sinking into a chair by the smoldering fire, Roxi held her head in her hands and sobbed. She'd never forgive herself for not keeping a better watch on the dog. Beth, their vet, had told her sighthounds didn't do well off leash, and she'd ignored the warning thinking Selah was different. But how could she have gotten out of the tent?

Jan sat down and reached her arm around her. "It's gonna be okay."

She lifted her tear streaked face, unable to speak.

"Father," Jan whispered, gently rubbing her hand across Roxi's back, "You know where Selah is. I ask you to help us find her. Keep her safe, and comfort Roxi and help her to know You're watching out for her dog."

The prayer made Roxi cry again, but a sliver of hope came, too. Last night she'd asked God for help and she'd finally understood, at least a little bit, why Jan's faith meant so much to her. She wasn't alone. Roxi clung to that. She got up and headed toward the woods again. She'd search until she couldn't stand.

That's when she noticed Ethan and Tony talking in whispers over by the cabin. They glanced at her, then quickly looked away. Roxi marched over to them.

"Have you seen my dog?"

Ethan looked up at his older brother. Tony shook his head.

But there was something about the way he smirked. Roxi stepped close enough that he had to look her in the face.

"Where's my dog?"

"How should I know?"

"Why are you two whispering over here?"

Tony took a half step back. "None of your business."

He'd seemed full of himself when they'd met, but they'd had little interaction since. She wondered what Morgan had said to her children about her. Had they googled her name and read about the bookstore murder?

"Listen," she said. "I'm not expecting you to like me, but that dog means the world to me. I just want to find her."

She glanced at their faces and Ethan lowered his head.

"You haven't seen her?"

When Ethan looked up again, she saw his gaze dart toward the Elliot SUV, then quickly come back to rest on her. She turned around and faced the vehicle. With its blacked out windows she couldn't seen anything inside.

Tony turned to Roxi as Skylar came to stand beside her. "You ever read Poe?" he asked.

"Who?"

"Edgar Allen—"

"What does that have to—"

"*The Purloined Letter.*" Tony walked away. "You should read it."

Roxi gave Skylar a shrug, surprised Tony knew anything about literature. All she knew about Poe was how valuable his first editions were.

Skylar got a funny look on her face, then sighed. "Check the car," she said.

"What?"

"The stolen letter was hidden in plain sight." Skylar went to the SUV's passenger door. When she opened it, Selah flew out, launching herself at Roxi.

Laughing and crying at the same time, Roxi dropped to her knees as she hugged the dog. Skylar yelled the news to the others, but Roxi honed in on Tony's retreating back. She jumped up and ran after him. Grabbing his arm, she jerked him around, and before he could do a thing, she punched him hard with the side of her fist.

The blow sent him to the ground, and for a moment time froze.

"Don't you ever, *ever* do that again," she said.

Tony stared up at her, holding his face. His mouth gaped in shock. He stumbled to his feet right as his mother came rushing over.

She shouldn't have done it. This guy was Jan and Keith's nephew. Roxi picked up Selah and walked over to Keith's pickup. Setting the dog inside, she climbed in with her, turned on the engine and slammed her foot on the gas pedal.

36

Brynn sat up and felt her stomach start to wretch. But as she took in deep breaths, the nausea slowly subsided. She pulled down her covers, barely remembering lying down. There were her clothes, neatly folded on a chair by the bed.

Brynn scrambled for the pile. With weak fingers she probed the empty pockets of her jeans. Had the bag fallen out at the campfire?

Brynn dressed as fast as her aching body and foggy mind would allow. She had a vague impression of May and Christy helping her into the house last night, and shame washed over her. Had they gone through her clothes?

She cracked the bedroom door and peered down the hall as another round of nausea hit. This time she knew it wouldn't pass. Just making it to the toilet in time, Brynn fell to her knees and spit bile into the bowl. She barely had a chance to catch her breath before a second wave overcame her.

Brynn clutched the toilet, fingers shaking. She deserved this. She'd brought it on herself. Overcome, she cried into the toilet at the realization of who she really was. She could never get back those wasted years, those unfulfilled dreams. And here she was falling back into the very same hole, not only hurting herself but others, too.

A cool hand pressed against her forehead, holding her hair out of her face.

"Let it all out," Christy said softly.

She coughed and gagged into the toilet. What must this woman think of her?

"You're gonna be okay," Christy's voice soothed.

The bathroom filled with the rancid smell of vomit, and Brynn hated that Christy was seeing this. When the nausea let up a little Christy rose and got her a warm washcloth.

"I'm sorry," Brynn finally said. "I . . . I really screwed up."

Christy flushed the toilet, helping Brynn to her feet. She opened the medicine cabinet and produced a bottle of mint mouthwash.

"This'll help take the taste away."

Brynn nodded, still feeling weak. "I really am sorry."

Christy held up her hand. "I'm not the one you need to talk to."

"She's gonna want me out of here."

"Talk to her, Brynn."

She blew her nose, then gargled with the mouth wash. She felt a little more human by the time she walked into the kitchen followed closely by Christy. May sat at the table with a cup of something hot, but she pushed it aside when they entered. The disappointment in her eyes spoke volumes.

Any explanation Brynn gave now would sound stupid, so she held her tongue. Sitting on the table in front of May was the bag of oxy she'd bought from Shane. What would happen if she grabbed it and popped two before they could stop her?

"I'm sorry," she finally said.

"These yours?" May picked up the bag.

They'd found them in her pockets. No sense denying it. Brynn nodded.

"Where'd you get them?"

"Does it matter?"

May's brow furrowed. "Does it *matter?*"

"I just—"

"Shane, right?"

She stared down at her feet.

"Do you know why I fired him?"

Brynn couldn't look at May.

"Because I couldn't trust him, either." May shifted in her chair. "Listen, Brynn. I was ready to give you another chance because I thought maybe, just maybe, you really did get a bum deal and wanted to change. But I guess I was wrong about that, too."

"I *do* want to change."

May waved her hand in the air. "Last night proves you don't."

She started to speak, but May stopped her.

"You didn't have to go with him. You didn't have to buy these." May flicked the bag with her finger. "But you made your choice, and I'm sorry to say it, but I'm going to have to make mine."

This wasn't supposed to happen. She was going to prove her worth here. Her sisters would be proud of her. Her life would mean something.

"Couldn't I have one more chance?" Her plea came out sounding desperate, but Brynn didn't care.

May ran her fingers through her hair, and Brynn saw the circles under her exhausted eyes. It was clear she'd only made things harder for May, and even when she wanted to do something right she couldn't.

"I get the party," May said. "If you want to live like that, it's not my business. But I can't have someone doing drugs on my property."

She wanted to protest that a few pain pills wasn't that big of a deal, but stopped herself. That's what she'd said before Mom died. May had every right to be angry. Brynn nodded and watched her hopes for a family drift away like a leaf in a swift stream. She glanced at Christy standing beside her, then back to May. Together the three of them could've been like a triple-strand cord. Instead they were being torn apart before they even got started.

Christy stepped toward the table. "May . . ."

Shaking her head, May stood up. "No, this is over. It was a bad idea to begin with. Brynn, you have till tonight to make arrangements."

Swallowing, Brynn nodded. The words came like the judge's gavel on the day of her sentencing, and she didn't wait to hear anymore. She walked past May out the door to the Airstream. There were no arrangements to make. Besides these women, she had no one.

She climbed into the trailer and locked the door, sinking to the sofa in a daze. She was an addict with a record who couldn't even stay straight for a week.

Brynn reached for her sleeping bag. She'd tucked it and the tent under the dinette table when May had first brought her out here. Kneeling on the worn carpet, she stuffed her hand into the down of the bag until her fingers touched the leather of her grandfather's gun holster.

"I'm sorry, Mom," she whispered. "I did what you asked, but he's gone."

Lifting her eyes to the trailer's stained ceiling, she tried to picture her mother before the cancer ate away every shred of her life and dignity. Was she really up there in heaven? If so, Brynn longed to be with her.

37

May scratched Lacey's withers with her fingernails. Horses often groomed each other at that spot, and it was a safe bet that most enjoyed being touched there. But the mare showed no signs of pleasure and instead moved to the other side of the pen.

"Not in the mood, huh?" May approached her again. "It's alright, girl. How about some work in the round pen this morning?"

Her response was a snort that sent horse snot all over her sleeve.

"Thanks," May said, slipping the rope halter over the horse's nose and carefully knotting it. Lacey had been pacing all over her pen when May first brought her grain out to her, and she'd hoped breakfast would help calm her down. But she hadn't even finished her hay. A run in the round pen would be a good idea. May wanted to build some trust between them.

Opening the gate, the mare caught on more quickly than yesterday. She didn't bolt past her, but it still took five minutes of maintaining control of her feet before they could walk through.

May headed toward the round pen with Lacey. The mare was a respectful distance behind her, but the whites of her eyes showed, and her head was high, a sure sign of a tense state of mind.

"Easy, girl. It's okay."

All it took was Christy opening the back door and letting it slam behind her for Lacey to spook. Jumping sideways, the mare burned the lead rope through May's fingers so fast she couldn't hold it.

Tearing across the yard, the mare ran first toward the house, then did a sliding stop and turned to race the other way, straight for the pasture gate.

May knew better than to run after her. It would only scare the frightened animal more. Instead, she slowly and evenly walked toward the horse hoping she wouldn't try to jump anything. But Lacey wasn't slowing down.

She was gonna try to clear the gate.

No, no.

May did run then. If she could get in front of her she might have a chance to direct her away from the gate. But she couldn't possibly outrun a horse. May stopped and watched as Lacey reached the gate in record time, hesitated for a split second, then took a flying leap and cleared it.

Christy came running, and together they watched Lacey gallop across the pasture, lead rope flying. May tilted her head back and groaned. That was their biggest pasture, and if the horse decided she didn't want to be caught, it could take all morning to round her up.

May headed toward the barn, and Christy went to get Jim. He was good with a lariat.

Brynn came bursting out of the Airstream. "What happened?"

"Lacey jumped the fence," May said. "We're going after her."

"I can help," Brynn said.

"No!" May spun around, pointing at Brynn's chest. "You stay right there, you hear me?"

Brynn dropped her head and retreated back to the Airstream. May felt a pang of guilt at her own harshness, but she couldn't be worrying about where Brynn was, too.

❦

May guided Spirit alongside the gelding Christy was riding as they scanned the fields for Lacey. "You haven't said a thing this whole ride."

"Neither have you."

"I've been a little pre-occupied."

"Where's Brynn supposed to go?" Christy asked.

"That's not really my problem."

Christy scowled. "Something's not right about this. I feel like we should help her."

May rested a hand on her thigh as they walked along on their horses. She didn't understand it, but she had to admit she felt the same way. It was completely irrational. She was running a ranch, not a halfway house.

"If she leaves, how are we gonna know she's okay?" Christy asked.

"I guess we're not." The statement sunk like a stone between them. "You think I should've handled it differently?"

Her sister shielded her eyes with her hand to search the pasture one last time. So far they'd been out for two hours with no sign of Lacey. May kept hoping they'd find her happily grazing in the cottonwoods, or by the stream, or somewhere. Had she jumped another fence?

"I'm not sure," Christy said.

"She had drugs."

"I know."

"But you still think I shouldn't have fired her?"

Neck reining her horse around a scrub, Christy didn't

respond. May was impressed at how much her sister had improved as a rider. Only a few short years ago she could barely stay in a saddle.

"She just reminds me of myself," Christy said softly.

"I can't keep someone here I don't trust!" May urged Spirit around the other side of the scrub. "We don't have the money anyway. For the life of me, what was Ruth thinking?"

"Why would Ruth hire someone if you couldn't afford it?"

"I have no idea."

"See, that makes no sense."

"Tell me about it, I don't—"

"Ruth was one of the wisest women I know." Christy turned toward her. "You honestly think she would've done something like that without a really good reason?"

"Like what?"

"I don't know."

May rode silently beside her sister. When May had asked Ruth why she'd hired the girl, all she'd said was that Brynn deserved a chance. But hadn't they learned their lesson when they tried that with Shane?

"I know there are times when business is business," Christy said. "But I don't think this is one of them."

May shook her head. "Then why didn't you say something earlier?"

"I tried to, but it's your ranch."

They were nearing the house, and the horses picked up their paces at the prospect of fresh hay and water. *Her ranch.*

There were people who would give an arm and a leg to own this property. Last year a developer offered them more for it than she'd make in the next twenty years. But this place was so much more than a plot of land. The grass was dry and golden this time of year, and it glowed with a brilliance money could never buy. She could never sell. They'd have to pry her off with a backhoe first.

She scanned the fields for Lacey. The rolling hills made it impossible to see very far, and she was starting to get concerned they hadn't found her yet. Where in the world could the mare have gone?

"She can stay with me," Christy said, her focus on the house.

May gave her sister a sideways glance. "So you can drag her home drunk again?"

"If that's what it takes."

"Why, Chris?" At the gate, May dismounted and unhooked the chain. "She did this to herself."

"That how you felt when I first came here?"

She held the gate open for Christy to ride through, her sister's words hitting like a punch. "You were different."

"Was I?"

"You're my sister," May muttered, closing the gate and remounting Spirit.

"I gave you reason after reason to kick me out," Christy said, twisting in her saddle to look at May. "You found me drunk too, remember? I hurt you so much more than Brynn has, but you didn't give up on me. It's why I'm here today."

She'd tried so hard to be a good witness to Chris when she first came back into her life. The challenge had driven her to her knees almost every night, and she'd grown closer to God during that time than she'd ever been before.

May glanced away, her eyes stinging. She still prayed. She still read her Bible. But lately she did it out of habit. Had she forgotten, already, all God had done for her?

"What should I do?" May sighed as they approached the yard.

There was a pickup parked outside the Airstream. Roxi was leaning against the driver's door, her arms crossed. Her little dog sat in the front seat. When Roxi spotted them, she quickly came over.

"Aren't you supposed to be camping?" May asked, dismounting and giving Spirit a rub on the neck.

"Where's Brynn?"

She waved at the Airstream. "In there, I think."

"She's not. I looked."

"The house?" Christy said.

Roxi shook her head. "No one answered when I knocked."

May exchanged a look with Christy. All three of their trucks and Christy's Honda were still here, so Brynn couldn't have taken a vehicle.

May loosened Spirit's cinch, trying to stay calm.

The teen crossed her arms. "What's going on?"

"Maybe she went for a walk," May said, hoping Brynn hadn't left for good already.

"Is Brynn alright?" Roxi seemed genuinely upset.

"She's . . . didn't you hear about last night?"

"No."

May looked to Christy for help, but her sister just shrugged.

"Jan and Keith called us after eleven," May said. "We found a bunch of kids up on the north end of your ranch."

"What does that have to do with Brynn?"

"She was there."

Roxi stared at May, digesting the words. "What do you mean?"

Was she really going to have to spell this out? When the light still didn't dawn in Roxi's eyes, May added, "She was drunk. We had to help her back."

"Okay, but where is she now? She left her book behind."

"I have no idea," May said.

Christy dismounted. "What book?"

Roxi spun toward the horse pens. "And where's Lacey?"

May grimaced, then explained what happened.

"Is she okay? Could she hurt herself out there?"

Squinting, May scanned the pasture again not wanting to

tell the girl that the horse certainly could hurt herself out there. She'd planned on taking her truck back out to search some of the other pastures after talking with Brynn, because she really needed to find that horse. The lead rope had a breakaway snap, but it could still be dangerous if the mare got tangled up in something.

"Roxi, what book are you talking about?" Christy asked.

The girl glanced back at the Airstream. "I think it was a Jane Austen. It looked ancient. Didn't she show it to you?"

May and Christy's eyes met.

"No . . . she didn't," Christy said slowly.

"I thought maybe she got it at the book sale."

Christy passed her reins to May, heading for the Airstream at a jog. Roxi followed her inside. All May could do was stare after them, trying to calm her growing dread. When Christy came back out, a book in her hands, May only had to look once at her anguished expression to know.

Christy ran across the yard and pressed the book into May's hands.

"Is it . . ."

"Yes," Christy whispered. Holding her hand to her mouth, she could barely speak. "She was here. Right . . . right under our noses."

Christy took the book from her again and paged forward to the inscription on the flyleaf. She held her finger on the page, turning it so May could read.

To my daughter Brynn,
One of my biggest regrets is that I never got to see you take your first steps or do any of the "firsts" a child does. I wasn't there for you, and I'm sorry. I hope someday you can forgive me. I'll always love you.
Love, Dad

May blinked. She thought back to every interaction she'd had with Brynn, from their first meeting to the confrontation in the kitchen.

It couldn't be.

38

Brynn promised herself she wouldn't look back. But she did anyway.

At the end of the long ranch driveway, with her backpack hanging from her shoulder, she stared down the road at what could've been her home if she'd only been stronger.

She gazed at the pastures. It was better this way. She was making the right choice. She wasn't a good person like May or an overcomer like Christy. Now they could live their lives again without the complication of an illegitimate half-sister.

Brynn walked faster. Once they figured out who she was, she wasn't a hundred percent certain they wouldn't try to find her, and the first place they would look would be on this road.

She needed to get out of here.

⌒

May unsaddled Spirit in a daze, barely able to comprehend what was becoming clearer with each passing minute. She quickly shut the gelding in a stall in case she needed him later, threw him a flake of hay, and met Christy and Jim in the barn door-way.

"No horses missing except Lacey," May said.

"So she's on foot."

May fought tears. "She was in my house, Chris. And I kicked her out!"

"You didn't know."

"I should have. Somehow."

Christy grabbed her shoulders. "This is not your fault."

May couldn't look Christy in the eyes. She was being kind, but May knew the truth. It most definitely was her fault. She could've shown some compassion or noticed how wounded Brynn was.

There was no other explanation. She'd turned away their sister.

✎

Brynn stared down at the cut wires of the fence where only hours ago she and Shane had crossed into the field. No one would look for her here. At least not for awhile, and that's all she needed.

Ducking under a branch, she stepped over the wire. Someone would eventually come up to repair it, and that's when they'd find her. By then, it wouldn't matter.

Brynn stopped at the remains of the fire. She couldn't see the road, which was a good thing. That meant no one could see her, either.

The sun was dipping toward the horizon but wouldn't set for several more hours. Maybe she should wait until dark. But if she waited, she wasn't sure she'd still have the guts to go through with this. May and Christy were probably back by now. She'd thought about leaving a note, but the book would be enough. There was nothing more to say anyway.

Brynn dropped her pack. It thumped into the dirt, and she

crumpled down beside the mound. She stared at the blackened logs that had blazed brightly last night. She'd taken her first pills because of an evil disease that had cruelly attacked her mother. Nothing in life had prepared her for that. Not even Mom's attempts to explain it away and encourage her to keep living.

She pulled her legs under herself. At least Mom eventually got to be free of her broken and decimated body. Brynn was the one left behind to pick up the pieces of a fractured life that would never be the same. She remembered the social worker at the hospital trying to comfort her, saying things like "It will get better with time," and "Eventually the pain will lessen."

She tossed a pebble into the fire pit. It had been six years. Nothing had gotten better, and her pain was still a phantom limb that ached every time she thought of her mother. She rocked back and forth, tears falling. "I can't do it anymore, Mom. I miss you too much."

Reaching for her pack, she unzipped it and pulled out the .22 still in its holster. The leather was cracking in spots, much of the carving worn smooth. Mom had first taught her how to use the weapon when she was twelve. They'd gone off into the woods to shoot at glass jars like Mom and her grandfather had done years before.

Slipping the Smith & Wesson from the holster, Brynn pulled out the box of bullets.

39

Before May could drive off, Roxi caught up with her and tried to encourage her with a smile.

"You find Brynn," Roxi said. "I'll find Lacey. I promise I'll be careful, and Jan and Keith will help me."

May's eyes were red, and for a moment her brow wrinkled, but then she gave Roxi a firm nod and started her engine. "Use any of the horses in the main corral."

Christy and Jim soon left in Christy's Honda. Roxi knew they'd be combing the roads, hoping Brynn wasn't already on a bus headed who-knew-where.

Standing in the middle of the ranch yard, Roxi watched the clouds of dust following the vehicles. She'd had a feeling something was up with Brynn, but she never would've guessed that she was May and Christy's sister.

Since it was too hot to leave Selah in her truck, Roxi brought her inside the house to temporarily stay with May's dog, Scribbles.

"Be nice, girl," she said as Selah started wagging her tail while Scribbles sniffed her. Then Scribbles barked, and both dogs took off across the kitchen and down the hall in a flurry of happy fur. Roxi smiled, then called Jan.

Soon Skylar, Jan, and Keith pulled into the ranch yard

towing a trailer loaded with two of their own horses, Sally for Roxi and a calm gelding for Skylar. Jan and Keith would ride two of May's horses. They quickly saddled up and began the search. Jan and Roxi headed in one direction, Keith and Skylar in the other.

"Most likely she'll come back to the barn on her own," Jan said after a few minutes riding.

"I hope so," Roxi said.

"Do we know which way she went?"

Shaking her head, Roxi scanned the field. "She could be anywhere."

∽

With trembling fingers, Brynn loaded the gun. As the bullet dropped into the chamber, she let out the air she'd been holding and stared down at the weapon in her hand. This was her ticket to seeing Mom again.

She flipped the cylinder closed and stared up at the Spanish Peaks. She'd never intended to end up in jail or hooked on drugs. Never intended for any of this to happen. Brynn rested her finger on the trigger, the gun still pointed toward the fire. She'd told Shane the truth last night—no one would care if she was gone. It had been that way for six years, and it was still true now.

But would it be different if May and Christy had known she was their sister?

She rubbed her thumb up and down the gun's wooden grip, sweat dripping down her back. Her bones ached, and so did her head. Closing her eyes, Brynn felt the weight of the gun between her fingers.

She pressed the barrel against her temple.

40

L et's split up," Roxi suggested. Keith had loaned her his cell phone again, so she wasn't worried about getting lost. "I'll call you if I see her."

Jan agreed to meet back at the ranch house in two hours, and she headed over the hill toward the woods on the other side of the property. Roxi would travel the fence in the direction of the Mercer's ranch.

She was now alone, but at least she was riding a familiar horse. Roxi encouraged Sally into a trot, trying not to bounce in the saddle while paying close attention to Sally's ears. She had a feeling the horse would probably spot Lacey before she did. She tried not to think about worst case scenarios, but she kept imagining Lacey lying in a ditch somewhere with a broken leg, or tangled up in the fence unable to break free.

Under her breath she prayed, asking God to help her find Lacey and keep the horse safe. "And while you're at it," she muttered, "please take care of Brynn."

A moment later she spotted something she'd hoped she wouldn't find. Roxi slowed her horse. One of the wooden fence posts lay snapped at the base, and the wires it had supported were tangled on the ground with it.

She quickly dismounted and examined it more closely,

kicking at the post. The wood was rotten. It wouldn't have taken much to knock it over.

Roxi noticed a clump of dark fur caught on one of the barbs. She pulled it off, rolling it between her fingers. It had to be Lacey's. And staining her fingertips was more than dirt. She sniffed at the clump and detected the metallic scent of blood.

She grabbed the cell and called Jan.

⸚

Brynn steadied her hand. Gritting her teeth, she pictured Mom's face before she got sick. Healthy. Vibrant. Smiling. Happy. That's what waited for her. One squeeze of her finger, and this hellish existence would be a distant memory, and she could run into her mother's arms forever. There was nothing keeping her here.

She rested her elbow on her leg for stabilization. Would it be quicker under her chin or in her mouth? Brynn closed her eyes and let out a cry, pushing the barrel into her temple so hard her head throbbed from the pressure. She couldn't miss.

The sound of pounding hooves made her eyes fly open.

She scanned the field but saw nothing. Was she hallucinating? Repositioning herself, she knelt before the ashes. Unbidden, Roxi's face flashed through her mind. For whatever reason, the girl seemed to look up to her. What would blowing her brains out say to Roxi?

Wiping her sweaty palm on her jeans, she raised the gun to her head again. She couldn't think about Roxi. The Mercers would look after her. She'd be okay.

Brynn raised her face to the blue sky. A soft wind blew her hair into her face, and strands stuck to her forehead. She hoped God would forgive her for this. Those nights she'd partied, those pills she'd consumed, those people she'd lied to and stolen from . . . would He accept her into heaven now?

"Give me one good reason why I shouldn't do this!"

41

Roxi carefully led Sally over the downed barbed-wire fence so she wouldn't cut herself. She was on Jan and Keith's property now.

Remounting, she scanned the new pasture for any signs of the black bay mare. A whoosh of wind blew through the pine trees nearby, but she heard nothing else.

Roxi clicked with her tongue, and Sally started obediently into a trot again. After a few strides she came to an abrupt stop that sent Roxi flying forward in the saddle.

Sally's ears pointed straight ahead. The horse stood stock still, then let out a piercing whinny. Roxi grabbed her saddle horn. "What is it, girl?"

She whinnied again.

A faint whinny answered back.

Roxi sat straight up, heart pounding. She shielded her eyes with her hand, searching for the other horse. Lacey! It had to be.

Then she saw her, up by the far edge of the pasture. She looked like a wild mustang with the wind tousling her mane and tail into a vision of power and elegance.

Roxi tapped her horse with her heels. She didn't want to scare Lacey off, but she needed to get up there fast. They trotted across the field, and Lacey stood poised, ears and head erect. Staring right at her.

When she was a few yards away, Roxi jumped off Sally. She led her by the lead and halter she wore under her bridle to one of the trees nearby where Roxi tied the rope to a lower branch. Sally immediately lowered her head to graze and Roxi knew she'd be okay until she caught Lacey.

Roxi slowly approached Lacey. "Careful now," she whispered to herself. Before she got very far, Lacey trotted toward her, snorted, then nickered.

She froze.

Instead of running away, or even going to Sally, Lacey came and stood right in front of her. For a moment they stared at each other, Roxi looking up into Lacey's soft eyes. A lead rope dangled from her halter, and flies gathered at the bloody gash on her front leg.

"You okay, girl?"

Roxi slowly picked up the lead rope, then touched the mare's forehead. When she did, Lacey let out a sigh. She pressed her nose into Roxi's arm and just rested there, breathing on her. Was it really because she looked like the mare's old owner?

Roxi couldn't move or even speak. The horse's earthy scent surrounded her, and in that moment Roxi knew God had answered her prayer. A lump formed in her throat as she stroked Lacey's neck.

She jumped when the mare's head shot up, and she sounded off with another piercing whinny. Roxi spun around.

She followed Lacey's gaze, seeing nothing at first. Then she saw something over by the edge of the forest. What in the—

It looked like a person lying on the ground.

At the sight of Roxi and the horse, Brynn dropped her gun hand to her lap. Her fingers shook. Covering her mouth, Brynn held back a sob. Had God really heard her? Was this His answer?

She sucked in short breaths, tears dripping down her cheeks. Roxi glanced her way and waved at her, but Brynn couldn't respond. She stared at the gun in her hand. It was as if a blindfold was suddenly torn from her eyes. She'd come so close. So close . . .

"Everyone's looking for you!" Roxi called across the distance.

Dragging over her pack, Brynn tucked the gun inside before Roxi could see it.

The girl approached, leading Lacey. Slowly Brynn stood to her feet. Her legs barely held her, and she couldn't hide that she'd been crying.

When Roxi got closer, Brynn focused on the horse. "Is she hurt?"

"I think the barbed wire got her leg," Roxi said, pointing out the bloody gash. "But Brynn . . . what about you? Are you okay?"

"I'm fine." She tried to dry her eyes with her fingers.

"You don't look fine."

Brynn turned away from the girl and stared across the field. "They're looking for me?"

"Yeah. They found your book." Roxi bent to examine Lacey's other legs. "So you're really their sister?"

For a second she hesitated. Admitting the truth would change everything, but in that moment Brynn realized change was exactly what she needed.

May had traveled every road she could think of, scanning and searching for a glimpse of Brynn. It was as if the young woman had simply vanished. She drove down Main Street, remembering when they'd first met at the ranch and how gruff she'd been with her. She'd begrudgingly given her a job, but only because Ruth insisted.

She was about to turn around and head home when she saw Shane standing in front of the coffee shop. May slammed on her brakes, spun the wheel, and did a u-turn right in the middle of the intersection. She slid to a stop in front of The Perfect Blend.

Shane began walking away from her, but May flung open her door and ran up to him, grabbing him by the arm. "I need to talk to you."

He jerked out of her grasp. "I've got nothing to say."

She realized he probably thought she was going to blast him for the party. Had she treated him unfairly, too? She'd been justified in firing him, but was there some way she could've handled it better? For the first time in awhile May tried to see him as more than a troublemaker.

Shane's posture was stiff, like he was braced for a fight, and she cringed that anyone would look at her and feel that way.

"It's not about last night," May said. "Well . . . in a way it is."

"She told you, didn't she?"

"She's gone, Shane."

He stared at her for a moment, then dropped his cigarette on the sidewalk. "What's that got to do with me?"

"Do you know where she is?"

"Why would I?"

Taking a deep breath, she lowered her voice. "I really need to find her."

"Why, so you can fire her, too?"

May tried to take the words in stride. "I just need to find her, okay?"

He pulled out a pack of cigarettes and lit another one. The smoke curled around his head.

"Shane, have you seen her?"

"No."

"Come on. Any ideas?"

He shrugged. "You're her sister. Find her yourself."

May stared at him. "What did you say?"

"I don't blame her for–"

She grabbed him by the arm again. "Did she tell you I was her sister?"

Shane twisted away from her. "Yeah, she told me."

"Last night?"

He took a long drag from his cigarette. "I was trying to cheer her up, alright? That's why we were there in the first place."

May sighed. How could Brynn have told Shane, but not her and Christy?

"I figured you knew by now," Shane muttered.

She turned toward her truck. She had a feeling Shane was telling the truth. He really didn't know where Brynn was. "Please call me if you see her," May said over her shoulder.

Shane nodded. He started to say something, then seemed to change his mind and walked into the coffee shop.

42

By the time May got back to the ranch, she was ragged. She hadn't eaten anything since breakfast, and now the sun was dropping. It seemed like ages ago when Harvey told her she had another sister. A sister she probably would never see again.

May got out of her truck and slowly walked over to Lacey's empty enclosure. She could practically see the headline in the newspaper: *Local Trainer Loses Horse.* That would be great for business. Everything she'd worked for, all the prayers for guidance and wisdom . . . where was God in this? How could He have allowed so many troubles?

The Mercer's truck was still here, so they were probably still searching for Lacey. Christy and Jim had gone as far as Walsenburg to make sure Brynn wasn't hitchhiking along the road, but they weren't back yet. May saddled up Spirit to go help with the search for the missing mare. The ride would help her think.

Once they were out in the field, the Scripture she'd long ago memorized flitted through her mind. *The righteous cry out, and the Lord hears them.* She'd said those words from the Psalms many times, but now she doubted them. She was hardly righteous, and it sure didn't feel like God was listening.

Spirit's ears pricked toward something in the distance.

She didn't see or hear anything, but May had learned long

ago to trust her horse's keen senses. Spirit wouldn't have alerted if there wasn't something out there.

A faint snort carried through the air, and May squinted to see movement far in the distance. She urged Spirit into an easy trot in the direction of whatever it was.

Brynn was on Sally, followed closely by Roxi riding Lacey bareback with nothing but her halter and lead as bridle and reins. The teen kept stroking the big mare's neck and cooing words of affection. Jan had caught up with them shortly after Roxi had found her, and Brynn had managed to fake it so they wouldn't guess what almost happened. For all they knew, she was just upset about having to leave.

Exhausted, Brynn forced herself to focus on staying on her horse. They must've traveled a few miles already. If she'd guessed right, they were on May's land by now.

Suddenly, all three horses' ears perked up. Another rider approached. Brynn realized it was May about the same time the horses relaxed. Even before the gray gelding came to a complete stop beside them, May dismounted and rushed over.

Brynn slid out of her saddle, her feet hitting the ground hard enough to send a jolt of pain up her legs. Her sister had every right to be angry, every right to–

May pulled her into a firm hug. Brynn went rigid at first, expecting to be yelled at. But then she hung onto May and cried against her shoulder. This was her sister. Her *sister*. How could she have thought it was right to keep that secret?

"I'm so sorry," May said, holding her.

Brynn pulled away, surprised May was crying too. She'd been sure no one cared.

"We found your book."

She lowered her gaze to the ground. "I didn't know how you'd take it."

"We knew we had a sister," May said. "We just didn't know it was you."

Brynn lifted her eyes, searching May's face. They *knew*?

Squeezing her shoulders, May let her go. "Dad never told us. We only found out the other day."

"I never met him," she whispered.

"That was his loss." May looked at her, her face brimming with compassion. "And ours, Brynn."

There were so many questions, neither of them seemed to know where to begin.

"What now?" Brynn finally asked.

"Let's get back to the house."

May walked over to Roxi and Lacey, giving the mare a pat on the neck. "Good job," she said. "Where'd you find her?"

"At our place, believe it or not," Roxi said. "I left you a voicemail."

Jan added, "She tore down a fence to get there. We tried to repair it, but the post was broken."

"I'm just glad she's okay. I'll fix that tomorrow." May glanced up at the sinking sun. "Let's get everyone home."

With May's help, Brynn climbed up on her horse again and the four of them started across the field. They passed a stand of cottonwoods, and Brynn replayed every moment she'd had with the Williams sisters. May was completely justified in firing her, sister or not.

"Were you really leaving?" Hurt tinged May's voice.

The leather saddle creaked with each of the horse's steps, and Brynn readjusted her seat. "I . . . I didn't think you'd want a sister like me."

A hoof hit a stone. Lacey snorted.

"I can see why you'd think that," May said. "But it's not true. I just hope you can forgive me for pushing you away."

"You did what you had to do."

"I should've realized there was more going on. I should've trusted Ruth."

Brynn's headache had returned almost as bad as when she'd held the gun to her temple. But at the last gate she still got down and opened it for all of them. May rode Spirit through and up to the barn, quickly dismounting and untacking him. Roxi slipped off Lacey's back and led her up the barn aisle. Jan went to find first aid supplies to clean Lacey's wound.

"I'll call Beth," May said. "See if she can come out tonight."

Brynn was fading fast. Removing her backpack from where they'd tied it behind her saddle, she let May take Sally, then walked into the barn herself. Roxi held Lacey's halter while Jan started washing the cut with a soapy rag.

"She's okay," Roxi said, nodding at her. "But I'm not so sure about you."

Brynn had no words. She hadn't told the teen what she'd unwittingly prevented.

If Roxi had shown up a minute later . . .

May took Brynn's pack and guided her toward the house with one arm around her, and Brynn allowed herself to be led away. She just wanted to curl up in a ball. Her sisters now knew the truth, but things were far from over.

Inside, Christy, Jim, Skylar, and Keith met them in the kitchen. Christy took one look at her and grabbed her in a fierce embrace.

It was a long time before Christy let go.

43

Brynn slept for a few hours in Ruth's bedroom, but by nine o'clock that evening she was wide awake. She could hear Christy and May's low voices in the kitchen, and Brynn knew she had to come clean.

She re-dressed into her dusty clothes. The Tylenol Christy gave her had helped the headache, but her body still felt like a truck ran over it.

Brynn came down the hall with her backpack hanging from her shoulder. This wasn't going to be easy. They knew she was their sister now, but she still had a record. She'd still bought drugs from Shane. May had still fired her.

Her sisters sat at the kitchen table. They both smiled when she walked into the room.

"Can I get you something to eat?" Christy asked.

She shook her head. With the way her stomach felt, she had no idea when she'd ever want to eat again.

May slid out the chair next to her, and Brynn sat down, resting the pack on the floor by her leg. She looked from sister to sister.

"I don't expect you to welcome me into your lives," Brynn said. "I didn't even know about you until I came here. I was just looking for my father, and I didn't know he was married."

Christy scooted her chair closer. "Did you really think we wouldn't want to know you're our sister?"

She shrugged. "Not if it meant your father had an affair."

The words came out a little too abruptly. May and Christy looked at each other, and Brynn wished she could take them back.

"Tell us about your mom," Christy said.

"Her name was Laura Taylor. I think she was a waitress when I was born."

"They probably met on one of Dad's business trips."

"I . . . I don't know." Brynn sighed. "She told me he abandoned us."

Mom had always said her father didn't care, and Brynn had believed it as a young girl. Had Mom ever regretted not telling her that her father had another family? Was that why she'd asked Brynn to find him, so he could tell her what really happened?

Christy gave Brynn a sad smile. "Dad was an alcoholic for as long as we can remember. He was never abusive, he just drank too much. Mom sometimes did, too. When your mother and he . . . that was about the time things started getting really bad."

"How'd you find out about me?"

May was staring down at her hands. "He confided in an old family friend who's been like a father to us ever since Dad died. Remember when I went up to Colorado Springs right before Doc sent you to the hospital? I was showing him our Jane Austen books. He's a lawyer and was the executor of Aunt Edna's estate. Which reminds me . . ." May abruptly stood and left the room, probably to get the books.

Glancing out the window into the darkness, Brynn wondered how Lacey was doing. She had no doubt she would've pulled the trigger if Roxi and that mare hadn't shown up, and it was hard to wrap her mind around the fact that they'd saved her life.

"Brynn." The space between Christy's eyebrows narrowed. "What were you doing out there?"

It was time. Rustling in her bag, Brynn felt for the .22. She pulled it out and set it on the table in front of her. The metal thunked softly on the wood, and she watched Christy's face. Her expression didn't change.

Brynn picked the gun back up and carefully opened the cylinder. Removing the bullet, she placed it in Christy's palm, folding her sister's fingers over it. Their eyes met.

"Oh, Brynn."

May walked into the kitchen, the Jane Austen books under her arm. She started to say something, then stopped when she saw the gun sitting on the table. Brynn stared up at May, pleading with her eyes for her sister to understand.

Sinking into her chair, May lined up the Jane Austens in the middle of the table side by side. The paper labels on the spines were all the same faded pink, but the corners of Brynn's volume were worn to the boards.

"A complete set," Christy whispered, thankfully breaking the moment.

The symbolism of the books wasn't lost on Brynn, but she still couldn't bring herself to believe having these two as sisters was possible. They were much older than her and ten times wiser.

May glanced at Christy.

"Before we go any further, I need to say something." Brynn rubbed her forehead and let out a sigh. "I took money from you, May. The rest of what you had in your box. That's how I bought the pills from Shane."

May gave a slight nod. "I figured."

"I'll pay you back."

"Let's deal with that later."

Brynn dove in further. "I mostly told you the truth. My mom did die when I was seventeen, and that's when I first started taking pills. It was the only way I could handle watching her suffer."

She paused, gauging their reactions. They were waiting for her to continue. "I was a good Christian girl," Brynn said. "I knew better, but soon I had to have them. I stole from my friends, sold everything I had. I even broke into someone's house." She clenched her hand. "When I got out of jail for that, I told myself I was never using again. I didn't lie to you about that, May. I went through rehab in prison. I really was clean when I first came here. But when Ruth died . . . it brought back all the old feelings."

"She knew who you were, didn't she?"

"I asked her not to say anything." Brynn tried to keep her voice from cracking. "I didn't mean to relapse; I just fell back into it."

"Because of Shane," May said.

"No, because of me." She glanced over at the stove. Wisps of steam curled from the teapot's spout, and she went over to pour herself a cup. She didn't even like tea, but she needed a distraction. She grabbed a mug from the sink not caring that it was dirty. She could still see the gun resting on the table, and the reality of what she'd almost done was raw.

Standing in front of the sink, she tried desperately to keep herself together. If she'd gone through with it, would she have even made it to heaven?

When Christy and May came to stand on either side of her, she closed her eyes. "I didn't mean to hurt either of you."

Christy wrapped her arm around her. She hadn't felt loved in so long, but in that moment Brynn could feel the depth of their love, and it overwhelmed her.

"You're not alone," Christy said. "Not anymore."

Then Christy prayed, and her words of comfort, peace and restoration caused Brynn to remember her desperate plea up on the hill. Her vision blurred, and May handed her a wad of napkins for tissues as they sat back down at the table.

"I'm sorry," Brynn whispered, blowing her nose. "It's just . . . I turned my back on God. It doesn't seem right to talk to Him now."

May shook her head. "But He didn't turn His back on you. And I think He especially delights in forgiving His children."

"I don't know if I even *am* His child anymore."

It was a daring statement to utter, but Brynn somehow felt these women could handle it. Her gaze rested on the gun. Could she really be a believer if she'd thought suicide was an option?

"Brynn, He chose you first," Christy said with a smile. "If you accepted Jesus, you were adopted and became his daughter. Nothing you do can change that. And nothing can change that He wants you back."

She tried to smile too. She'd come all the way out here to Elk Valley searching for her father. Well, it looked like she'd found Him. He just wasn't Who she'd expected.

44

Brynn climbed into Christy's Honda the next morning, still feeling sick to her stomach. She must've taken more pills over the last two weeks than she'd realized for the withdrawal to bother her like this. She leaned against the headrest. Why couldn't she stop thinking about where May had tossed those oxys?

Christy jumped in the driver's seat, giving her an encouraging grin.

"I feel like crap," Brynn said.

She also wondered where Christy put the gun.

Rubbing at her forehead, Brynn groaned. "How am I gonna do this?"

Christy started the engine, patting Brynn on the leg. "One day at a time."

"Oh, is that all?" She tried to laugh, but it didn't come out sounding all that jovial.

They pulled away from the ranch house, and Brynn twisted in her seat to see May standing on the back stoop watching them leave.

"You positive she's okay with this?"

Nodding, Christy kept driving.

Brynn wasn't so sure, but tried not to worry about it as they headed into Elk Valley. When they parked behind The Book Corral, neither of them moved to leave the car.

"When I first stopped drinking I was miserable." Christy turned off the engine but still held the wheel with one hand. "I even asked Jim to get rid of my stash for me because I couldn't do it myself."

"I don't have any more pills, if that's what you're asking."

Christy laughed. "I know. Why do you think I packed your bag?"

Staring at the dashboard, Brynn realized Christy probably understood more of what she was feeling than she'd thought.

"I get what you're going through." Christy pulled her keys from the ignition. "And you can't do this by yourself."

Brynn exited the Honda and followed Christy inside. The storeroom was just like before, stacked with boxes and clutter, the computer sitting dormant on Christy's small desk.

"I'm sorry you couldn't open up today."

Christy turned on the lights. "You're more important than any of this."

"Did you ever suspect who I was?"

The question made her sister pause in the doorway that separated the storeroom from the rest of the bookstore. Christy glanced her way. "I knew there was something about you, but I couldn't put my finger on it."

"I wondered if seeing that photo in the paper . . ."

Snapping her fingers, Christy rushed over to the desk and pulled a copy of *USA Today* from a stack of mail ready to topple. "You thought you were famous before. Take a look at this."

She folded several pages over each other, then handed it to Brynn, poking at the headline:

Rare Discovery at Colorado Book Sale.

The article was similar to the one in the Pueblo paper, and the same photo of her and Christy ran with the piece.

"We do look alike, don't we?"

"I hope so," Brynn said.

"Same gap between our front teeth." Christy pointed at the photo. "Dad had it, too."

Christy took Brynn up to the bedroom she'd slept in the other day before the book sale. "This'll be yours. Sorry about the mess. I can clear out some of these boxes."

Brynn tossed her pack to the floor. "I lived in a tent for six months. This is great."

"I'd like to hear more about that."

They both sat on the edge of the bed, and Brynn gathered her thoughts. It had been so long since she'd shared much about herself with anyone. Six long years, in fact. It felt weird, but she couldn't say she minded Christy caring enough to ask.

"Mom died, and I couldn't stay in our apartment." She fingered the hole in the knee of her jeans. "It was rented anyway. Some girlfriends let me crash at their place, but by then I was using pretty heavily. Most of Mom's life insurance went to pay bills. The rest went up my nose. My friends eventually kicked me out."

Christy frowned.

"It was my fault," Brynn said. "I stole all kinds of stuff from them, and they couldn't trust me anymore. I had a tent, some gear. It made sense, and since it was summer it wasn't too bad."

Leaning back onto her elbows, Christy thought for a moment. "Six years ago I wasn't in much better of a place."

"Really?"

"I'll tell you all about it soon, but right now I want to know when were you arrested."

Brynn fell back onto the bed beside Christy. She hadn't expected her to be that direct.

"We're not all that different, Brynn. I've been arrested, too."

Her eyebrows rose. "You have? What—"

"Like I said, I'll tell you all about me later."

That was fair enough. Christy was letting her live here so she deserved to know, but it still wasn't easy spilling about her past like this. "I tried to buy heroin from an undercover cop. I got nailed for that, plus breaking and entering, and evading arrest. Enough for five years. I was almost nineteen."

Christy didn't let on if she was surprised or not. "I wish I could've helped you sooner."

She did, too. More than Christy could know. Having a big sister would've changed everything.

"I hate imposing on you like this."

"Oh, don't worry, I plan on putting you to work." Christy poked her in the arm with a chuckle. "But seriously. I'm glad you're here."

Brynn smiled.

❧

Christy was true to her word and, over the next few days, she kept Brynn busy stocking shelves, alphabetizing the entire History section, packing and shipping online orders, and helping her learn bookselling terms so she could eventually enter books in the database. Keeping her mind busy helped with the cravings, and she had a feeling it was no accident Christy made sure she was never alone for more than a few minutes.

After closing up on Wednesday evening, they pigged out on linguini Alfredo while watching old episodes of *Once Upon A Time* on Christy's laptop.

Brynn offered to do the dishes so Christy could retire early with the newest novel from an author named James Scott Bell.

Once the dishwasher was running, she took out the trash. Christy kept a big plastic can underneath the steps, and Brynn dumped the bag in it, pausing at the bottom of the stairs. Her fingers squeezed the railing, and she thought about how only a few days ago she'd held a gun in that same hand.

She sat down on the steps, staring up at the half moon. Ruth had been right about her sisters. They were part of the good, and she'd almost missed out.

Closing her eyes, Brynn sniffed in the night air. Cigarette smoke drifted to her nose, and she paused. There was no reason she should be smelling cigarettes.

"Long time no see."

The voice startled her.

Brynn swung around to see Shane's shadowy form leaning up against the back door of the bookstore. The cigarette between his lips glowed, then faded.

"What are you doing here?"

He blew more smoke in her direction. "I heard you moved to town."

She stood up. "Shane, it's ten o'clock."

"We were out a lot later than that the other night."

"Yeah, and I was being stupid."

The cigarette glowed again. "I'm sorry I left you."

Shane stepped from the darkness, and in the waning moonlight she couldn't see much of his expression.

"How 'bout a redo? I know this place outside town that's quiet, and we wouldn't have to worry about anyone showing up."

They hadn't spoken since the party on the hill. That was probably for the best, but she couldn't deny she'd found Shane intriguing. If things had been different, they could've been friends.

"I can't." Her voice was barely above a whisper.

Shane glanced up at Christy's apartment. "So she got to you."

"Yeah, and I'm glad."

Reaching into his pocket, he pulled out a small bundle, and before she could protest he'd pressed it into her hand. She knew exactly what it was.

"Shane, I–"

"You don't owe me for these."

"That's not–"

"We had a nice thing going." Even in the moonlight she saw him smile. "Maybe we can keep it up, you know?"

Brynn's throat tightened. She didn't want to hurt him, but everything about this guy was a temptation. "Shane, you're better than this. We both are."

He stared at her for a moment, then started to laugh.

"What?"

"And I can't take these."

"So save 'em for a rainy day."

Even as her senses tingled at the thought, she shook her head, holding the baggie out to him. *One day at a time. One day at a time.*

He crossed his arms. "Seriously?"

"Don't you see what these have done to us?" She waved the bag in front of him.

"Says the girl who just last week was popping 'em like candy."

Brynn let out a shaky breath, surprised at the emotions he was stirring inside of her. For the first time in years she was seeing clearly, but it didn't make saying no any easier. "And the next day I almost killed myself."

She let the words sink in. When he didn't speak, she knew he got it. Stepping closer, she grabbed hold of his hand and held it in both of hers. His fingers were warm. "Shane, this isn't gonna get us anywhere. You could walk away, too. It's worth it."

He just stared down at her. She couldn't read his eyes. Then slowly he pulled his hand away and melted back into the darkness.

Brynn threw the pills in the trash can and climbed the stairs to the apartment. She was shaking. As she walked down the hall to her bedroom, she heard Christy's voice. It sounded like she was on the phone.

"You wanna talk to Brynn?" Christy asked, and she knew it was May on the other end.

Christy then said, "Oh, okay. That's fine."

Brynn snuck past the doorway, not wanting to hear more.

⌒

Part of the deal to stay at Christy's was that Brynn had to attend meetings for recovering addicts with her. Held at church, Brynn wasn't keen on going but knew it was the only way she could stay straight.

As they walked across the parking lot, Christy gave her a sideways hug. "I promise it won't be as bad as you're thinking."

She smiled, but all she could think about was that the last time she'd been here she'd been buying drugs from Shane. Deciding to keep that detail to herself, she took a deep breath and followed Christy inside.

Brynn walked into the small meeting room with the circle of green chairs and wished she could've been anywhere else. What was she supposed to say to these people? Oh, hello? You're an addict, too? That's nice. So am I.

Christy walked toward a group chatting by the window, and Brynn made a beeline for the carafe of coffee and plates of cookies in the corner, hoping to avoid talking to anyone before the meeting started.

"Welcome." The deep voice came from beside her, and for a second she hoped he was talking to someone else. A quick glance, and she realized she was the only one standing on this side of the room.

Brynn turned and came face to face with bald-headed Pastor Walt, the guy who'd caught her in the parking lot. Her mouth went dry. Surely, he remembered her.

Extending a beefy hand, Pastor Walt's smile was so broad dimples appeared in his cheeks. She shook it once.

"Hi," was all she could manage.

"I'm glad to see you here, Brynn."

He remembered her name, too. Great.

"I . . . I'm here with Christy." She pointed in her sister's direction.

"That's terrific." Pastor Walt grabbed a chocolate chip cookie from the tray. He stuffed the whole thing in his mouth, chewed three times, then finished it off with a swallow that made his throat bulge.

He grinned and waved at the station. "Sugar and caffeine addictions are allowed."

Filling a Styrofoam cup with coffee, she added a splash of cream. Christy kept a pot on 24/7, and she was still learning to drink the stuff black like her sister.

Brynn picked up an oatmeal cookie. "Did you know what I was doing? With Shane?"

There was that dimpled grin again. "What do you think?"

"So, you're here because . . ."

"I've been clean for twenty years. Now I help others get the same track record."

She focused on her coffee wondering if she should apologize, explain her relationship with Christy, or say something else about her behavior.

Pastor Walt seemed to sense her turmoil. He touched her arm in a fatherly way, then gestured toward the chairs. "The past is the past. Dead and buried. We're all about new beginnings here, Brynn."

She managed a smile, remembering how Ruth had said almost the same thing. "Good, because I need one."

45

May asked Brynn and Christy back to the ranch for dinner the next evening.

"It's gonna be fine," Christy said as she parked in between Jim and May's trucks.

Brynn still hadn't told Christy about overhearing that phone call. May clearly hadn't wanted to talk to her, and she wondered if it was because she was having second thoughts about her.

They found Jim in the kitchen wearing an apron and pouring boiling pasta into a colander. Christy laughed when she saw him.

He paused mid pour. "What?"

Christy held her hand to her mouth, probably trying to contain her amusement.

"Where's May?" Brynn asked.

"She should be in here helping me," Jim said, with a slight roll of his eyes. "Can you go out and tell her dinner's in ten?"

Brynn hesitated.

He waved at the door. "She's in the barn."

Reluctantly, Brynn walked outside, scanning the pens for signs of Lacey. But the mare's enclosure was empty. Had she gone back to Skylar already?

Pausing outside the huge sliding door of the barn, she reminded herself that May knew everything, and she had seemed to accept her. But Brynn knew that of her two sisters, she'd most disappointed May.

She found May and Lacey in the aisle. May was dabbing ointment on Lacey's front leg.

"How's she doing?" Brynn asked.

May glanced up. "Pretty good."

"Is it healing okay?"

Gesturing toward the leg, May nodded. "Beth says in another week we'll barely even notice it."

"That's great." Brynn came closer and stroked Lacey's nose. She felt the horse press gently into her palm.

May handed her a grooming brush. "Why don't you get the other side?"

"Jim said dinner would be ready soon."

"We won't be long."

She took the brush and ran it down Lacey's neck. "I was kinda scared to come back here."

May stopped brushing. She rested her hand on Lacey's back where the saddle would've gone. "It's me, isn't it?" Her voice was low.

"I know I let you down."

May stared at Lacey's back for a long moment, and Brynn wondered if she'd said the wrong thing.

"You know, I used to pray every day." May's shoulders dropped. "I asked God to give me opportunities to share Him with others. To help people. But when He finally gave me a chance, I blew it."

She stared down at the brush in her hand.

"I blew it, Brynn, and I guess I've sort of been avoiding you because of it."

Dust rose around May as she continued to brush Lacey. Brynn thought about all that had happened to May in the past few weeks. The life her sister had known and loved had been uprooted. And Brynn had only added to it all.

May let out a sigh, meeting her gaze again. "Because of me you almost . . . I . . . I don't know how I'll ever forgive myself."

Brynn came around to her sister's side of the horse. "I lied to you. Nothing was your fault."

"Would you really have done it?"

She stroked the mare's side. "I was about to, but Roxi and this one here stopped me. Please don't beat yourself up. What matters is that everything turned out okay."

Relief washed over May's face, and they finished grooming Lacey in comfortable silence, then walked up to the house together.

"You're welcome here anytime," May said. "And I mean that. I know Christy needs your help right now, but I'd love to get to know you better."

She took in a deep breath of summer air. So much had changed in such a short time. Christy was right. She really wasn't alone anymore.

✑

"Is this too much?" Christy asked, studying her reflection in the bathroom mirror.

Brynn rested her hand on Christy's freckled shoulder and took in the silky blue dress with spaghetti straps. It flowed effortlessly over Christy's frame, modest yet worthy of the runway. It would've cost her a fortune, but Pastor Walt's wife, who had her own internet fashion line, had graciously loaned it to Christy for the occasion. With her rich brown hair pinned up, Christy the bookstore owner would be a gracious hostess for the auction.

"It's perfect," Brynn said.

Holding up a pair of silver earrings made to look like tiny stacks of books, Christy's brow wrinkled. "Too cutesy?"

With a laugh, Brynn picked up a comb and ran it through her own hair. "You're over thinking."

"I'm just so nervous."

"I can tell."

"And I haven't dressed up like this in years!"

"You look beautiful."

Christy smiled over at her. "Well thank you, little sister."

"Jim won't know what hit him."

Puckering her lips, Christy applied a thin layer of lip gloss as a faint blush crept to her cheeks. "This could make or break us, you know."

Brynn warmed at the way Christy used the word "us". It had been two months since she'd moved in, and already Christy was letting her handle some of the day-to-day aspects of the business. They'd attended another book sale together, and Brynn had soaked everything in. She never would've pictured herself entering the book business, but she was really enjoying it.

"I still can't believe *Anne of Green Gables* is this valuable," Brynn said.

Christy elbowed her. "And you found it."

Tossing the lip gloss on the counter, Christy squirted her neck and wrists with perfume, then sighed. "Well, that's as good as we're gonna get."

Trying to hide another smile, Brynn glanced down at the slacks and blouse she'd bought with her first paycheck. They suddenly looked way too casual. Christy was the star here, but Brynn realized she also represented the bookstore. Should she have worn a dress, too?

Wrapping her arm around her, Christy pointed at the mirror. They stood side by side, Brynn an inch or two taller, but their resemblance was obvious.

"I'm really proud of you," Christy said.

She tried to shrug off the praise.

"You're learning things quicker than I ever did."

"I have a good teacher."

Christy made eye contact with Brynn's reflection. "If things go well today, we might have a few more options for the future, and I've been thinking."

"Oh?"

"I heard the real estate office next door's moving to a bigger building soon. Their old space will be for sale."

"So you could expand."

"In more than one way. Brynn, I know you said you gave up your painting, but there are a lot of talented artists in this town. Unfortunately, there's only one gallery, and that's a dinky place over by the Safeway. If we knocked out some walls and had a gallery right alongside the books, I bet we could draw in customers to both." Christy picked up the lint roller and ran it over Brynn's blouse for her. "The thing is, I don't know a thing about art."

Brynn surprised herself by not instantly protesting like she always had before when someone mentioned her art. For the first time, thinking about it didn't hurt. Brynn's mind whirred. She'd worked at a gallery before. She knew all about acquisitions and exhibitions.

Christy offered her a lighter shade of lip gloss. "Will you think about it?"

"Okay."

Her older sister beamed, and Brynn felt how much Christy's approval meant to her. She wasn't used to someone looking out for her, but Christy had taken it upon herself.

They headed downstairs. To sell *Anne of Green Gables*, Christy had partnered with a local auctioneer who had connections in the rare book world. Today they would hold a reception and auction off the rare book, live, in the bookstore. Bids could be placed in person, online, or over the phone, and bidders had registered from all over the world.

"Where should I put this?" May's voice called out as they walked into the front room. Her back was turned, and she held up a folding table. Jim's muffled response came from in between the shelves. The two had been busy setting up chairs and clearing as much space as possible all morning. The reception was to start at noon.

"How can I help?" Brynn asked.

Jim poked his head from behind a bookshelf. He started to respond to her, but then she saw his eyes drift to Christy.

"Wow," he said, and Christy blushed again.

Brynn leaned over and whispered, "Told you," before heading over to where May was working. "Dressed up" for her meant wearing her best pair of jeans and a fringed leather vest.

Pulling May aside, Brynn guided her over to the front window. "What do you think?"

May took in the new display "A View on the Classics". Placed front and center on an old wooden desk they'd borrowed from the antique store down the street, was the three volume *Sense and Sensibility* set. It was sandwiched in between two decorative horse head bookends, and Brynn had hand drawn the title and description on a card stock plaque large enough for passers by to read.

The Austens weren't for sale yet, but that didn't keep them from drawing in customers. Brynn had also stacked other classics like *Jane Eyre*, *Wuthering Heights*, and *Moby Dick* on the chair and under the desk. To keep with the theme, an old spyglass and binoculars were used as props.

"Did you do this?"

Brynn gave a little shrug. "It wasn't hard."

"Looks great."

An hour later Brynn stood beside Christy, and they both stared down at *Anne of Green Gables* displayed on a fancy stand by the auctioneer's podium.

"Hope it sells for a mil," Brynn said, and Christy laughed.

Glancing around the now-packed room, Brynn saw many familiar faces. May and Beth were chatting with the owner of The Perfect Blend coffee shop who'd donated the refreshments.

Jan, Keith and Roxi were standing in the back waiting for the fun to begin. She caught Roxi's attention and waved. The teen waved back. She still hadn't told Roxi what she'd prevented up on the hill that day. Now that Brynn was living in Elk Valley and Roxi was spending a lot of time at May's ranch, she had a feeling they'd get to know each other better in the future.

Twenty minutes before the auction started, excitement electrified the air. It reminded Brynn of that first book sale, only even more was at stake today. They'd estimated the book could fetch as much as a hundred grand with the right buyer.

Christy groaned. "Oh, no."

"What?"

"I forgot my camera. It's out in my car."

Brynn glanced at the clock, knowing Christy needed to stay inside. "I'll get it."

"Would you?" Christy dug in a drawer behind the front counter for her keys. "I really want to get a shot of the crowd."

She took the keys. "Give me two minutes."

Brynn managed to squeeze through the people and out the front door, then quickly scanned the street for Christy's Honda. She'd parked out here so May and Jim could use her personal space behind the store.

Spotting it, she dashed across the street. By the time she found the camera, which in the chaos that was Christy's car had slipped under a seat, it was nearly time for the auction to begin. Brynn ran across the street again.

A car horn blared. Tires screeched as a blue Cadillac with several antennae sticking up from its roof slammed its brakes to avoid hitting her.

"Sorry!" Brynn held up her hands in apology.

The driver waved her away, but at the curb, Brynn looked back at the car. It seemed familiar. She watched as the Cadillac pulled up and parked. Oh, great. The driver was going to ream her out. But as Brynn saw the gray-haired old woman emerge, a huge smile lit up her face.

"Lord have mercy!" Crazy Gladys said when she spotted Brynn. "Didn't your mama teach you to look both ways?"

She wasn't sure if Gladys recognized her. But when the woman came closer, her grin spread ear to ear. "Well I'll be a ring-tailed gallywompus."

Brynn didn't know exactly why, but she walked up and gave the old woman a big hug.

Gladys returned it with a laugh. "Well, it's good to see you again, too."

Brynn gestured toward the Cadillac. The five antennae should've clued her in. "What in the world brings you out here?"

"Storms, my dear." Gladys winked. "Always storms."

"But we haven't had any."

"Well, almost always. I'm passing through on my way to Iowa."

"By way of Elk Valley?"

With another laugh, Gladys glanced up at the bookstore. "I do have other interests, you know. I'm on the store's e-mail list, and I heard about this shindig. Thought it would be fun to see a real live book auction. Planned my route so I could swing by."

"Really? Do you know the owner, Christy?"

"Met her last time I was passing through. Even bought a painting from her."

Brynn's heart gave an extra thump. "Painting? Of what?"

Gladys got a glowing look on her face. "The Savior Himself. Never seen a more striking rendition."

She was relieved Ruth's art had been truly appreciated.

Gladys placed her hand on Brynn's arm. "I prayed for you, girl. Did everything turn out okay with your father?"

"How long do you have?"

"Oh, I've always got time for a good story."

Brynn held up Christy's camera. "You'll never guess the ending to this one. Let's get inside, and I'll tell you the whole thing."

The room was abuzz with chatter when they walked in. Brynn quickly took several shots of the crowd for Christy, then led Gladys up to the front where she could have a good view. Brynn had just enough time to fill her in on what happened after she gave her that ride in Monument before the auctioneer approached the podium.

All chatter ceased. Brynn glimpsed Christy standing by the new acquisitions bookshelf. She clutched a nearly shredded napkin, and Jim had his arm around her.

Next to the podium, a high-school-aged guy with hair died blonde on the tips hunched over a laptop. He was the auctioneer's nephew and would be in charge of the online bidding.

A news crew stood off to the side, flashing pictures and filming.

At the auctioneer's nod, Christy stepped up to the front of the room.

"Thank you all so much for coming out," she said shyly. "As you know, we're here today because of a very noteworthy book."

Picking up *Anne of Green Gables* carefully with both hands, Christy held it so the crowd could see. "This novel by L. M. Montgomery has become a well-loved classic to thousands of young and old readers alike. Anne with an 'e' captured our hearts. So you can imagine the interest a first edition gathers. You all are proof of it."

Christy placed the book back on its stand, catching Brynn's

eye. She waved for her to come up and join her. Brynn shook her head, only to have Gladys jab her in the side with a bony elbow. "Get up there, girl."

Reluctantly, Brynn walked up.

"This is my sister, Brynn." Christy gestured at her like she was a display, too. "We have her to thank for all this, because it was actually she who found this book."

Everyone started clapping, and Brynn glanced down at the shoes Christy had lent her. They pinched in the toes but were nicer than anything she had.

"But this isn't just any first edition," Christy continued. "We have researched and verified that we have here a first edition with its original dust jacket. That is an extremely rare find, as I'm sure most of you know."

Brynn could hear Christy's voice grow stronger and steadier as she talked about her beloved books. Her words came naturally now. Standing side by side with this woman, Brynn felt her shoulders straighten. She'd played a part in this. If she hadn't taken that extra look at the book table, they might not be here today.

"So are you ready to begin?"

A roar of clapping responded. Brynn laughed as she returned to Gladys.

"This is just grand!" Gladys said, letting off a shrill whistle through her teeth that almost made Brynn cover her ears.

The auctioneer started the bidding at ten thousand. A wave of dread passed over Brynn when he hovered there as no bids came. But then the nephew's hand shot up indicating they had an online bid, and they were off.

Everything happened so fast Brynn could barely keep up, her eyes darting to the auctioneer, the nephew, Christy, Gladys . . . within ten seconds the bid was up to thirty thousand.

"And who'll give me thirty five? Thirty five?"

A minute later the bid was fifty thousand.

Brynn shot a look at Christy, who was frozen in place. The bidding plowed on in thousand dollar increments. Gladys clutched her arm at sixty thousand.

"Oh, my word," Gladys whispered.

"Tell me about it," Brynn whispered back.

People were starting to hesitate at seventy grand, but right as the auctioneer was about to close, his nephew called out, "Seventy five!"

Someone gasped.

"Seventy five going once! Twice! Thrice!"

The auctioneer paused, scanning the crowd. Brynn did, too.

"Sold for seventy five thousand dollars to . . ." he glanced down at his nephew, who muttered something up at him. "A buyer in Nova Scotia!"

The room filled with chatter again, chairs slid, and Crazy Gladys shook her head. "Well I'll be . . . doesn't that just beat all?"

Brynn stood on her toes trying to catch Christy's attention, but her sister was inundated with well wishers clapping her on the back, shaking her hand, hugging her. After a moment their eyes briefly met, and Brynn smiled. Her sister smiled back.

"Thank you," Christy mouthed.

Brynn gave her a small salute.

46

Roxi stood in the middle of Lacey's pen, stroking the mare's onyx neck. She almost hadn't come today, but Jan had finally persuaded her. She needed to say goodbye. Over the past few weeks, she'd been making the trek over to the Triple Cross Ranch daily to watch May work with the horse. She'd taught Roxi how to lunge her, and she'd even gotten to ride Lacey once in the round pen. Under May's gentle yet firm hand, Lacey had blossomed. She was still a lot of horse, but the wildness in her eyes had calmed, and May felt it was time for her to go back home.

"It's not like you're saying goodbye forever."

Roxi turned to see Brynn standing outside the paddock.

"I know, but it won't be the same." She and Skylar were getting along, but they were still from different worlds, and even though Morgan told her she could come over anytime, Roxi couldn't see herself hanging out at their place.

Roxi sighed. Her daily visits with Lacey were over. She scratched the mare's blaze trying not to get emotional.

Brynn opened the gate and came inside the pen with her. "She's pretty special, isn't she?"

"Yeah."

They stood together for a few moments quietly admiring

Lacey. She glanced at Brynn wondering how things were going for her. Except for at the auction, she hadn't seen her much since she'd moved in with Christy.

"You look happy," Roxi finally said, glad the sadness that had hovered over her new friend had faded.

Brynn cleared her throat. "You were right about dreaming. Maybe it is time for me to start again."

"So it's true about the art gallery."

"We'll see. All I know is I can't stop thinking about it."

Roxi smiled, stroking Lacey's neck.

"What about you?" Brynn asked.

"I've had better days than this one." She gave Lacey a kiss on the nose.

"I've been wondering . . ." Brynn waved a fly away from Lacey's eye. "Why did you come out all that way looking for her that day?"

She thought back to when she'd found Brynn on the edge of the pines, and how distraught she'd looked. She didn't remember Brynn saying much. She'd just gathered up her backpack and come with them. They'd thought maybe she had a bad hangover. Later she and Jan guessed there was more to the story, but they hadn't wanted to pry by asking.

With a shrug, Roxi rubbed the inside of Lacey's ear with her thumb. Some horses hated to have their ears touched, but she'd found the mare loved it. Lacey tilted her head into Roxi's touch, and she hesitated with her answer. She wasn't like Jan who could talk about God as comfortably as she talked about her horses, but maybe she could say something. "I prayed," she finally said. "Does that sound weird? I asked God to show me where to go."

Brynn dug at the dirt with her boot toe, and Roxi was surprised to see her eyes misting.

"It's not weird," Brynn said. "Not at all."

Skylar and Morgan arrived with their truck and trailer right on time, and Roxi felt her shoulders deflate. She wrapped her arms around Lacey's neck and breathed in the horse's smell.

They loaded her into the trailer without incident, and Roxi and Jan hopped into their truck to follow the Elliots back up to Pueblo. She needed to see Lacey all settled in. It might help in the coming days when she missed her.

"She's gonna be fine," Jan said as they pulled out onto the road.

Roxi couldn't take her eyes off the back of the trailer. She could see Lacey's shadowy form and guessed she was happily munching breakfast from the hay net. What if all their hard work was for nothing, and Skylar treated Lacey as harshly as before? She had no control over that, but she sure wished May could've trained Skylar, too.

At least Skylar was keeping her, and Roxi could still visit. Leaning her cheek against the warm glass of the truck window, she settled in for the forty-five minute drive.

But she sat up straight again when they turned onto the road. "Is this the right way?"

She was still learning all the back roads of Elk Valley, but she was pretty sure they should've turned the other direction out of May's ranch.

"Yep," Jan said.

They must be taking a route she didn't know. Roxi was thoroughly confused when the caravan slowed at the driveway of Lonely River Ranch.

"Did you forget something?"

"Not exactly."

"Then what . . ."

Morgan turned their truck and trailer down the long drive

toward the simple ranch house. Jan followed, bumping over the ruts.

"What are we doing?"

"I think you better ask Skylar."

As soon as they were parked, Roxi was the first to jump out. Skylar quickly joined her, but Morgan stayed in the truck.

Skylar handed Roxi a manila folder. "These are her papers."

"Skylar, what's going on?"

A soft nicker came from the trailer. Skylar turned and unlocked the back, opening the trailer door wide. "I've never connected with her. You obviously have, and for the first time since I bought her, she actually looks happy."

Roxi's heart beat faster.

"I want you to have her," Skylar said.

"You're kidding, right?"

Skylar rolled her eyes. "Seriously? Why else would we bring her to your ranch?"

"But—"

"Don't worry. Mom's letting me make this decision."

All Roxi could do was stare into the trailer at Lacey's sleek, muscular body.

Jan came and stood beside her, giving her shoulder a nudge. "It was hard to keep a secret, let me tell you."

Not sure whether to laugh or cry, she ended up doing both. Skylar backed Lacey out of the trailer and handed Roxi the mare's lead rope.

"Congratulations!" Skylar beamed. "You're now the proud owner of a Quarter Horse Appendix."

"A . . . what?"

"Look it up."

"But she's yours," Roxi protested.

"Not anymore."

Fumbling with the folder and lead rope, Roxi gazed into Lacey's face with the star and blaze she knew so well. The mare was still chewing some hay, her ears erect. She whinnied when she caught sight of Sally standing at the corral fence, and Jan laughed.

"I think she's already made a friend."

Skylar waved and jumped back into the truck. "Have fun!"

It happened so fast Roxi didn't have time to think. As the Elliots' truck disappeared in a cloud of dust, she laughed. "Is this for real?"

Jan patted Lacey's rump. "Looks like."

"Then I guess we're both home now, girl," Roxi whispered, resting her forehead against the mare's warm neck.

"That you are," Jan said.

Roxi had just finished settling Lacey in the small paddock next to Sally when May's truck pulled into the yard. Roxi dropped the empty water bucket she was carrying and ran over to her.

"Did you know about this?"

With a grin, May shut her door. "For two weeks."

"I can't believe it!" She turned to watch the mare trot around the perimeter of her pen calling to Sally. "I never dreamed . . . okay, I did dream, but . . . she's really mine?"

"Lock, stock and barrel."

Together they walked over to the pasture. Sally was just trotting over to Lacey to greet her from across the fence. They sniffed noses, and then Lacey arched her neck and squealed. Sally just stared at her.

"That always cracks me up when they do that," May said.

"She sounds like a pig."

May laughed, resting her boot on the bottom rail of the fence. "Were you surprised?"

"Oh, yeah." Lacey squealed again, then took off across her pasture, black tail and mane flying.

"I've watched you with her." May nodded in Lacey's direction. "You've got potential, and I could use an assistant."

She paused, unsure if she'd heard correctly.

"Interested?" May asked.

Roxi didn't know when she'd smiled so much.

❧

Brynn walked into Ruth's art studio that evening after supper. She imagined Ruth sitting at the easel, dipping her brush into a mound of bright green oil paint, doing what she loved.

The old woman's sketchbook still lay where she'd left it that terrible day. Brynn reverently picked it up, flipping through the pages, once again amazed at Ruth's skill. When she got to the last page her heart caught in her throat. This is what she'd been working on in that horse's pen. Her last drawing.

It depicted the backs of three women, their arms wrapped across each other's shoulders. Beneath them Ruth had written these words:

A cord of three strands is not quickly broken.

Brynn stared at the rendering for a long time, then carefully flipped over the page and took a pencil from the jar beside the easel. She tucked the book under her arm and walked outside to the back of the barn where she and Ruth had talked that first night. Sitting on a feed bucket, Brynn watched the cows and horses grazing beneath the Spanish Peaks.

Fiddling with the pencil, Brynn eyed the blank page, then pulled up the sleeve of her t-shirt and studied the Phoenix. It rose from the ashes. Just like she needed to do.

She took in a deep breath of summer air and started to sketch.

About the Author

C. J. has loved to read since she was a kid dragging home bags of books from the library. When she was twelve she started dreaming about becoming a published author. That dream came true when her first novel *Thicker than Blood* won the 2008 Jerry B. Jenkins Christian Writers Guild Operation First Novel contest. It became the first book in the Thicker than Blood series, which also includes *Bound by Guilt*, *Ties that Bind*, and *Running on Empty*. She has also written *Jupiter Winds*, the first book in a teen space adventure series. C. J. lives in Pennsylvania with her family and their menagerie of dogs and a Paint mare named Sky.

Visit her Web site at www.cjdarlington.com

TIES THAT BIND
Q & A

Thanks to Nora St. Laurent, Christy Lee Taylor, Rick Estep, Deanna Rupp, Mary Crawford, and Jennifer Erin Valent for the great questions. Due to space, I wasn't able to include all of them. Visit my website for a more exhaustive Q&A: www.cjdarlington.com

What inspired you to write Ties that Bind?

What would it be like to enter society again after years behind bars? For a long time I was intrigued with the idea of writing about someone just released from prison. What sort of troubles would they face? I began to ask myself "what if" questions, and Brynn Taylor was born. After I finished writing my novel *Bound by Guilt*, I was curious what happened to my main character Roxi Gold after the events of the story. It was fun to bring these two young ladies together in *Ties that Bind*.

How much of the used book world you portray is real and how much is made up?

The Book Corral is a fictional bookstore (as is Dawson's Book Barn), but everything else is based on reality. For several years I traveled the country going to book sales like the ones I describe. People sometimes assume that book dealers are very academic, considerate people who like nothing better than sitting around sipping tea discussing their latest reads. That type does exist, but more often than not I encountered many like those I wrote about in this story.

The first editions described are also real. In fact, the copy of *Sense and Sensibility* pictured on the cover of *Ties that Bind* was a set Peter Harrington Books in England actually sold a few years ago. They graciously allowed me to use their photo.

What character in Ties that Bind do you relate to the most and why?

There are bits and pieces of me in all the characters I write, but in *Ties that Bind* I think I relate closest to May. She has a strong faith, but it's really being tested in this story.

Two years ago, someone very close to me died, and I admit it shook my faith. I couldn't understand how something like that could happen to this person, a strong believer, who trusted God to the very end. You'll probably pick up on some of the questions I felt in this story, but like May, I survived, and so did my faith. In her, I also see someone who really desires to be a good witness of Christ's love, but isn't perfect and sometimes messes up. God forgives her just as much as he forgives the unbelievers in the story.

What do you hope readers take away from Ties that Bind?

I came at this story a little differently than my previous novels. I often write about characters who don't know Christ, but in *Ties that Bind* I wanted to write about someone who *had* known the Lord at one point in her life but drifted away from her childhood faith. Through Brynn's journey I wanted to show that this type of character is also deeply loved by God. He desires for his children, no matter how far they've traveled away from him, to come back into His arms. God's love and forgiveness is not only for those who've sinned big in their lives, but it's there just as strongly for those who've drifted away. I think sometimes it's harder for people who grew up knowing the Lord to ask for His forgiveness.

Through *Ties that Bind* I hope all of us will see just how far and long is the reach of God's love. No one is ever too far gone.

DISCUSSION QUESTIONS

If your book club reads *Ties that Bind* and is interested in talking with me via Skype or speakerphone, please contact me via e-mail at cj@cjdarlington.com, and I'll do my best to arrange something with you. Thanks for reading!

1. If you were Brynn's friend, how would you help her come to terms with her shattered faith because of her mother's suffering? What Scriptures could you share?

2. How many examples of forgiveness did you notice in the story? Share a time in your life when you forgave someone who didn't necessarily deserve it. How did the experience affect you?

3. How does May's horse training philosophy reflect her beliefs about God?

4. Are you a Jane Austen fan? If so, what's your favorite novel and why?

5. Who was your favorite character in *Ties that Bind* and what made you enjoy them the most?

6. What spiritual principles are at work in Jan and Keith's family?
7. Do you think Brynn's life would've been different if she'd had a relationship with her father as a child? Why or why not?

8. Why is Brynn so afraid to tell May and Christy who she is? Do you think her fears are justified?

9. How does Roxi affect Brynn's life through the story? Have you ever found out after the fact that you affected someone's life unknowingly?

10. Do you think May and Christy will sell the *Sense and Sensibility* set? What would you do?

11. Which character do you think has the most influence on Brynn for the Lord? Why is that?

12. What would you say is the most important theme of *Ties that Bind*?

13. Roxi has to decide whether or not to accept what Jesus did for her on the cross. Have you accepted God's gift of forgiveness and invited Him into your life? If so, share your experience. If not, there's no better time than now!

Want to read more?

Mountainview Books, LLC presents:

RUNNING ON EMPTY
by C. J. Darlington

Turn the page to read an excerpt!

1

Elk Valley, Colorado

Del Mangini recounted the wrinkled bills in her wallet as if the act could multiply them. Nineteen dollars. That had to be enough.

She approached the shortest of the checkout lines behind a tanned, fortyish woman in pink running gear. Del eyed the mountain of fresh vegetables, bags of fruit, and huge pack of T-bones the woman loaded onto the conveyer belt.

Her stomach growled, and by the woman's surreptitious glance she knew she wasn't the only one who heard it. Del stared down at her Goodwill-bought sneakers with the knot-repaired laces, embarrassment rising up her neck. She'd skipped breakfast and lunch to put three gallons in her ancient Chevy Malibu.

Plunk!

A bag of raw, organic almonds landed on Del's foot. She slowly picked it up.

"Excuse me, but those are mine." The woman snatched the nuts from her and tossed them on the belt.

Del tried to pretend she didn't care, but it had been months since she'd eaten anything that didn't come out of a can or box, and the proof lay in her grocery basket: loaf of Wonder bread, two boxes of spaghetti, quart of 2% milk, store-brand cornflakes, crunchy peanut butter, and her one splurge—a jar of pesto marinara sauce. If she added a little water, she could stretch it to last a week.

The teenage checker's scanner beeped like a pulse monitor, and when it was finally Del's turn, she lifted her basket onto the belt and watched as each price flashed on the screen.

"Total's twenty three seventeen." The checker popped her gum.

"But . . . I thought the pasta was on sale."

"Ended yesterday."

"Are you sure?"

"I can check." The teen reached for the phone receiver beside the register.

Del glanced at the fidgeting line behind her, clearly imagining their unvoiced thoughts about the sorry-looking young woman quibbling about a fifty-cent savings. She shook her head and pushed the marinara sauce to the side. "It's okay. I'll just come back for this later."

The clerk shrugged, and with a punch of a few buttons brought the total down. Del handed over her bills and escaped from the grocery store knowing she wouldn't be back. Couldn't be, actually. She headed across the parking lot. A flash of pink caught her eye, and she spotted the woman in the running suit loading her groceries into a shiny Escalade. Her back was turned, her cart unattended. One quick sprint and Del knew she could grab one of those bags before the woman would catch her.

She walked closer.

The woman swung around, and Del spun on her heels. What was she *doing*? She should be mapping out the next business to ask for a job, not thinking about stealing someone's groceries.

But how was she going to get through the month on nineteen dollars' worth of food?

She climbed into her rusted car. If she sold it she might get a couple hundred to keep her floating, but then where would she be? She couldn't walk everywhere.

Closing her eyes, desperation built in her chest as it had every day she watched her meager cash supply dwindle and every job opportunity slip through her fingers. She should've just slept with Eric.

Del blew air through her lips in frustration. It had been three months since she caught him swiping cash from the bank deposit at It's Only Natural Foods where they both worked. He swore he'd tell the owner, who happened to be his grandmother, that it was Del if she didn't give him what he really wanted. She refused, and the next day she was fired. Del tried to tell her side of the story and convince the owner she'd done nothing wrong, but she didn't believe Del.

In a town the size of Elk Valley, word spread like the wildfires that swept up the west slope of the Spanish Peaks last year, and no one in town would hire her. But even without her tarnished reputation, she didn't have much chance anyway. Her resume consisted of random fast food jobs and a stint helping a now-dead old cowboy break mustangs.

As she reached to start the engine, the Chevy's passenger door opened and a man climbed into her car, sat down, and slammed the door shut.

"Hey!" She pulled back her fist to punch him with all she had.

He raised his hands. "I'm sorry! I'm sorry! I should've knocked."

"Get out of my car!"

The man kept his hands up as if in surrender. He wore dark jeans, a red Rockies T-shirt, and a ball cap with a bill so frayed she could see the cardboard along its edge.

"I said get out!"

"Please just listen to me."

Did he have a gun? Was this a carjacking? She should get out and run. But something about him made her pause. If he wanted the car, wouldn't he have demanded that already?

"I'm going to reach into my shirt pocket," he said, pulling out a business card then slowly lowering his hand. "Are you Del Mangini?"

She stared at the man. With a ruddy complexion and graying stubble on his chin he looked like he was probably pushing fifty. "Who are you?"

"So I was right."

"You've got ten seconds to tell me what this is about before you're going to regret you set foot in my car."

He gave her a hesitant smile. "Right. I'm David Kirsch. A PI."

"What?"

"Private investigator."

"I know what PI—"

"I've been trying to find you for a month."

Great. Like she didn't have enough on her plate. She gripped her door handle hard. This guy was probably packing, but would he dare threaten her during business hours at a grocery store? Maybe, maybe not. Daylight hadn't stopped those thugs the cops picked up in Walsenburg a few months ago when they'd shot and nearly killed a woman for her purse.

"You've been trying to find *me*?"

"Not the easiest thing."

Maybe she should run after all.

"Why?" Del asked, scanning the parking lot. The lady in pink was gone. A guy her age was gathering up the shopping carts and pushing a huge line of them toward the entrance. If she screamed he would hear.

"I need to find your mother."

Del swung toward this strange man who'd violated her privacy. Kirsch tried to hand her the business card. She didn't take it.

"My mother?"

"Yes."

She laughed. "You're kidding, right?"

Kirsch's head tilted ever so slightly, and his expression remained serious. Okay, so he wasn't kidding.

"And why do you need to find her?" Del asked.

"Can't say."

"Who hired you?"

"That's confidential."

"I think you got your wires a little mixed up."

A faint smile played on Kirsch's lips again. "I'm good at what I do."

Yet it took him a month to find her. Somehow she found satisfaction in that. She had intended to drop off the radar from her old life in Pennsylvania, and apparently it worked.

"Not *that* good, because I'm your dead end." Del fingered her keys. Her stomach still gnawed for food.

Kirsch leaned forward, trying to catch her eye again. "Come on."

"Okay, you got me. I'll tell you where she is."

The PI stared at her, like he was trying to figure out if she was bluffing. "I'd appreciate it."

"Pennsylvania."

Kirsch blinked. She wondered if his ego was crushed for being so far off.

"At a place called Green Meadows," Del said.

Kirsch pulled out a smartphone and started tapping notes into it. "Thank you."

"Cemetery," Del said.

He looked up.

"I meant a literal dead end. My mother's buried there."

Clearing his throat, Kirsch paused with his finger hovering over the phone. "I'm sorry, but—"

"Time to leave, Sherlock. Now."

"But—"

"I obviously can't help you."

"Your *biological* mother."

It was Del's turn to stare.

"I know your adoptive parents passed away." Kirsch's expression was sympathetic. "Apologies for not being clear on that, but I'm trying to find your birth mother."

"My birth mother is buried in that cemetery."

"Are you sure?"

"What do you mean am I sure?"

"What was her name?"

"Listen, I don't know what game you're—"

"They didn't tell you, did they?"

The air in the car suddenly seemed to thin, and Del felt like she was on the summit of Mount Everest struggling for oxygen. She knew what he was implying, but she didn't want to entertain it. Her parents loved her, meant the world to her, and had died heroes.

Kirsch tapped again on his phone then turned it toward her. A woman's photo stared back, and Del had to do a double-take. The woman's dark blonde hair was wilder than her own, which she kept at shoulder length, but even she couldn't deny the resemblance.

"Her name's Natalie," Kirsch said.

"You're pulling my leg, right?"

"I think you know I'm not."

Del paged through memory after memory of her parents, a cognitive slideshow. Had they ever mentioned something, anything, to mean they weren't her real parents? She came up empty. So she didn't look like them. That was no big deal, right? She'd always assumed she took after some distant relative to explain why she'd ended up five foot two with parents who both played basketball in college. Or why two Mediterranean beauties had ended up with a towhead child.

Kirsch set his business card on the console between them. Embossed with silver lettering, probably on purpose to make himself look more legit. But any lug could buy cards online. This could bee one big con. But what would be the purpose in that?

"Are you sure you have the right girl?" Del asked.

He slipped his phone into his shirt pocket. "Like I said, I'm good."

"Get out of my car."

Kirsch gave one nod, as if he knew their conversation really was over, and exited as quickly as he entered. She watched him walk across the parking lot and climb into a black pickup. He touched the bill of his cap then drove away.

She flipped the locks and sat frozen in her seat.

FIND RUNNING ON EMPTY AT YOUR FAVORITE ONLINE RETAILER.

Visit the Mountainview Books, LLC website for news on
all our books:

www.mountainviewbooks.com